Praise for
The Mrs. Murphy Series

THE TAIL OF THE TIP-OFF

"You don't have to be a cat lover to enjoy Brown's eleventh
Mrs. Murphy novel.... Brown writes so compellingly...
[she] breathes believability into every aspect of this smart
and sassy novel." —*Publishers Weekly* (starred review)

"Rita Mae Brown's series remains one of the best cat
mysteries.... Brown keeps the series fresh."
—*The Post & Courier* (Charleston, SC)

"The animals' droll commentary provides comic
relief and clues helpful in solving the crime."
—*The Washington Post*

"A tightly woven mystery, peopled with the delightful
characters of small-town Virginia...a real three-point
play: an intriguing mystery, great characters, and an
engaging sense of humor." —*I Love a Mystery*

"A fast-paced plot and enough animated feline
personalities to keep readers entertained."
—*Daily News* (New York)

"A not-to-be-missed exciting cozy."
—*The Midwest Book Review*

"Nobody can put words in the mouths of animals
better than Rita Mae Brown...fast-paced action...
Harry and her menagerie are simply great."
—*Abilene Reporter-News*

CATCH AS CAT CAN

"This latest is as good as its predecessors . . . thoroughly enjoyable." —*Winston-Salem Journal*

"Brown's proven brand of murder and mayhem played out against a background of Virginia gentility and idealized animals is once again up to scratch." —*Publishers Weekly*

"Any new Mrs. Murphy is a joyful reading experience, and *Catch as Cat Can* is no exception. . . . An adult mystery that appeals to the child in all of us."
—*The Midwest Book Review*

"The[se] mysteries continue to be a true treat."
—*The Post & Courier* (Charleston, SC)

"An entertaining read in a fun series." —*Mystery News*

CLAWS AND EFFECT

"Reading a Mrs. Murphy mystery is like eating a potato chip. You always go back for more. . . . Whimsical and enchanting . . . the latest expert tale from a deserving bestselling series."
—*The Midwest Book Review*

"Mrs. Murphy, the incomparable feline sleuth with attitude, returns to captivate readers. . . . An intriguing and well-executed mystery . . . Grateful fans will relish this charming addition by a master of the cozy cat genre."
—*Publishers Weekly*

"As charming as ever." —*The Tennessean*

"With intricate plot twists that will keep readers guessing right up until the end, *Claws and Effect* once again blends murder and mayhem with animal antics." —*Pet Life*

"Another charming and elegantly spun yarn."
—*The Providence Sunday Journal*

"Excellent series . . . Another murder in Crozet would be
most welcome." —*Winston-Salem Journal*

PAWING THROUGH THE PAST

"This is a cat-lover's dream of a mystery. . . . 'Harry' is
simply irresistible. . . . [Rita Mae] Brown once again
proves herself 'Queen of Cat Crimes.' . . . Don't miss out
on this lively series, for it's one of the best around."
—*Old Book Barn Gazette*

"Apparently eight's the charm for Rita Mae Brown
and her cat, Sneaky Pie, whose latest adventure just
may be the best in this long-running series."
—*Booklist*

"Another delightful mystery . . . Once again, Rita Mae
Brown proves she can capture the ambiance of life in a
small southern town and, more impressively, get readers
to accept thinking, mystery-solving cats and dogs."
—*The Virginian-Pilot*

"Cleverly crafted . . . Fans of the Mrs. Murphy series
will want to immediately read this novel, while newcomers
will search for the previous books."
—*The Midwest Book Review*

"A delightful cozy mystery, all the more so because of
the active role the pets take in solving the crime . . . [The]
puzzling mystery will shock and delight you."
—*Romantic Times*

"Rita Mae Brown's books are always well written, always
entertaining, always full of interesting people becoming

involved with plots, plans, and emotional entanglements. *Pawing Through the Past* is no exception."
—*I Love a Mystery*

CAT ON THE SCENT

"Rita and Sneaky Pie know how to grab a reader. This fun-loving and delightful mystery is a must even if you're not a cat lover." —*The Pilot* (Southern Pines, NC)

"These provocative mysteries just glow."
—*Mystery Lovers Bookshop News*

"Features all the traits of purebred fun....
The antics of the animals, Brown's witty observations, the history-revering Virginians, and the Blue Ridge setting make this a pleasurable read for lovers of this popular genre."
—*BookPage*

"Animal antics and criminal capers combine captivatingly in *Cat on the Scent*."
—*The San Diego Union-Tribune*

"A charming and keen-eyed take on human misdeeds and animal shenanigans...Told with spunk and plenty of whimsy, this is another delightful entry in a very popular series." —*Publishers Weekly*

"A fine murder mystery...For fans of Mrs. Murphy and her pals, both two- and four-legged, *Cat on the Scent* smells like a winner." —*The Virginian-Pilot*

"Charming." —*People*

Pay Dirt

Or, Adventures at Ash Lawn

RITA MAE BROWN

& SNEAKY PIE BROWN

ILLUSTRATIONS BY WENDY WRAY

BANTAM BOOKS   NEW YORK · TORONTO · LONDON · SYDNEY · AUCKLAND

PAY DIRT
A Bantam Book

PUBLISHING HISTORY
Bantam hardcover edition published December 1995
Bantam mass market edition / November 1996
Bantam mass market reissue / April 2004

Published by
Bantam Dell
A Division of Random House, Inc.
New York, New York

This is a work of fiction. Names, characters, places, and incidents either are the product of the author's imagination or are used fictitiously. Any resemblance to actual persons, living or dead, events, or locales is entirely coincidental.

Library of Congress Catalog Card Number: 95-20021
No part of this book may be reproduced or transmitted in any form or by any means, electronic or mechanical, including photocopying, recording, or by any information storage and retrieval system, without the written permission of the publisher, except where permitted by law.
For information address: Bantam Books, New York, New York.

ISBN 0-553-57236-9

Manufactured in the United States of America
Published simultaneously in Canada

OPM   20 19 18 17 16 15 14

Dedicated to Joan Hamilton & Larry Hodge
and all my horse pals at Kalarama Farm

Cast of Characters

Mary Minor Haristeen (Harry), the young postmistress of Crozet, whose curiosity almost kills the cat and herself

Mrs. Murphy, Harry's gray tiger cat, who bears an uncanny resemblance to authoress Sneaky Pie and who is wonderfully intelligent!

Tee Tucker, Harry's Welsh corgi, Mrs. Murphy's friend and confidante; a buoyant soul

Pharamond Haristeen (Fair), veterinarian, formerly married to Harry

Mrs. George Hogendobber (Miranda), a widow who thumps her own Bible!

Market Shiflett, owner of Shiflett's Market, next to the post office

Pewter, Market's fat gray cat, who, when need be, can be pulled away from the food bowl

Susan Tucker, Harry's best friend, who doesn't take life too seriously until her neighbors get murdered

Big Marilyn Sanburne (Mim), queen of Crozet

Rick Shaw, Albemarle sheriff

Cynthia Cooper, police officer

Paddy, Mrs. Murphy's ex-husband, a saucy tom

Simon, an opossum with a low opinion of humanity

Herbert C. Jones, Pastor of Crozet Lutheran Church, a kindly, ecumenical soul who has been known to share his sermons with his two cats, Lucy Fur and Elocution

Hogan Freely, President of Crozet National Bank, a good banker but not good enough

Laura Freely, a leading guide at Ash Lawn, she is Hogan's wife

Norman Cramer, a respected executive at Crozet National Bank, whose marriage to Aysha Gill set Crozet's gossip mill churning

Aysha Gill Cramer, a newlywed, who watches over her husband like a hawk

Kerry McCray, Norman Cramer's still-flickering old flame, who is beginning to smolder

Ottoline Gill, Aysha's mother, who keeps an eye out for social improprieties—and an eye on her new son-in-law

Introduction

While researching Virginia's historical shrines for my mysteries, I've learned even more about human history but nil about ours.

One of you nonfiction pussycats reading this ought to write the animal history of America. All life-forms are important, but it's hard to get enthusiastic about fish, isn't it—unless you're eating one.

Do pay attention to the fact that humans had to create government because they can't get along with one another. Cats don't need Congress. There's enough danger in life without listening to a gathering of paid windbags. From time to time you might remind your human that he or she is not the crown of creation s/he thinks s/he is.

Ta-ta

SNEAKY PIE

Pay Dirt

Cozy was the word used most often to describe the small town of Crozet, not *quaint, historic,* or *pretty.* Central Virginia in general, and Albemarle County in particular, abounded in quaint, historic, and pretty places, but Crozet was not one of them. A homey energy blanketed the community. Many families had lived there for generations, others were newcomers attracted to the sensuous appeal of the Blue Ridge Mountains. Old or new, rich or poor, black or white, the citizens of the town nodded and waved to one another while driving their cars, called and waved if on opposite sides of the street, and anyone walking along the side of the road was sure to get the offer of a ride. Backyard hedges provided the ideal setting for enriching gossip as gardeners took respite from their labors. Who did what to whom, who said what to whom, who owed money to whom, and, that glory of chat, who slept with whom. The buzz never stopped. Even in the deepest snows, a Crozetian would pick up the phone to transmit the latest. If it was really juicy, he or she would bundle up and hurry through the snow for a hot cup of coffee, that companion to steamy gossip shared with a friend.

The hub of the town consisted of its post office, the three main churches—Lutheran, Baptist, Episcopal, and one small offshoot, the Church of the Holy Light—the schools—kindergarten through twelfth—Market Shiflett's small grocery store, and Crozet Pizza. Since a person worshiped at one church at a time, the goings-on in the other three might remain a mystery. The small market provided a handsome opportunity to catch up, but you really had to buy something. Also, one had to be careful that Market's fat gray cat, Pewter, didn't steal your food before you had the chance to eat it. Schools were a good source, too, but if you were childless or if your darlings were finally in college, you were out of that pipeline. This left the post office the dubious honor of being the premier meeting place, or Gossip Central.

The postmistress—a title which she preferred to the official one of postmaster—Mary Minor Haristeen rarely indulged in what she termed gossip, which is to say if she couldn't substantiate a story, she didn't repeat it. Otherwise, she was only too happy to pass on the news. Her unofficial assistant, Mrs. Miranda Hogendobber, the widow of the former postmaster, relished the "news," but she drew the line at character assassination. If people started dumping all over someone else, Mrs. Hogendobber usually calmed them down or plain shut them up.

Harry, as Mary Minor was affectionately known, performed her tasks wonderfully well. Quite young for her position, Harry benefited from Miranda's wisdom. But Harry's most valuable assistants were Mrs. Murphy, her tiger cat, and Tee Tucker, her Welsh corgi. They wallowed in gossip. Not only did the goings-on of the humans transfix them, but so did the shenanigans of the animal community, reported by any dog accompanying its master into the post office. Whatever the dogs missed, Pewter found out next door. When she had something to tell, the round gray cat would run to the back door of the post office to spill it. Over the last few years, the cats had banged on the door so much, creating such a racket, that Harry installed a pet door so the friends could come and go as they pleased. Harry had designed a cover she could lock down over the animals' entrance, since the post office had to be secured each night.

Not that there was much to steal from the Crozet post office—stamps, a few dollars. But Harry diligently obeyed the rules, as she was a federal employee—a fact that endlessly amused her. She loathed the federal government and barely tolerated the state government, considering it the refuge of the mediocre. Still, she drew a paycheck from that bloated government on the north side of the Potomac, so she tried to temper her opinions.

Miranda Hogendobber, on the other hand, vividly remembered Franklin Delano Roosevelt, so her perception of government remained far more positive than Harry's. Just because Miranda remembered FDR did not mean, however, that she would reveal her age.

On this late July day the mimosas were crowned with the pink and gold halos of their fragile blossoms. The crepe myrtle and hydrangeas rioted throughout the town, splashes of purple and magenta here, white there. Not much else bloomed in the swelter of the Dog Days, which began on July 3 and finished August 15, so the color was appreciated.

So far, less than two inches of rain had fallen that month. The viburnums drooped. Even the hardy dogwoods began to curl up, so Mrs. Hogendobber would sprinkle the plants early in the morning and late in the evening to avoid losing too much moisture to evaporation. Her garden, the envy of the town, bore testimony to her vigilance.

The mail sorted, the two women paused for their morning tea break. Well, tea for Harry, coffee for Miranda. Mrs. Murphy sat on the newspaper. Tucker slept under the table at the back of the office.

"Is this a honey day or a sugar day, Mrs. H.?" Harry asked as the kettle boiled.

"A honey day." Miranda smiled. "I'm feeling naturally sweet."

Harry rolled her eyes and twirled a big glob of honey off the stick in the brown crockery honey pot. She then removed the teabag from her own drink, wrapping the string around it on the spoon to squeeze the last drops of strong tea into her cup. Her mug had a horse's tail for a handle, the rest of the cup representing the horse's body and head. Miranda's mug was white with block letters that read WHAT PART OF NO DON'T YOU UNDERSTAND?

"Mrs. Murphy, I'd like to read the paper." Miranda gently lifted the tiger cat's bottom and slid the paper out from underneath.

This action was met with a furious grumble, ears swept back. *"I don't stick my paws on your rear end, Miranda, besides which there's never anything in the paper worth reading."* She thumped over to the little back door and walked outside.

"In a mood." Miranda sat down and looked over the front page.

"What's the headline?" Harry asked.

"Two people injured on I-64. What else? Oh, this Thread-needle virus threatens to affect our computers August first. I would be perfectly happy if our new computer were fatally ill."

"Oh, now, it's not that bad." Harry reached for the sports page.

"Bad?" Mrs. Hogendobber pushed her glasses up her nose. "If I do one little thing out of sequence, a rude message appears on that hateful green screen and I have to start all over. There are so many buttons to punch. Modern improvements—time wasters, that's what they are, time wasters masquerading as time savers. I can remember more in my noggin than a computer chip can. And tell me, why do we need one in the post office? All we need is a good scale and a good meter. I can stamp the letters myself!"

Seeing that Miranda was in one of her Luddite moods, Harry decided not to argue. "Not everyone who works in the postal service is as smart as you are. They can't remember as much. For them the computer is a godsend." Harry craned her neck to see the photo of the car wreck.

"What a nice thing to say." Mrs. Hogendobber drank her coffee. "Wonder where Reverend Jones is? He's usually here by now. Everyone else has been on time."

"A thousand years is as a day in the eyes of the Lord. An hour is as a minute to the rev."

"Careful now." Miranda, a devout believer although those beliefs could occasionally be modified to suit circumstances, wagged her finger. "You know, at the Church of the Holy Light we don't make jokes about the Scripture." Miranda belonged to a small church. Truthfully, they were renegades from the Baptist church. Twenty years ago a new minister had arrived who set many parishioners' teeth on edge. After much fussing and fuming, the discontents, in time-honored tradition, broke away and formed their own church. Mrs. Hogendobber, the stalwart of the choir, had been a guiding force in the secession. When the offending minister packed his bags and left some six years after the rebellion, the members of the Church of the Holy Light were so enjoying themselves that they declined to return to the fold.

A tiny rumble at the back door announced that a pussycat was entering. Mrs. Murphy rejoined the group. A louder rumble indicated that Pewter was in tow.

"Hello," Pewter called.

"Hello there, kitty." Mrs. Hogendobber answered the meow. When Harry first took over Mr. Hogendobber's job and brought the cat and dog along with her, Miranda railed against the animals. The animals slowly won her over, although if you asked Miranda how she felt about people who talk to animals, she would declare that she herself never talked to animals. The fact that Harry was a daily witness to her conversations would not have altered her declaration one whit.

"Tucker, Pewter's here," Mrs. Murphy said.

Tucker opened one eye then shut it again.

"Guess I won't tell her the latest." Pewter languidly licked a paw.

Both eyes opened and the little dog raised her pretty head. *"Huh?"*

"I'm not talking to you. You can't be bothered to greet me when I come to visit."

"Pewter, you spend half your life in here. I can't act as though it's the first time I've seen you in months," Tucker explained.

Pewter flicked her tail, then leapt on the table. *"Anything to eat?"*

"Pig." Mrs. Murphy laughed.

"What's the worst they can say if you ask? No, that's what," Pewter said. *"Then again, they might say yes. Mrs. Hogendobber must have something. She can't walk into the post office empty-handed."*

The cat knew her neighbor well because Mrs. Hogendobber had whipped up a batch of glazed doughnuts. As soon as her paws hit the table, Harry reached over to cover the goodies with a napkin, but too late. Pewter had spied her quarry. She snagged a piece of doughnut, which came apart in marvelous moist freshness. The cat soared off the table and onto the floor with her prize.

"That cat will die of heart failure. Her cholesterol level must be over the moon." Mrs. Hogendobber raised an eyebrow.

"Do cats have cholesterol?" Harry wondered out loud.

"I don't see why not. Fat is fat. . . ."

On that note the Reverend Herbert Jones strode through the door. "Fat? Are you making fun of me?"

"No, we've been talking about Pewter."

"Relatively speaking, she's bigger than I am," he observed.

"But you've kept on your diet and you've been swimming. I think you've lost a lot of weight," Harry complimented him.

"Really? Does it show?"

"It does. Come on back here and have some tea." Mrs. Hogendobber invited him back, carefully covering up the doughnuts again.

The good reverend cleaned out his postbox, then swung through the Dutch counter door that divided the public lobby from the back. "This computer virus has everyone's knickers in a twist. On the morning news out of Richmond they did a whole segment on what to expect and how to combat it."

"Tell us." Harry stood over the little hot plate.

"No. I want our computer to die."

"Miranda, I don't think your computer is in danger. This seems to be some sort of corporate sabotage." Reverend Jones pulled up a ladderback chair. "The way I understand it, some person or persons has introduced this virus into the computer bank of a huge Virginia corporation, but no one knows which one. The diseased machine has to be a computer that interfaces with many other computers."

"And what may I ask is interface? *In* your face?" Miranda's tone dropped.

"Talk. Computers can talk to each other." Herb leaned forward in his chair. "Thank you, honey." He called Harry "honey" as she handed him his coffee. She never minded when it came from him. "Whoever has introduced this virus—"

Miranda interrupted again. "What do you mean, virus?"

The reverend, a genial man who loved people, paused a moment and sighed. "Because of the way in which a computer understands commands, it is possible, easy, in fact, to give one a command that scrambles or erases its memory."

"I don't need a virus for that," Miranda said. "I do it every day."

"So someone could put a command into a computer that says something like, 'Delete every file beginning with the letter *A*.'" Harry joined in.

"Precisely, but just what the command is, no one knows. Imagine if this is passing throughout the state in a medical data bank. What if the command is 'Destroy all records on anyone named John Smith.' You can see the potential."

"But, Herbie"—Miranda called him by his first name, as they had been friends since childhood—"why would anyone want to do such a thing?"

"Maybe to wipe out a criminal record or cancel a debt or cover up a sickness that could cost them their job. Some companies will fire employees with AIDS or cancer."

"How can people protect themselves?" Mrs. Hogendobber began to grasp the possibilities for mischief.

"The mastermind has sent faxes to television stations saying that the virus will go into effect August first, and that it's called the Threadneedle virus."

"Threadneedle is such an odd name. I wonder what's the connection?" Harry rubbed her chin.

"Oh, there will be a connection, all right. The newspeople are researching like mad on that," he confidently predicted.

"One big puzzle." Harry liked puzzles.

"The computer expert on the morning show said that one way to protect your information base is to tell your computer to disregard any command it is given on August first."

"Sensible." Miranda nodded her head.

"Except that most business is transacted by computer, so that means for one entire day all commercial, medical, even police transactions are down."

"Oh, dear." Miranda's eyes grew large. "Is there nothing else that can be done?"

Herbie finished his tea, setting the mug on the table with a light tap. "This expert reviewed the defenses and encouraged people to program their computers to hold and review any commands that come in on August first. If anything is peculiar, your review program can instruct the computer to void the suspicious command. Naturally, big companies will use their own computer experts, but it sounds as though whatever they come up with will be some variant of the review process."

"I always wanted to put VOID on my license plate," Harry confessed.

"Now, why would you want to do a thing like that?" Mrs. Hogendobber pursed her lips, seashell pink today.

"Because every time my annual renewal payments would go through to the Department of Motor Vehicles, their computer would spit out the check. At least, that's what I thought."

"Our own little saboteur."

"Miranda, I never did it. I just thought about it."

"From little acorns mighty oaks do grow." Mrs. Hogendobber appeared fierce. "Are you behind this?"

The three laughed.

"You know, when I was a young doctor I had a big Thoroughbred I used to hunt named On Call," Herb reminisced. "When someone phoned my office the nurse would say, 'Oh, I'm sorry, the doctor isn't in right now. He's On Call.'"

Harry and Miranda laughed all the more.

"So what's the scoop, Pewter?" Tucker asked, then turned her attention to Mrs. Murphy. *"I suppose you already know or you'd have pulled her fur out."*

With that faint hint of superiority that makes cats so maddening, the tiger twitched her whiskers forward. *"We had a little chat on the back stoop."*

"Come on, tell me."

Pewter sidled over to the dog, who was now sitting up. *"Aysha Cramer refused, to Mim Sanburne's face, to work with Kerry McCray for the homeless benefit."*

Mim Sanburne considered herself queen of Crozet. On her expansive days she extended that dominion to cover the state of Virginia.

"Big deal." Tucker was disappointed.

"It is. No one crosses Mim. She pitched a hissy and told Aysha that the good of the community was more important than her spat with Kerry," the rotund kitty announced.

"Oh, Aysha." Tucker laughed. *"Now Mim will give her the worst job of the benefit—addressing, sealing, and stamping the envelopes. They all have to be handwritten, you know."*

"And all this over Norman Cramer. Mr. Bland." Pewter giggled.

The animals caught their breath for a moment.

"Boy, it's a dull summer if we're laughing about that tired love triangle," Mrs. Murphy said wistfully.

"Nothing happens around here," Tucker carped.

"Fourth of July parade was okay. But nothing unusual. Maybe

someone will stir up a fuss over Labor Day . . ." Pewter's voice trailed off. "*We can hope for a little action.*"

Mrs. Murphy stretched forward, then backward. "*You know what my mother used to say, 'Be careful what you ask for, you might get it.'*"

The three friends later would remember this prophecy.

2

Ash Lawn, the Federal home of James and Elizabeth Monroe, reposes behind a mighty row of English boxwoods. When the fifth president and his lady were alive, these pungent shrubs probably rose no higher than waist level. The immense height of them now casts an eerie aura yet lends an oddly secure sense to the entrance. The formal entrance isn't used anymore; people must pass the small gift shop and arrive at the house by a side route.

The warm yellow clapboard creates an accessibility, a familiarity—one could imagine living in this house. No one could ever imagine living in the beautiful and imposing Monticello just over the small mountain from Ash Lawn.

Harry walked among the boxwoods and around the grounds with Blair Bainbridge, her new neighbor—"new" being a relative term in Crozet; Blair had moved there more than a year ago. A much-sought-after model, he was out of Crozet as much as he was in it. Recently returned from Africa, he had asked Harry to give him a tour of Monroe's home. This irritated Harry's ex-husband, Fair Haristeen, D.V.M., a blond giant who, having repented of his foolishness in losing Harry, desperately wanted his ex-wife back.

As for Blair, no one could divine his intentions toward Harry. Mrs. Hogendobber, that self-confessed expert on the male animal, declared that Blair was so impossibly rugged and handsome that he had women throwing themselves at him every moment, on every continent. She swore Harry fascinated him because she seemed immune to his masculine beauty. Mrs. Hogendobber got it more than half right despite arguments to the contrary from Harry's best friend and her corgi's breeder, Susan Tucker.

Mrs. Murphy chose the shade of a mighty poplar, where she scratched up some grass, then plopped down. Tucker circled three times, then sat next to her as she eyed the offending peacocks of Ash Lawn. The shimmering birds overran the Monroe estate, their heavenly appearance marred by grotesquely ugly pinkish feet. They also possessed the nastiest voices of birddom.

"Oh, how I'd like to wrestle that big showoff to the ground," Tucker growled as a huge male strutted by, cast the little dog a death-ray eye, and then strutted on.

"Probably tough as an old shoe." Mrs. Murphy occasionally enjoyed a wren as a delicacy, but she shied off the larger birds. She prudently flattened herself whenever she perceived a large shadow overhead. This was based on experience because a redtailed hawk had carried off one of her tiny brothers.

"I don't know why President Monroe kept these birds. Sheep, cattle, even turkeys—I can understand turkeys—but peacocks are useless." Tucker jumped up and whirled around to bite something in her fur.

"Fleas? It's the season." Mrs. Murphy noticed sympathetically.

"No." Tucker grumbled as she bit some more. *"Deer flies."*

"How can they get through your thick fur?"

"I don't know, but they do." Tucker sighed, then stood up and shook herself. *"Where's Mom?"*

"Out and about. She's not far. Sit down, will you. If you go off and

chase one of those stupid birds, I'll get blamed for it. I don't see why we can't go into the house. I understand why other people's animals can't visit, like Lucy Fur, but not us." The younger of Reverend Jones's two cats, Lucy Fur, was aptly named as she was a hellion.

"Bet Little Marilyn would let us through the back door." Tucker winked. She knew Mim Sanburne's daughter loved animals.

"Good idea." The cat rolled in the grass and then bounded up. *"Let's boogie."*

"Where'd you hear that?" Tucker asked as they trotted to the side door. A bench under a small porch made the area inviting. No humans were around.

"Susan said it yesterday. She picks up that stuff from her kids. Like 'ABC ya' for when you say good-bye."

"Oh." Tucker found the semantics of the young of limited interest, since every few years the jargon changed.

Underneath Ash Lawn's main level, docents dressed in period costumes spun, wove, boiled lard for candles, and cooked in the kitchen. Little Marilyn—Marilyn Sanburne, Junior, recently divorced and taking back her maiden name—was the chief docent at Ash Lawn this day. Although only in her early thirties, the younger Marilyn had contributed a great deal financially to Ash Lawn as well as to the College of William and Mary. The college maintained the house and grounds of James Monroe and provided most docents. Little Marilyn was a proud alumna of William and Mary, where she had switched majors so many times, her advisers despaired of her ever graduating. She finally settled on sociology, which greatly displeased her mother, and therefore greatly pleased Little Marilyn.

As Harry had graduated from Smith College in Massachusetts, she was not one of the inner circle at Ash Lawn, but the staff was good at community relations, so Harry and her animals felt welcome there. Of course, everyone at Ash Lawn knew Mrs. Murphy and Tucker.

The other docents that July 30 were Kerry McCray, a pert strawberry-blonde and Little Marilyn's college roommate; Laura

Freely, a tall, austere lady in her sixties; and Aysha Gill Cramer, also a friend of Little Marilyn's from William and Mary. As Aysha had been married only the previous April, in a gruesome social extravaganza, it was taking everyone a bit of time to get used to calling her Cramer. Danny Tucker, Susan's sixteen-year-old son, was working as a gardener and loving it. Susan was filling in at the gift shop because the regular cashier had called in sick.

A scheduling snafu had stuck Aysha and Kerry there at the same time. The two despised each other. Along with Little Marilyn, the three had been best friends from childhood all the way through William and Mary, where they pledged the same sorority.

After graduation they traveled to Europe together, finally going their separate ways after a year's time. They wrote volumes of letters to each other. Kerry returned to Crozet first, getting a job at the Crozet National Bank, which had started locally at the turn of the century but now served all of central Virginia. Little Mim followed soon after, married badly, and then divorced. Aysha had returned to Albemarle County only six months ago. Her impeccable French and Italian were not in demand. Career prospects were so limited in this small corner of the world that marriage was still a true career for young women, providing they could find a suitable victim.

The friends picked up where they had left off. Aysha, a bit chubby when she was younger, had matured into a good-looking woman bubbling with ideas.

Little Marilyn, recovering from her divorce, was still blue. She needed her friends.

Kerry, engaged to Norman Cramer, often invited Aysha and Little Marilyn out with them for dinner, the movies, a late night at the Blue Ridge Brewery.

Weedy and timid, Norman possessed a handsome face framing big blue eyes. He, too, worked at the Crozet National Bank as the head accountant. Excitement was not Norman's middle name, so everyone was knocked for a loop when Aysha snaked him away from Kerry. No one could figure out why she wanted him except that she was in her thirties, disliked working, and marriage was an easy way out.

Her mother, Ottoline Gill, far too involved in her daughter's life, seemed thrilled with her new son-in-law. Part of that may have been shock from ever having a son-in-law. She had despaired of Aysha's future, declaring many times over that a girl as beautiful and brilliant as her darling would never find a husband. "Men like dumb women," she would say, "and my Aysha won't play dumb."

Whatever she played or didn't play, she captivated Norman with the result that Aysha and Kerry were now bitter enemies who could barely speak to each other in a civil tone of voice. Norman, away from Aysha's scrutiny, would be pleasant to Kerry, although she wasn't always pleasant back.

Marilyn sent Aysha to work downstairs, packing Kerry out to the slave quarters. It eased the tension somewhat. She knew each one would seek her out in the next day to complain about the mix-up. Kerry would be easier to console than Aysha, who liked nothing better than to have someone at an emotional disadvantage. However, Aysha enjoyed being a docent for Ash Lawn and Marilyn would mollify her, for her sake as well as the good of the place. Bad enough to have Aysha fuss at her, but coping with that harridan of a mother was real hell. And if Ottoline picked up the cudgel, then Marilyn's own mother, Mim, would become involved, too, if for no other reason than to put the pretentious Ottoline in her place.

Mrs. Murphy, tail to the vertical, felt the cool grass under her paws. Grasshoppers shot off before her like green insect rockets. They'd jump, settle, then jump again. Usually she would chase them, but today she wanted to get inside the historic home just to prove she wouldn't be destructive.

As the day drew to a close, most of the tourists had left. A few lingered in the gift shop. The staff of Ash Lawn began closing up. Harry and Blair had entered the house to see if Marilyn needed any help.

A distant roar grew louder. Then a screech, burp, and cutoff announced that a motorcycle had pulled into the parking lot, not just any motorcycle, but a gleaming, perfect black Harley-Davidson. The biker was as disheveled as his machine was gorgeous. He wore a black German World War II helmet, a black leather vest studded with chrome stars, torn jeans, heavy black biker boots, and an impressive chain across his chest like a medieval Sam Browne belt. Wraparound black sunglasses completed the outfit. He was unshaven but handsome in a grungy fashion.

He sauntered up the brick path leading to the front door. Tucker, now on the side of the house by the slave quarters, stopped and began barking at him. Both animals had left the side door to see what was going on.

"Shut up, Tucker, you'll spoil my strategy," the cat warned. She was lying flat by the public entrance just waiting for it to swing open when the visitor entered so she could dart in. Whoever opened the door would let out a yelp as she zipped between their legs. Then they'd have to chase her or cajole her. Harry would have a fit and fall in it. Someone would think to bribe her with food or perhaps fresh catnip from the herb garden. Mrs. Murphy had it all planned. Then she glanced up and saw the Hell's Angel marching toward the door. She decided to stay put.

He opened the door and Little Marilyn greeted him. "Welcome to the home of James and Elizabeth Monroe. Unfortunately our hours are ten to five during the summer and it's five-thirty now. I'm terribly sorry, but you'll have to come back tomorrow."

"I'm not going anywhere." He brushed right by her.

Laura heard this exchange from the parlor and joined Marilyn. Harry and Blair remained in the living room. Aysha was downstairs in the summer kitchen and Kerry was closing up the slave quarters.

"You'll have to leave." Little Marilyn pursed her lips.

"Where's Malibu?" His guttural voice added to his visual menace.

"In California." Blair strode into the front hall.

The biker sized him up and down. Blair was a tall man, broad-shouldered, and in splendid condition. This was no push-over.

"You the resident comedian?" The biker reached into his vest and pulled out a little switchblade. He expertly flipped it open with one hand and began to pick his teeth.

"I am for today." Blair folded his arms across his chest. Harry, too, stepped into the hall behind Blair. "These ladies have informed you that Ash Lawn will be open tomorrow morning. Come back then."

"I don't give a frig about this pile. I want Malibu. I know she's here."

"Who's Malibu?" Harry wedged forward. It occurred to her that the biker's pupils were most likely dilated or the reverse, and he wore sunglasses to cover that fact. He was on something and it wasn't aspirin.

"A thieving slut!" the biker exploded. "I've tracked her down and I know she's here."

"She couldn't possibly be here," Marilyn replied. "All of us who work here know one another and we've never heard of a Malibu."

"Lady, you just never heard the name. She's cunning. She'll hypnotize you, take what she wants, and then strike like a snake!" He pointed his two front fingers at her like fangs and made a striking motion.

Out of the corner of her eye Harry saw Aysha enter through the back door. She could see Kerry out back also on her way to the main house. The biker didn't see them. Harry backtracked, her hands behind her, holding them up in a stop signal. Blair by now had his hand on the biker's shoulder and was gently turning him around toward the front door.

"Come on. You won't find her today. Half the staff's already gone home." Blair's voice oozed reassurance. "I know what you mean, some women are like cobras."

The two men walked outside. Mrs. Murphy stared up at them. The biker smelled like cocaine sweat and grease. She put great store by smell.

The gruff man's voice quivered a touch. "This one, man, this one, oh, you don't know the things she can do to you. She plays with your body and messes with your mind. The only thing she ever really loved was the dollar."

Blair realized he would have to walk this fellow with the stoned expression all the way to his bike because he wasn't budging off the front porch. "Show me your bike."

Mrs. Murphy darted from bush to bush, keeping the men in sight and hearing every word. Tucker dashed ahead of her.

"Tucker, stay behind them."

"You're always telling me what to do!"

"Because you act first and think later. Stay behind. That way if Blair needs help this guy won't know you're there. The element of surprise."

"Well—" The dog realized the cat had a point.

"She wanted to make enough money to sit home, to be a lady." He laughed derisively. "I thought she was joking. A *lady?*"

Blair arrived at the sleek machine, resting on its kickstand. "Bet she hums."

"Yeah, power to burn."

Blair ran his hand over the gas tank. "Had a Triumph Bonneville once. Leaked oil, but she could sing, you know?"

"Good bike." The fellow's lower lip protruded, a sign of agreement, approval.

"Started out with a Norton. How 'bout you?"

"Liked those English bikes, huh?" He leaned against the motorcycle. "Harleys. Always Harleys with me. Started out with a 1960 Hog, 750cc, in pieces. Put her back together. Then I put together a Ducati for a buddy of mine, and before I knew it, I had more work than I could handle."

"BMWs?"

The biker shook his head. "Not for me. Great machines but no soul. And that piston instead of a chain drive—you shift gears on one of those things and it's a lurch. Kill your crotch." He laughed, revealing strong, straight teeth. " 'Course there's no more chains, you know. They use Kevlar." He pointed to the space-age material that had replaced the chain.

"My dad had an Indian." Blair's eyes glazed. "What I wouldn't give for that bike today."

"An Indian. No shit. Hey, man, let me buy you a beer. We've got some serious talking to do."

"Thanks, but my date is waiting for me back at the house. Take a raincheck though." Blair inclined his head back toward Ash Lawn, where Harry stood at the end of the entrance walk. She wanted to make sure Blair was okay.

"I'm staying at the Best Western."

"Okay, thanks." Blair smiled.

"I'm not going anywhere until I find that bitch."

"You seem determined. I'm sure you will."

The biker tapped his head with his fist. "Box of rocks, man, box of rocks, but I never give up. Until then, buddy." He hopped on his machine, turned the key, a velvet purr filling the air. Then he slowly rolled down the driveway.

Mrs. Murphy watched him recede. *"Motorcycles were invented to thin out the male herd."*

Tucker laughed as they fell in with Blair.

"What were you doing out there?" Harry asked as the other women came out of the house and crowded around Blair.

"Talking about motorcycles."

"With that certain?" Marilyn was incredulous.

"Oh, he's not so bad. He's searching for his girlfriend and he's staying at the Best Western until he finds her. I might even have a beer with the guy. He's kind of interesting."

Both Kerry and Aysha had been informed of the search for Malibu.

Laura said, "You're not afraid of him?"

"No. He's harmless. Just a little loaded, that's all."

"Long as you're not Malibu, maybe he is harmless." Harry laughed.

"Can you imagine anyone named Malibu?" Aysha's frosty tone was drenched in social superiority.

"Think my life would improve if I rechristened myself Chattanooga?" Kerry joked for the others' benefit. She wanted to smash in Aysha's face.

"Intercourse. Change your name to Intercourse and you'll see some sizzle." Harry giggled.

"Ah, yes." Laura Freeley's patrician voice, its perfect cadence, added weight to her every utterance. "If I recall my Pennsylvania geography, Intercourse isn't far from Blue Ball."

"Ladies"—Blair bowed his head—"how you talk."

3

The John Deere dealership, a low brick building on Route 250, parked its new tractors by the roadside. These green and yellow enticements made Harry's mouth water. Probably a thousand motorists passed the tractors each day on their way into Charlottesville. The county was filling with new people, service people who bought enormous houses squeezed on five acres—riding mowers were their speed. They probably didn't lust after these machines sitting in a neat row. But country people, they'd drive by at dusk, stop the car, and walk around the latest equipment.

Harry's tractor, a 1958 John Deere 420S row crop tractor, hauled a manure spreader, pulled a small bushhog, and felt like a friend. Her father had bought the tractor new and lovingly cared for it. Harry's service manual, a big book, was filled with his notations now crowded by her own. The smaller operator's manual, ragged and thumbed, was protected in a plastic cover.

Johnny Pop, as Doug Minor dubbed his machine, still popped

and chugged. Last year Harry bought a new set of rear tires. The originals had finally succumbed. Given this proven reliability, Harry wanted another John Deere, the Rolls-Royce of tractors. Not that she planned to retire Johnny Pop, but a tractor in the seventy-five-horsepower range with a front end loader and special weights for the rear wheels could accomplish many of the larger, more difficult tasks on her farm that were beyond Johnny Pop's modest horsepower. The base price of what she needed ran about $29,000 sans attachments. Her heart sank each time she remembered the cost, quite impossible on a postmistress's wage.

Mrs. Murphy and Tucker waited in the cab of her truck, another item that needed replacing. The Superman blue had faded, the clutch had been repaired twice, and she'd worn through four sets of tires. However, the Ford rolled along. Most people would buy a new truck before a tractor, but Harry, being a farmer first, knew the tractor was far more important.

She strolled around the machines, not a speck of mud on them. Some had enclosed cabs with AC, which seemed sinful to her, although if you ran over a nest of digger bees, that enclosed cab would be a godsend. She liked to dream, climb up to touch the steering wheel, run her fingers along the engine block. That's why dusk appealed to her. It wasn't so much that she didn't want to talk to the salesmen. She'd known them for years, and they knew she hadn't a penny. She hated to waste their time since she wasn't a serious customer.

She opened the door of her truck; a tiny creak followed. She leaned onto the seat but didn't climb in right away.

"Well, kids, what do you think? Pretty fabulous?"

"They look the same as last time." Tucker was hungry.

"Beautiful, Mom, just beautiful." Mrs. Murphy would occasionally ride in Harry's lap when she drove Johnny Pop. *"I vote for the enclosed cab myself and you can put a woven basket with a towel in it for me. I believe in creature comforts."*

"Ah, well, let's go home." She climbed into the truck, cranked the motor, and pulled onto the highway, heading west.

In fifteen minutes she was at the outskirts of Crozet. She passed the old Del Monte food packaging plant and decided to pull into the supermarket.

"I want to go home." Tucker whined.

"If you want to eat, then I've got to get you food." Harry hopped out of the car.

Tucker inquisitively looked at the cat. *"Do you think she understood what I said?"*

"Nah." Mrs. Murphy shook her head. *"Coincidence."*

"I bet I could jump out the window."

"I bet I could, too, but I'm not running around this parking lot, not the way people drive." She put her paws on the window frame and surveyed the lot. *"Everyone must need dog food."*

Tucker joined her. *"Mim."*

"Bet it's her cook. That's the farm car. Mim wouldn't do anything as lowly as shop for her own food."

"Probably right. Well, there's the silver Saab, so we know Susan is here. . . ."

"Aysha's green BMW. Oh, hey, there's Mrs. Hogendobber's Falcon."

"And look who's pulling in—Fair. Um-um." Tucker's eyes twinkled.

Hurrying down the aisle with a basket on her arm, Harry first bumped into Susan.

"If you're not buying much, you could have gone to Shiflett's Market and saved yourself the checkout line."

"He closed early tonight. Dentist."

"Not another root canal?" Harry counted items in Susan's cart. "Are you having a party or something? I mean, a party without me?"

"No, nosy." Susan pushed Harry on the shoulder. "Danny and Brookie want to have a cookout. I said I'd buy the food if they did the work."

"Danny Tucker behind the barbecue?"

"Well, you see, he's got this new girlfriend who wants to be a chef, so he thinks if he shows an interest in food beyond eating it, he'll impress her. He's talked his sister into helping him."

"Talked or bribed?"

"Bribed." Susan's big smile was infectious. "He's promised to drive her and a friend to the Virginia Horse Center over in Lexington and then he'll look at Washington and Lee University, without Mom, of course."

Mrs. Hogendobber careened around the aisle, her cart on two wheels. "Gangway, girls, I'll miss choir practice."

The two women parted as Miranda roared through tossing items into her cart with considerable skill.

"Great hand-eye," Susan noted.

Nearly colliding with Mrs. Hogendobber, since she entered the aisle from the opposite end, was Aysha Cramer, with her mother, Ottoline. "Oh, Mrs. Hogendobber, I'm sorry."

"Beep! Beep!" Mrs. Hogendobber expertly maneuvered around her and was off.

Ottoline, wearing an off-the-shoulder peasant blouse that revealed her creamy skin and bosoms, plucked the list out of Aysha's cart. "If you're going to waste time talking, I'll work on this list."

Aysha shrugged as her mother continued on and turned the corner. She rolled her cart over to Harry and Susan. "We know she's not DWI."

Mrs. Hogendobber didn't drink.

"Choir practice," Susan said.

"I hope I have as much energy as she does at her age," Aysha said admiringly. "And just what is her age?"

"Mentally or physically?" Susan rocked her cart back and forth.

"Mother says she's got to be in her sixties, because she was in high school when mother was in eighth grade," Aysha volunteered.

Of course, Ottoline the raving bitch never said anything nice about anyone unless it reflected upon her own perceived glory, so Aysha's recounting was a bogus edition of Mrs. Gill's true thoughts.

As if on cue, Ottoline sashayed down the aisle in the opposite direction from which she had left. She dumped items in the cart, nodded curtly to Harry and Susan, only to continue down the aisle, calling over her shoulder, "Aysha, I'm pressed for time."

"Yes, Mumsy." Then she lowered her voice. "Had a fight with the decorator today. She's in a bad mood."

"I thought she'd just redecorated," Susan said.

"Two years ago. Time flies. She's into a neutral palette this time."

"Better than a cleft palate," Harry joked.

"Not funny," Aysha sniffed.

"Oh, come on, Aysha." Harry couldn't stand it when Aysha or anyone behaved like a humorless Puritan.

Apart from the occasional lapse into correctness, Harry thought Aysha had turned out okay except for her unfortunate belief that she was an aristocrat. It was a piteous illusion, since the Gills had migrated to Albemarle County immediately following World War I. To make matters worse, they had migrated from Connecticut. Despite her Yankee roots, Aysha flounced around like a Southern belle. Her new husband, not the brightest bulb on the Christmas tree when it came to women, bought it. He called her "lovegirl." God only knows what she called him. Newlyweds were pretty disgusting no matter who they were.

Susan asked, "Aysha, you've heard about this Threadneedle virus. Tomorrow's the big day. You worried?"

"Oh, heavens no." She laughed, her voice lilting upward before she lowered it. "But my Norman, he's been to meetings about it. The bank is really taking this seriously."

"No kidding." Harry grabbed a few more cans of dog food.

"You can imagine if accounts were mixed up, although Norman says he believes the real target is Federated Investments in Richmond and this whole thing is a cover to get everyone in an uproar while they, or whoever, strikes FI."

"Why FI?" Susan asked the logical question.

"They've been having such hard times. New chairman, shake-ups, and hundreds of people have been let go. Who better but an FI employee to devise a scheme with computers as the weapon? Norman says that by August 2 FI will be in a bigger tangle than a fishing line."

"Ladies!" Fair, framed by a sale sign for charcoal briquets, waved from the end of the aisle.

Aysha smiled at Fair, then looked at Harry to pick up telltale signs of emotion. Harry smiled, too, and waved back. She liked her ex.

"Well, I'd better push on, forgive the pun." Susan headed out. "Danny will be the youngest coronary victim in Crozet if I don't get back with this food."

"Me too."

"Harry, are you cooking?" Aysha couldn't believe it.

Harry pointed to her cart. "Tucker and Mrs. Murphy."

"Give them my best." Aysha moved in the other direction, her laughter tinkling as she went.

Ottoline, hands on hips, appeared at aisle's end. "Will you hurry up?"

Harry reached the end of the aisle, where Fair waited for her. He was pretending to buy charcoal at a discount.

"How you doin'?"

"Fine, what about you?"

"Seeing more shin splints than I can count. Too many trainers are overworking their young horses on this hard ground." Shin splints, or bucked shins, are a common problem among young racehorses.

Harry owned three horses, one of which, still a bit new to her, had been given to her by Fair and Mim. Lately, Mim had warmed to Harry. In fact, the haughty Mrs. Sanburne seemed to have softened considerably over the past couple of years.

"We're doing pretty good at home. Come on by and let's ride up Yellow Mountain."

"Okay." Fair eagerly accepted. "Tomorrow's a mess, but the day after? I'll swing by at six. Ought to have cooled off a little by then."

"Great. Who do you want to take out?"

"Gin Fizz."

"Okay." She started off knowing that the cat and dog would be crabby from waiting so long.

"Uh, heard you and Blair Bainbridge were up at Ash Lawn yesterday. I thought he was out of town." Fair prayed he would be going out of town again soon—like tomorrow.

"He finished up that shoot and instead of stopping by to see his folks, he came directly home. He's pretty tired, I think."

"How can you get tired wearing clothes and twirling in front of the camera?"

Harry refused to be drawn into this. "Damned if I know, Fair, no one's ever asked me to model." She wheeled away. "See you day after tomorrow."

4

"Get out the shovels," Harry called to Mrs. Hogendobber as she trooped through the back door just as Rob Collier, the mail delivery man, was leaving by the front door.

He ducked his head back in. "Morning, Mrs. H."

"Morning back at you, Rob." She beheld the mammoth bags of mail on the floor. "What in the world?"

"Heck of a way to start August."

As the big mail truck backed out of the driveway, the two women, transfixed by the amount of mail, just stared.

"Oh, hell, I'll get the mail cart and start on bag one."

"I'll be right back." Mrs. Hogendobber hurried out the door and returned in less than five minutes, enough time for Harry to upend the big canvas bag and enough time for Mrs. Murphy to crash full force into the pile, sending letters and magazines scattering. Then she rolled over and bit some envelopes while scratching others.

"Death to the bills!" the cat hollered. She spread all four paws on the slippery pile, looked to the right, then to the left, before springing forward with a mighty leap, sending mail squirting out from under her.

"Get a grip, Murph." Harry had to laugh at the tiger's merry show.

"Here's what I think of the power company." She seized a bill between her teeth and crunched hard. *"Take that. And this is for every lawyer in Crozet."* She pulled her right paw over a windowpane bill, leaving five parallel gashes.

Tucker joined the fun, but not being as agile as Mrs. Murphy, she could only run through the mail and shout, *"Look at me!"*

"All right, you two. This is the only post office in America where people get mail with teeth marks on it. Now, enough is enough."

Mrs. Hogendobber opened the back door just as Pewter was entering through the animal door. *"Hey, hey, wait a minute."*

Mrs. Murphy sat down in the mail debris and laughed as her fat friend swung toward her. Mrs. Hogendobber laughed too.

"Very funny." Pewter, incensed, wriggled out.

"Everyone's loony tunes this morning." Harry bent over to tidy the mess but thought the cat had the right idea. "What is that incredible smell?"

"Cinnamon buns. We need sustenance. Now, I was going to wait and bring these over for our break, but Harry, we'll be working through that." She checked the big old railroad clock on the wall. "And Mim will be here in an hour."

"Mim will have to come back." Harry threw letters in the mail cart and wheeled it to the back side of the mailboxes. "Unless you've got some scoop, turn on the radio." Harry winked as she snatched a hot cinnamon bun and started the sorting.

"I'm not listening to country and western this morning."

"And I don't want to be spiritually uplifted, Miranda."

"Don't fuss." Mrs. Hogendobber clicked on the dial.

The announcer bleated the news. "—an eight-million-dollar

loss for this quarter, the worst in FI's sixty-nine-year history. One thousand five hundred employees, twenty-five percent of the famed company's work force, have been let go—"

"Damn." Harry shot a postcard into Market Shiflett's box.

"I imagine those people being handed their pink slips are saying worse than that."

The news continued after a commercial break for the new Dodge Ram. The deep voice intoned, "Threadneedle, the feared computer virus, was already striking early this morning. Leggett's department store has reported some small problems, as has Albemarle Savings and Loan. The full extent of the scramble won't be known until the business day gets under way. But the early birds are reporting light trouble."

"You know, if some computer genius out there really wanted to perform a service for America, he or she would destroy the IRS."

"We are overtaxed, Harry, but you're becoming an anarchist." Miranda wiped a bit of vanilla icing that dripped off her lips, hot coral today to match her square hot coral earrings. Mrs. H. believed in dressing for success, fifties style.

"Ten percent across the board if you make over one hundred thousand and five percent if you make under. Anyone making less than twenty-five thousand a year shouldn't have to pay tax. If we can't run the country on that, then maybe we'd better restructure the country—like FI, we're becoming a dinosaur. . . . Too big to survive. We trip over our own big feet."

Mrs. Hogendobber flipped up another bag. "I don't know—but I do agree we're making a mess of things. Now, what's she doing here?" She saw Kerry McCray coming through the door.

"Hope you don't need your mail," Mrs. Hogendobber called out.

"I tore it up anyway." Mrs. Murphy licked her lips.

"Did you really?" Pewter was impressed.

"Sure, look at this." Mrs. Murphy pushed over an envelope bearing neat fang marks on the upper and lower corners.

"Bet it's a federal offense," the gray cat sagely noted.

"Hope so," Mrs. Murphy saucily replied.

"I'm not here for the mail," Kerry said. "Just wanted to tell you that the Light Opera series at Ash Lawn is doing *Don Giovanni* on Saturday and really, you've got to come. The lead has such a clear voice. I don't know music like you do, Mrs. Hogendobber, but he is good."

"Why, thank you for thinking of me, Kerry. I will try to swing by."

Harry stuck her head around the mailboxes. "So, Kerry, you been out with the lead singer yet?"

Kerry blushed. "I did show him the University of Virginia."

"You just keep being yourself, honey. He'll soon fall head over heels."

Kerry blushed again, then left, crossing the street to the bank.

"Where does the time go?" Harry shot envelopes into the boxes a bit faster.

"You're too young to worry about time. That's my job."

Harry snagged another cinnamon bun. Pewter had the same idea. "Hey, piggy. That's mine."

"Oh, give her a bite."

"Miranda, you were the person who didn't like cats. The one who thought they were spoiled and sneaky and, as I recall, speaking of time, this was not but two years ago."

Pewter, golden eyes glowing, trilled at Miranda's feet, open-toed wedgies today à la Joan Crawford. *"Oh, Mrs. Hogendobber, I looove you."*

"I'm gonna puke," Mrs. Murphy growled.

"Now this little darling wants the tiniest nibble." Mrs. Hogendobber pinched off some sweet, flaky dough liberally covered with vanilla icing. The cinnamon scent flooded the room as the bun was broken open. "Here, Pewter. What about you, Mrs. Murphy?"

"I'm a carnivore," Mrs. Murphy declined. *"But thank you."*

"I'll eat anything." Tailless Tucker wagged her rear end furiously.

Mrs. Hogendobber held a bit aloft, and Tucker stood on her hind feet, not easy for a corgi. She gobbled her reward.

The rest of the day held the usual round of comings and goings, everyone expressed an opinion on the Threadneedle virus, which like so many things reported on television was a fizzle. People also expressed opinions on whether or not BoomBoom Craycroft, the sultry siren of Crozet, would set her cap again for Blair Bainbridge now that he had returned from Africa and she from Montana.

At five to five Mrs. Sanburne reappeared. She'd stopped by at eight-thirty A.M., her usual. Post offices close at five, but this was Crozet, and if anyone needed something, either Harry or Mrs. Hogendobber would stay late.

"Girls," Mim's imperious voice rang out, "Crozet National Bank was infected with the virus."

"Our little bank?" Harry couldn't believe it.

"I ran into Norman Cramer, and he said the darned thing kept inserting information from other companies, feed store companies. Dumb stuff, but they immediately countered with the void commands and wiped it out quickly."

"He's a smart one, that Norman," Mrs. Hogendobber said.

"Sure fell hook, line, and sinker for Aysha. How smart can he be?" Harry giggled.

"I've never seen a woman *work so hard* to land a man. You'd have thought he was a whale instead of a"—she thought for a minute—"small-mouthed bass."

"Three points, Mrs. Sanburne," Harry whooped.

"My favorite moment was when I played through on the eleventh at Farmington. Aysha, who never so much as looked at a golf club in her life, was caddying for Norman and his golf partner, that good-looking accountant fellow, David Wheeler. Anyway, there she was at the water fountain. She put the golf balls in the fountain. I said, 'Aysha, what are you doing?' and she replied, 'Oh, washing Norman's balls. They get so grass stained.'"

With that the three women nearly doubled over.

Pewter lifted her head as she lay on the back table. Mrs. Murphy was curled next to her, but her eyes were open.

"What do you think of Norman Cramer?"

Mrs. Murphy shot back, *"A twerp."*

"Then why was Aysha so hot to have him?" Tucker, on the floor, asked.

"Good family. Aysha wants to be the queen of White Hall Road by the time she's forty."

"Better make it fifty, Murphy, she's got to be in her middle thirties now." Pewter touched the tiger with her hind paw. Murphy pushed her back.

"Have you seen *Don Giovanni* yet?" Mrs. Hogendobber inquired of Mim. "I was thinking about going tomorrow, Friday."

"Loved it! Little Marilyn can't stand opera, but she did endure. Jim fell asleep, of course. When I woke him he said his duties as mayor of our fair town had worn him out. The only event Jim Sanburne doesn't sleep through that involves music is the Marine Corps band. The piccolo always jolts him awake. Well, I've got a bridge party tonight—"

"Wait, one question. What's the lead singer look like?" Harry was curious.

"She was wearing a wig—"

"I mean the male lead."

"Oh, good-looking. Now, Harry, don't even think about it. You've got two men crazy over you. Your ex-husband and Blair Bainbridge, who I must say is the best-looking man I've ever seen in my life except for Clark Gable and Gary Cooper."

Harry waved off Mim. "Crazy for me? I see Fair from time to time and Blair's my neighbor. Don't whip up a romance. They're just friends."

"We'll see," came the measured reply. With that she left.

Harry washed her hands. The maroon post office ink was smeared into her fingertips. "We should change our ink color every year. I get bored with this."

"And you complain about taxes . . . think what it would cost."

"That's true, but I look at stamps from other countries and the postmark inks, and some of them are so pretty."

"Long as the mail gets there on time," Miranda said. "And when you consider how much mail the U.S. Postal Service moves in one day, one regular business day, it's amazing."

"Okay. Okay." Harry laughed and held up her hands for inspection. "I wouldn't want to waste any valuable ink on my fingers."

"Let's say you have rosy fingertips of a color not found in nature."

"Okay, I'm out of here."

5

The battery flickered on Harry's truck, so she stopped by the old Amoco service station which, a long time ago, was a Mobil station. The ancient Coke machine beckoned. She slipped the coins in and then "walked" the curvaceous bottle through to the end, where the metal jaws opened as she pulled the bottle to freedom. She liked the old machines because you could lift the top up and put your hand into the cool chest. Also, the new soda dispensers were so bright and full of light, she felt she ought to wear sunglasses to use them. A nickle bought a Coke when she was tiny. Then it jumped to a dime when she was in grade school. Now they cost fifty cents, but if one traveled to a big city, the price tag was easily seventy-five. If this was progress, Harry found it deeply depressing.

Usually she headed straight home after work, but the horses grazed on rich pasture. She didn't need to feed grain in the summer. The twilight lingered with intensity. Why hurry?

She absentmindedly nosed the recharged vehicle north up Route 810.

"Where are we going?" Tucker rested her snout on the windowsill.

"Another one of Mom's adventures." Mrs. Murphy curled up behind the long stick shift. She liked that part of the seat best.

"The last time she did this, we ended up in Sperryville. I'm hungry. I don't want to go for such a long drive."

"Whine, then. Get those sweet doggy tears in your eyes. That arouses her maternal instincts." Mrs. Murphy laughed.

"Yeah, well, I can overdo, you know. I've got to save that for special occasions." Tucker was resigned to her fate.

Harry clicked on the radio, then clicked it off. The Preparation H ad disturbed the soft mood of the fading light which blended from scarlet to hazy pink to a rose-gray laced with fingers of indigo.

She slowed at the turn to Sugar Hollow, a favorite spot in western Albemarle County for hikers and campers. The hollow led into a misty crevice in the mountain. No matter how hot the day, the forested paths remained cool and inviting. One could drive a car a few miles into the hollow to a parking lot, then walk.

A roar made Harry hit the brakes so hard that Tucker and Mrs. Murphy tumbled off the seat.

"Hey!" The cat clawed back onto the seat.

A black blur skidded in front of them, hung the turn, and then violently sped down the darkening road away from Sugar Hollow.

Harry squinted after the cycle. It was the black Harley, the driver encased in black leather and on such a hot day. She'd gotten a good look at the bike when Blair had escorted the man out of Ash Lawn. No other motorcycle like it in the area, plus it had California plates.

"Bet he didn't find Malibu in Sugar Hollow either." Harry grimaced.

6

A cold front rolled huge clouds over the mountains together with a refreshing breeze. Although it was the beginning of August, the tang of fall tantalized. In a day or two the swelter would return, but for now Mother Nature, surprising as always, was giving central Virginia a respite.

Harry and Fair turned their horses back toward her barn. The black-eyed Susans swayed in the field along with white Queen Anne's lace and the tall, vibrant purple joe-pye weed. Tucker ran alongside the pair. Mrs. Murphy elected to visit Simon, the possum who lived in the hayloft. A large black snake lived there, too, and Mrs. Murphy gave her a wide berth. The owl slept up in the cupola. The cat and owl couldn't stand one another, but as they kept different schedules, harsh words were usually avoided.

Tucker, thrilled to have the humans all to herself, kept up no matter what the pace. Corgis, hardy and amazingly fast, herd horses as readily as they do cattle. This was a trait Harry had had to modify when Tucker was a puppy, otherwise a swift kick might have ended the dog's career although the breed is nimble enough to get out of the way. Tucker merrily trotted to the side of the big gray mare, Poptart. She hoped that her mother would flirt with Fair. Tucker loved Fair, but Harry had signed off flirting the day of her divorce. Tucker knew Harry was usually forthright, but a little flirting couldn't hurt. She wanted the two back together.

"—right over the ears. Funniest damn thing you ever saw, and when she hit the ground she yelled 'Shit' so loud"—Fair grinned in the telling—"that the judges couldn't ignore it. No ribbon for Little Marilyn."

"Was her mom there?"

"Mim *and* the old guard. All of them. Clucking and carrying on. You'd think she'd have the sense to get away from her mother and go out on her own."

Harry drawled, "Thirty-three is a long, long adolescence. She could have stayed in the house she had with her ex, but she said the colors of the walls reminded her of him. So she moved back to that dependency on Mim's farm. I know I couldn't do it."

"Sometimes I feel sorry for her. You know, everything and nothing."

"I do, too, until I have to pay my bills, and then I'm too jealous for sympathy." A cloud swept low over her head. Harry felt she could reach up and grab a handful of swirling cotton candy. "The hell with money on a day like this. Nature is perfect."

"That she is." Fair spied the old log jump up ahead that Harry and her father had built fifteen years ago, big, solid locust trunks lashed together with heavy rope that Harry replaced every few years. It was three feet six inches. It looked bigger because of the bulk. He squeezed Gin Fizz into a good canter and headed toward the jump, sailing over.

Harry followed. Tucker prudently dashed around the end.

"Who did win the class at the benefit hunter show?" Harry remembered to ask.

"Aysha, with her mother in full attendance and Norman cheering. You'd have thought it was Ascot."

"Good. Say, did I tell you that Aysha was a docent up at Ash Lawn when I was there the other day?"

"She did go to William and Mary, didn't she?" Fair recalled as he slowed to a walk.

"Kerry was there, too, a scheduling foul-up, and Laura Freely. Little Marilyn was in charge, of course, but what set the day off was that this biker came up and had to be escorted off the premises. . . ." She realized that in bringing up Ash Lawn, she would remind Fair that she'd been up there with Blair, which would provoke a frosty response. Her voice trailed off.

"A biker?"

"Hell's Angel type."

"At Ash Lawn?" Fair laughed. "Maybe he's a descendant of James Monroe. What were you and Blair doing up there anyway?"

"Oh—Blair had never seen it. He wanted to do something relaxing."

Fair's lips clamped together. "Oh."

"Now, Fair, don't get in a huff. He's my neighbor. I like him."

"Yeah, Fair, lighten up." The dog added her two cents.

"Are you serious about this guy, or what?"

Harry and her ex-husband had been a pair since kindergarten, and she knew his moods. She didn't want Fair to sink into one of his manly pouts. Men never admitted to pouting, but that's exactly what he did. Sometimes it took her days to pull him out of one. "Number one, I don't have to answer to you. I don't ask *you* questions." She decided to attack.

"Because I'm not seeing anyone."

"For now."

"That was then. I'm not seeing anyone and I don't want anyone but you. I admit my mistake."

"Make that plural," Harry wryly suggested.

"Well—I admit my mistakes and I repent them. You know you're going to get over this and we'll—"

"Fair, don't be directive. I hate it when you tell me what I'm going to do, and feel and think. That got us into trouble in the first place, and I'm not saying I don't have my share of faults. As wives go, I was a real bust. Can't cook, don't want to learn. Can't iron but I can wash okay. I keep a clean house but sometimes my mind is untidy, and I forgot your birthday more times than I care to admit. Never remembered our anniversary either, for that matter. And the more you'd withdraw from me, the harder I'd work so I wouldn't have to talk to you—I was afraid I'd blow up. I should have blown up."

He pondered that. "You know—maybe you should have."

"Done is done. I don't know what tomorrow will bring, and it's not going to bring togetherness if you get pushy."

"You're the only woman in the world who talks to me like that."

"I suppose the rest of them swoon, bat their lashes, and tell you how wonderful you are. Bet their voices coo."

He suppressed a grin. "Let's just say they shower me with attention. And I have to be nice about it. I can't cut them to shreds over it." He paused. "You make me so mad, I could—I don't know. But I'm never bored with you like I'm bored with the, uh, conventional model."

"Thank you."

"Will you go with me to Mim's party next Saturday?"

"Oh"—her face registered confusion—"I'd love to, but I already have a date."

"Blair?"

"As a matter of fact, yes."

"Dammit to hell!"

"He asked me first, Fair."

"I have to line up for a date with my wife!"

"Your ex-wife."

"You don't feel ex to me." He fumed. "I can't stand that guy. The other day Mim was carrying on about his curly hair. So what? Curly hair? That's a fine recommendation for a relationship."

"Apparently it is for Marilyn Sanburne." Harry couldn't help herself. She wished she were a better person, but his discomfort was too delicious.

"Then I am asking for Thanksgiving, Christmas, and New Year's Eve."

"What about Labor Day weekend?" she teased him.

"Laminitis conference in Lexington," he replied, referring to the hoof disease.

"I was only kidding."

"I'm not. Will you save me those dates?"

"Fair, let's just take it as it comes. I'll say yes to the next summer party—someone's bound to have one—and we can go from there." She sighed. "Given the way the days are clicking off, I ought to say yes to Thanksgiving."

"*Tempus fugit,*" he agreed. "Do you remember Mrs. Heckler singing her congratulations to us?"

"Yeah." She grew wistful. "Isn't it funny what we do remember? I remember that old sweater Dad would wear every homecoming."

"His Crozet football letter sweater." Fair smiled. "I don't think he ever missed a game. Your dad was a good athlete. He lettered in football, baseball, and didn't he play basketball too?"

"Yeah. In those days I think everybody did everything. It was better. Healthier. Tenth-graders now are dreaming of their endorsement contracts. Doesn't anybody play for fun anymore? Dad sure did."

"What year did he graduate?"

"Forty-five. He was too young for the war. Bothered him all his life. He remembered some of the boys who never came home."

"Thank God my father made it back from Korea—seems like no one remembers that war except the guys who fought in it."

"I'm glad he came back too. Where would you be?" She urged Poptart over next to Gin Fizz, reached over, and punched Fair in the arm.

"Love tap? Mother, can't you brush his hair with your fingertips or

something?" Tucker advised. Tucker had been watching too much TV. She declared it was to study human habits, but Mrs. Murphy said there was plenty of that to study in front of her face. Tucker loved the television because it put her to sleep.

"Tucker, don't yip so loud," Harry pleaded.

"You're hopeless!" The dog ran in front of them. She could see Mrs. Murphy sitting in the hayloft door. *"The soul of romance."*

"You or Mom?" Mrs. Murphy laughed.

"A fat lot you know about love," the dog replied.

"I know it can get you in all kinds of trouble."

7

Harry was the first to notice it because she walked to work that Monday morning. The Harley, like a raven with folded wings, was perched in front of the post office. Although Tucker and Mrs. Murphy accompanied her, she had no desire to be alone in the P.O. with that man even if Blair did think he was nonviolent.

She peeped into Market's store. "Hey."

"Hey, back at you," Market called to her.

Pewter thundered out the front door when it was opened, the flab on her belly swaying from side to side. She and Mrs. Murphy immediately ran around the back of the buildings. Tucker was torn whether to join them or stay. She finally followed the cats.

"Where's the biker?"

"The what?" Market wiped his hands on his apron and walked toward Harry behind the counter.

"The Hell's Angel who owns the Harley. If he'd been in your store, you would have noticed."

"Nobody like that this morning. Of course, it's just seven-thirty, so maybe he's out for his morning constitutional and I'll yet have the pleasure." Market offered her a sticky bun. "Is he really a Hell's Angel?"

"Sure looks like one."

"Well, then, Miss Priss, how do you know him? You been hanging around biker bars?" Market teased her.

"He roared up to Ash Lawn the other day when I was giving Blair the tour."

"A cultural Hell's Angel. Harry, you're pulling my leg."

"No, honestly." Harry's inflection rose with her innocence.

"Maybe it's a surprise from Fair."

"Sure, sure."

"Blair?"

"Market, what is this? You're getting as bad as the biddies around here, trying to get me tied down again."

"Better than being tied up." He paused. "Then again..."

"Have you been talking to Art Bushey?"

As Art was famed for his sense of humor, dwelling mostly on sexual topics, this was not a long-shot question.

"Oh, I'm pricing a new Ford truck over at Art's. I'd like to move up to a three-quarter ton."

"Better sell a lot of potato chips."

"Ain't that the truth."

"This roll is delicious. Are you using a new bakery?"

"Miranda. She's decided she needs pin money, as she puts it, and she's going to be bringing in whatever she whips up. She's such a good baker, I think this arrangement might work."

"Put in a Weight Watchers clinic down the street, and you'll have all your bases covered. There's no way you can eat her concoctions without carrying extra freight."

Aysha and Norman Cramer pushed open the door. Harry stepped aside.

"Hi." Aysha bubbled over. "Sweet'n Low, please. I'm manning, I mean womanning, the phones over at the Junior League charity roundup today. We'll be drinking lots of coffee."

"Norman, what about you?" Market pointed to a sticky bun.

Norman blinked. He blinked a lot, actually, Harry observed.

"I, uh, yeah, I'll try one," he said.

"Now, honey, I don't want any love handles." Aysha pinched him.

"Lovegirl, just a little eensy bite." He smiled. He had beautiful big white teeth.

Laura Freely and Mim entered.

Laura went over to the headache remedies while Mim asked Harry, "And why aren't you in the post office? You're five minutes late."

"Waylaid by a Miranda Hogendobber sticky bun," Harry replied.

Norman swallowed. "They're delicious."

"Don't tempt me!" Laura instructed. "And don't take any to my husband over there at the bank." She nodded in the direction of National Crozet across the street. "Hogan *looks* at sweets and he gains weight."

Mim hovered over the buns. The odor enticed even her considerable willpower. The swirls in the buns resembled tantalizing pinwheels. "What the heck?" She plunked down a dollar and grabbed two buns. "Does she bring these to work?"

Harry nodded. "She's been baking a lot these last few weeks. She didn't tell me she was going into business though. Guess I was the guinea pig."

"And you don't have an extra pound on your frame," Aysha complimented her.

"Oh, thanks."

Laura pushed her BC Powders on the counter. "If you did all the farm chores, you wouldn't have to worry either. Harry can probably eat three thousand calories a day and not gain an ounce."

"Speaking of fat, where's Pewter?" Norman, who liked cats, leaned over the counter to look for her.

"Walked out the front door to have a chat with Mrs. Murphy. Well, gang, time to sort your mail."

"Throw out my bills, will you?" Aysha laughed.

"I'm going to give you mine." Harry grinned and left.

She unlocked the front door. Mrs. Hogendobber hadn't come in the back yet. Rob Collier pulled into the front parking space before Harry closed the door. She let it hang open and joined him.

"Only one big bag today."

"Thank God. You about killed us last week."

He noticed the motorcycle. "Who owns that?"

"I don't know his name."

"California plates. A long way from home." Rob hopped out of the truck, bag over his shoulder, and began reminiscing about motorcycles. Motorcycles engendered male nostalgia. "Did I ever tell you about the little Vespa I had? No bigger than a sigh. I wanted to learn to ride a bike, a real bike. I was fourteen, so I gave Jake Berryhill fifty bucks for his brother's old Vespa. Still ran. I didn't get out of second gear for the first month. Then I got the hang of it, so I traded the Vespa in on a 250cc Honda. I thought I was macho man, and I rode that thing on the back roads 'cause I didn't have a license and I didn't have plates."

"How'd you get away with it?"

"Hell, Harry, there weren't but two deputies for the whole of Albemarle County then. They couldn't be bothered with a kid on a Honda." He continued. "Got my license on my sixteenth birthday. Delivered the paper. Saved up and traded up—500cc Honda." He dumped the bag behind the counter, waved to Miranda, and wistfully gazed at the Harley. "You know, I just might have to get me one. Yeah. Slid on your machine, cranked it, and the crank would always fly up and bark your shin. Roll that right wrist in, let out the clutch with your left hand, just nice and easy, pick up your feet and roll—just roll on to free-dom."

"Why, Rob, that's poetic," Miranda said.

He blushed. "Happy times." Then he sighed. "What happens? I mean, when is the moment when we get old? Maybe for me it was when I sold that 500cc."

"Honda dealer's in town. There's Harley dealers in Orange and Waynesboro," Harry said.

"Yeah, yeah. I'm going to think about it—seriously."

"While you're thinking, go next door and buy one of Miranda's sticky buns. She's entered the baking business."

"I'll do that." He backed out the door and walked over to Market's.

Miranda beamed. "Do you think it's a good idea?"

"Uh-huh." Harry's tone was positive.

Out back, Mrs. Murphy, Tucker, and Pewter craned their necks upward at the post office drain spout. Little cheeps reverberated from inside.

"*Heard it this morning,*" Pewter solemnly noted. "*Haven't seen anyone fly in or out. Of course, I would have caught anyone if they'd tried.*"

"*Dream on, Pewter.*" Tucker giggled.

"*I can catch a bird. I most certainly can,*" she huffed.

"*We aren't catching this one.*" Mrs. Murphy's whiskers pointed forward, then relaxed. "*Come on, time to sort the mail.*"

"*Is there any food in there?*" Pewter inquired.

"*You work in a market. Why do you always want to know if we have food at the post office?*" Tucker's tongue hung out. The day was already heating up.

"*Curious. Don't you know anything, Tucker? Cats are by nature curious.*"

"*Brother.*" The dog pushed open the animal door and entered the post office.

• • •

By noon the biker still had not appeared. Harry couldn't stand it anymore. She went out front and sat on the Harley. It did feel great, nice and lowdown. She checked around to make sure the Hell's Angel wouldn't charge out of a building and scream at her for touching his precious bike.

By three, still no sign of the owner.

"Harry, I'm calling Rick Shaw." Miranda picked up the phone.

Harry considered this a moment. "Wait a second. Let me go get the license plate number." She ran outside and scribbled the number on a scrap of paper.

Miranda dialed the sheriff's department. Cynthia Cooper picked up the phone. "Why aren't you in the squad car?"

Miranda's voice was distinctive. Cynthia knew the caller at once. "I was. What can I do you for?"

"A black Harley-Davidson motorcycle has been parked in front of the post office all day and the owner doesn't seem to be around."

"Do you know the owner?"

"No, but Harry does. Hold on a minute." Miranda handed the phone to Harry.

"Hi, Cynthia. Actually, I don't know the owner but I saw him at Ash Lawn last week."

"Do you suspect anything?"

"Uh, no, I guess we're just wondering why the bike has been here all day. Maybe he copped a ride in a car or something, but we're not a public parking lot. Want the license number?"

"Yeah, okay."

She read off the number. "California plates. Pretty ones."

"They are. Pretty state taxes too. If I paid that much, I'd want gold-plated tags. Okay, Skeezits, I'll run a check and get back to you," she said, calling Harry by her childhood nickname.

The phone rang in fifteen minutes. It was Cynthia.

"The bike belongs to Michael Huckstep, Los Angeles, California. He's a Caucasian—thirty-four years old."

"That was fast." Harry was impressed.

"Computers. If the bike is still there tomorrow, call me. Actually, I'll swing by tonight and check on it anyway, but call me in the morning. Sometimes people do take advantage of federal facilities. It will probably be gone tomorrow."

8

But it wasn't. The next morning, Tuesday, the Harley was right there.

Cynthia cruised on over and inspected the bike while Harry and Mrs. Hogendobber hurried to finish their morning sorting. Mrs. Hogendobber kept running in and out of the office, she was so afraid she'd miss something.

On her last pass into the post office she breathlessly informed Harry, "She's going to have them dust for prints—you know, in case it's stolen."

"Well, if it were stolen, don't you think he'd know it and report it?"

"Not if he's the thief."

Harry cocked her head. "Do criminals have legitimate driver's licenses?"

"Little Marilyn does. The way she drives is a crime." Miranda laughed at her own joke.

Unable to contain her curiosity any longer, Mrs. Murphy strolled out the front door on yet another pass by Miranda. Tucker, lying on her back, legs straight up in the air, was dead to the world. The cat chose not to wake her.

Cynthia, tall and slender, knelt down on the left side of the machine and wrote down the serial number.

Mrs. Murphy jumped on the seat of the motorcycle. She quickly jumped off since it was boiling hot. *"Ouch! Don't they make sheepskin seat covers for bikes?"*

The humans forgot the task at hand for a moment to gossip about Little Marilyn's latest beau—a man both Mrs. Hogendobber and Cynthia considered unsuitable. They moved on to BoomBoom Craycroft's summer vacation, their hope that Kerry McCray would find a decent guy following her loss of Norman, and the delightful fact that Miranda's baked goods were sold out by eight-thirty that morning.

The tiger, her coat shiny as patent leather in the sunlight, sniffed around the motorcycle. She was careful not to get too close, as the metal would be hot as well. A familiar whiff on the right saddlebag, jet black like the rest of the bike, made her stop. She stood on her hind legs, perfectly balanced, and sniffed deeper. Then she got as close as she dared and inhaled. *"Cynthia, Cynthia, there's blood on the saddlebag."*

"—Blair Bainbridge, but you know if BoomBoom lays siege to him again, he might give in. Men find her sexy." Cynthia couldn't help indulging in a light gossip.

"She won't turn his head." Mrs. Hogendobber crossed her arms over her large bosoms.

"They all look at BoomBoom." Cynthia never could understand why a good makeup job and big tits made idiots out of supposedly intelligent men.

"Hey, hey, will someone listen to me!"

"Aren't you a Chatty Cathy?" Miranda reached down to stroke the cat's pretty head.

"There's blood on the saddlebag. Want me to spell it for you?" The

cat yowled. She vented her frustrations concerning human stupidity.

"My, she is out of sorts." Cynthia brushed her hands on her pants.

"You're about as smart as a pig's blister." Mrs. Murphy spat in disgust.

"I've never seen Mrs. Murphy spit like that." Miranda involuntarily took a step backward.

The cat whirled around and thumped to the front door. She called over her shoulder, *"It's not chicken blood. It's human blood, and it's a couple of days old. If you all would use those pathetic senses of yours, you might even find it yourselves."* She banged on the door. *"Let me in, dammit. It's hot out here."*

Since Harry failed to rush right over, Mrs. Murphy, now in a towering rage, shot around to the back of the post office. She smacked open the kitty door, walked in, and whapped Tucker right on the nose.

"Wake up!"

"Ow." The dog raised her head, then dropped it. *"You are hateful mean."*

"Come outside with me. Now, Tucker. It's important."

"More important than sleeping in the air-conditioning?"

Mrs. Murphy whapped her again. Harry noticed. "Murphy, retrieve your patience."

"You can just shut up too. None of you know bugjuice. You rely on your eyes far too much, and they aren't that good anyway. Humans are weak, vain, and smelly!"

By now Tucker was on her feet and had shaken herself awake. *"Humans can't help being what they are any more than we can."*

"Come on." She vanished out the door.

Tucker joined her at the motorcycle. Both Miranda and Cynthia had ducked into the market.

"Here." The cat pointed.

Tucker lifted her nose. *"Oh, yes."*

"Don't touch the bike, Tucker, it's scorching."

"Okay." The corgi moved closer. Her head was tilted back, her eyes bright and clear, her ears forward. *"Human. Definitely human and fading."*

"I say four days."

"Hard to tell in this heat, but it sure has been a couple of days. It's only a drop or two. If the saddlebag were soaked, even they'd notice it. The aroma of blood is powerful."

"They don't like the smell, assuming they can smell it."

"If there's enough of it, even they can pick it up. I don't know why they don't like it. They eat meat just like we do."

"Yeah, but they eat broccoli and tomatoes too. Their systems are fussier." Mrs. Murphy brushed by Tucker. *"I trust your nose. I'm glad you came out with me."*

"Have you tried pointing this out to them?"

"Yes." The cat shrugged. *"Same old same old. They'll never get it."*

"Well, it's a few drops of blood. No big deal—is it?"

"Tucker, a Hell's Angel shows up at Ash Lawn, makes a scene asking for a woman named after a town. Blair gets him out of there. Right?"

"Right."

"Then he sideswipes us as he flies out of Sugar Hollow. And now his motorcycle has been parked in front of the post office for two days."

Tucker scratched her ear. *"Something's rotten in Denmark."*

9

Actually, something was rotten in Sugar Hollow. A platoon of grade-school hikers on a Wednesday nature trail excursion stumbled upon the remains of a human being. In the high heat the body shimmied with worms.

The stench made the kids' eyes water and some threw up. Then they ran like the dickens down the hollow to the nearest telephone.

Cynthia Cooper picked up the call. She met Sheriff Rick Shaw at the Sugar Hollow parking lot. The nature camp counselor, a handsome nineteen-year-old named Calvin Lewis, led the sheriff and his deputy to the grisly site.

Cynthia pulled out a handkerchief and put it over her mouth and nose. Rick offered one to Calvin. The young man gratefully took it.

"What will you use?" he asked.

"I'll hold my nose. Besides, I've seen more of this than you'll ever want to know." Rick walked over to the corpse.

Cynthia, careful not to touch the body or disturb the scene around it, scanned the blackened mess from end to end.

Then she and Rick walked away from the stench to join Calvin, who wisely had remained at a distance.

"Did you notice anything else when you found the body?" Rick asked.

"No."

Cynthia scribbled in her notebook. "Mr. Lewis, what about broken branches or a path made by the feet of the body if it was dragged through the underbrush?"

"Nothing like that at all. If we hadn't been looking for mushrooms—the class is identifying different kinds of mushrooms—I don't think we would have, uh, found . . . that. I smelled it and, uh, followed my nose. It was so strong everywhere that at first I couldn't pinpoint the smell. If I'd known, I would have made the kids stay back. Unfortunately some of them saw him. I didn't mean them to see it—I would have told them it was a dead deer."

Rick put his arm around the young man's shoulders. "Quite a shock. I'm sorry."

"The kids who saw it—I don't know what to tell them. They'll have nightmares for weeks."

Cynthia spoke, "There are a lot of good therapists in the area, people experienced with helping children through trauma." What she didn't say was that most therapists never got this close to raw life or rather, raw death.

After cordoning off the corpse, Rick and Cynthia waited for their team. Calvin rejoined his campers way down at the parking lot.

Rick leaned against a big fiddle oak and lit a cigarette. "Been a long time since I've seen something like this. A real worm's hamburger."

"Whole back blown away. A .357 Magnum?"

"Bigger." Rick shook his head. "Had to have made a loud report."

"People shooting off guns all the time." Cynthia bummed a cigarette off her boss. "Even if it isn't hunting season."

"Yeah. I know."

"A few more days and I think the animals would have been able to pull the arms off, and the legs too. At least the body is intact."

"Let's hope that's a help." He spewed out a stream of soothing blue smoke. "You know, there used to be stills up here. Clear mountain water. Just perfect. Those guys would blow you away pronto. The marijuana growers are more subtle. Here anyway."

"No still around here—at least, I don't think so."

He shook his head. "Not anymore, now that Sugar Hollow is public. Ever drink that stuff?"

"No."

"I did once. Take your head right off. It's not called white lightning for nothing." He glanced over his shoulder at the distant corpse. "Wonder what he got into."

"Guess we'll find out."

"Might take us a while, but you're right. Whenever there's a murder I hope it's an isolated expression of violence and not the start of some, you know..."

She knew he meant a serial killer. To date nothing of the kind had ever happened in their area. "I know. Oh, Christ, here come Diana Robb and the crew. If she sees me smoking, I'm going to get Health Lecture 101." Cynthia quickly smashed out her butt in the soft earth.

"Would it do any good?"

"Oh, sure it would—until I wanted the next cigarette."

10

A damp wind slid down the mountains. Harry jounced and jostled along on Johnny Pop. The manure spreader turned, flinging out wood shavings and manure. The sun seemed pinned to the top of the mountain, the shadows from the line of oaks lengthened. Sunrise and sunset were Harry's two favorite times of the day. And today the sweet smell of her red clover filled the air, making the sunset seem richer. Harry kept her fields in alfalfa, red clover, and timothy. She usually produced a very good hay crop from this.

The cat and dog slept in the barn. A full day at the post office wore them out. Tucker heard the noise of a heavy truck crunching down the driveway. She jumped up and awakened Mrs. Murphy.

"Who goes there?" Tucker bounded outside.

Blair Bainbridge's dually pulled into sight. Blair stopped and hopped out, shaded his eyes with his hand, saw Harry and sprinted out into the field.

"That's odd," Tucker said to herself. *"He always says hello."*

Mrs. Murphy, yawning in the doorspan, replied to Tucker's unspoken thought. *"Maybe he's realized he's in love with Mom."*

"Don't be sarcastic." Tucker sat down, stood up, sat down, finally stood up, and trotted toward the tractor.

Mrs. Murphy rolled over on her other side. She wasn't going anywhere. *"See you later, Alice Gator."*

Tucker tore after Blair, caught up with him, then blew past him.

Harry, seeing them both, cut the engine. One couldn't hear very well with Johnny at full throttle. "Blair. Hi."

Out of breath, he gasped, "There's been a murder."

"Who?" Harry's eyes enlarged.

"They don't know."

"How'd you find out?"

He put one hand against the seat of the tractor. "Accident."

"Accident or accidentally?" She smiled at herself because she realized that was exactly the kind of question her mother would have asked.

He caught his breath as Tucker circled the tractor. "Accident on 810 at Wyant's Store. I slowed down and noticed Cynthia Cooper just mad as hell, so I pulled over. It was a kid in an old Trooper, driving it like a car. He went off the side of the road, overcorrected, and then sideswiped Cynthia, who was coming from the opposite direction. I mean, she was steamed. The kid was crying, of course, begging her not to tell his parents."

"Is she okay?"

He nodded yes. "Kid too. Anyway, I stayed to help, not that there was much to do, but she isn't the type to get upset. She told me she'd just come out of Sugar Hollow, where a nature group had discovered a dead man. Said it was the grossest mess and she wouldn't be eating dinner tonight. She described what the man was wearing—Harry, I think it's the biker."

Harry jumped down. "What?"

He nodded again. "Heavy black boots, leather vest with symbols and studs—who else fits that description?"

"Blood on the saddlebags!" Tucker yipped.

"Well, he can't be the only man in the country with a black leather vest." She stopped a minute and shrugged. A chill overcame her. "Damn, he about ran me over coming out of Sugar Hollow. Covered from head to toe in leather."

"Better talk with Cynthia."

"Did you tell her what you thought?"

"Yeah." He stared at the huge tractor wheel. "He was a little strange. The wheel of fortune, you know."

Harry watched the sun vanish. "Someone's up and someone's down—or dead."

"Won't somebody listen to me? There's evidence on the motorcycle's saddlebags!"

"Tucker, hush, I'll feed you in a minute."

Dejected, Tucker sat on Blair's foot. Blair reached down to pet her.

Blair's lustrous hazel eyes bored into Harry's. "Do you ever get a feeling about somebody? A real sense of who they are?"

"Sometimes."

"Despite his appearance and his manner that day, I just felt he was an okay guy."

"Blair, he can't have been so okay, or he wouldn't be dead."

11

A small crowd gathered at the post office parking lot. Harry, Mrs. Hogendobber, Reverend Jones, Market Shiflett, Aysha, Norman, Ottoline, Kerry, the Marilyn Sanburnes—senior and junior, Blair, Mrs. Murphy, Tucker, and Pewter watched as the sheriff's men loaded the motorcycle onto a flatbed gooseneck. Hogan Freely, president of the Crozet National Bank, with his wife, Laura, walked over and joined the crowd.

Cynthia supervised.

Reverend Jones spoke for all of them. "Do you know anything, Cynthia?"

As Cynthia replied, Susan Tucker pulled in. "Wait, wait for me."

"What is this, a town meeting?" Cynthia half joked.

"Kind of." Susan slammed the door of the new Saab. "Fair's on call. He can't make it, but I'll see that your report gets to Fair and BoomBoom, who has a doctor's appointment."

"There's not much to report. A decayed body, a white male

most likely in his early thirties, was found in Sugar Hollow yesterday, late afternoon. We have reason to believe, thanks to Blair's accurate description, that the body is that of the owner of this motorcycle. We're running dental checks and we hope to know something soon. That's it."

"Are we in danger?" Mim asked the sensible question.

Cynthia folded her arms over her chest. "There's no way to accurately answer you, Mrs. Sanburne. We suspect foul play, but we don't know for sure. At this point the department isn't worried that there's a killer on the loose, so to speak."

But there was a killer on the loose. The little gathering felt safe because they didn't know the victim and therefore falsely believed they couldn't know the killer.

As Deputy Cooper drove off behind the truck with the motorcycle, the assembled folks squeezed into Market's for some drinks. The motorcycle had conveniently been removed during lunch hour. The sun beat down on them. An ice-cold drink and air-conditioning were welcome.

The animals scooted between legs.

"Come back here." Pewter led them to the back shelves containing household detergents. *"If we get up here we can see everything."* She jumped onto boxes from the floor to the top shelf. Mrs. Murphy followed her.

"Raw deal," Tucker grumbled.

"You can go behind the counter. Market's so busy, he won't notice."

"All right." Tucker, happier now that she could participate in gleaning information from the humans, worked her way back through the legs to the counter.

Susan, a born organizer, addressed the gathering. "Any of us that've seen the motorcycle before it was parked at the post office ought to write it down for Sheriff Shaw and Deputy Cooper. Obviously, anyone having contact with the deceased should do likewise."

"*Contact?* He barged into Ash Lawn and made such a scene!" Laura blurted out.

"Well, did you tell Deputy Cooper?" Mim inquired.

"No, but I will. I mean, how could I tell her? We just this instant found out—if it really is that same man. Could be someone else."

Miranda happily watched as people bought her doughnuts, brownies, and tarts—today's batch of goodies. Each day she baked larger quantities and each day they disappeared. She tore herself away from her own products to say, "Those of you who were up at Ash Lawn can go see Sheriff Shaw tomorrow. It would save him time if you go together."

"What happened at Ash Lawn?" Herbie Jones asked the obvious.

"This disheveled man, this dirty biker, pushed open the front door after we were closed—" Laura started to say.

"He wasn't that disheveled," Blair interrupted.

"Well, he certainly wasn't well groomed," Laura protested.

"Jeez." Market brought his hand to his face. "If you can't agree on how he looked, I can't wait to hear the rest of it."

"I was in the back, so I can't add anything." Aysha bought a lemon curd tart. She couldn't resist despite her mother's glowering gaze.

Harry added to the picture. "Blair and I were in the living room. We didn't see him come in but we heard him. He wasn't rude, really, but he was, uh, intense."

"Intense? He was cracked." Kerry put her hands on her hips. Kerry was a bit of an overreactor. She'd only come in from the slave quarters to catch the tail end of the incident. "He wouldn't leave, and Marilyn, who was in charge that day—"

"I asked him to leave," Little Marilyn chimed in. "He wouldn't go. He said he wanted Marin—"

"Malibu," Harry interrupted.

"Yes, that was it. He wanted this Malibu and he claimed she was at Ash Lawn. Well, of course she wasn't. But he was so insistent."

"Who's Malibu?"

"An old girlfriend," Blair told them.

"That doesn't tell us who she is." Mim, as commanding as ever, hit the nail on the head.

Ottoline sarcastically said, "With a name like Malibu, I suggest we look for someone in a tube top, high heels, short shorts, and with voluminous hair—bleached, of course."

12

The sheriff's office, drab but functional, suited Rick Shaw. He disliked ostentation. His desk was usually neat since he spent most of his time in his squad car. He disliked desk work as much as he disliked ostentation. Mostly he hated being stuck inside.

Today files cluttered his desk, cigarette butts overflowed in the large, deep ashtray and the phone rang off the hook. He'd been interviewed by the local television station, the local newspaper, and the big one from Richmond. Those duties he performed as a necessity. He wasn't a sheriff who loved seeing his face on the eleven o'clock news. Sometimes he'd make Cynthia juggle the interviews.

The coroner worked late into the night taking tissue samples.

No driver's license or identifying papers were found on the body. Cynthia knew the plates were registered to Michael Huckstep. But was the body that of Michael Huckstep? They could assume it was, but until they had a positive ID, they wouldn't know for certain. After all, someone could have killed Huckstep and posed as him.

Rick asked for a list of missing persons as well as stolen motorcycles to be made available to him. They were. Nothing on either California list matched the abandoned Harley or the dead man.

Cynthia scraped into the office. He held up his hand for her to wait. He dispensed with his phone call as soon as he could.

"Mim," he said.

Cynthia emptied the ashtray into the wastebasket. "She wants to be the first to know." She replaced the ashtray. "We went over the bike. Nothing there. No prints. Whoever drove it to the post office wore gloves."

"Bikers usually wear gloves."

"Wonder what he was doing in Sugar Hollow?"

Rick held up his hands as he twirled around in his swivel chair. "Sightseeing?" He twirled in the opposite direction, then stopped. "Makes me dizzy."

"If it weren't for drugs, we'd be out of work," she joked. "I bet he went in there to make a deal. Sugar Hollow is pretty but not exactly a tourist attraction. He was in there with someone who knows the county—I betcha."

She silently reached over, slipping a cigarette out of his pack, lit it, and spoke. "We searched his motel room. Blair said the biker told him he was staying at the Best Western. The manager, the night manager, and the maids haven't seen Mike Huckstep, the name under which he registered, in days. They don't pay much attention to people coming and going, I guess. No one agrees when they last saw him, but he seemed to be respectful and quiet when he checked in—and he paid in advance for a week."

"Anything in the room?"

"Three T-shirts and a clean pair of jeans. Not another thing. Not a notepad, a pencil, not even socks and underwear. No paperbacks or magazines. *Nada.*"

"I've been reading over the transcripts of your questioning of the Ash Lawn staff as well as Harry and Blair. You know"—he tipped back in his chair and swung his feet onto the folders on the desktop—"this doesn't compute."

"You mean their testimony?"

"No, no, that's fine. I mean the murder. It leads nowhere. Maybe it was a busted deal and the killer took his revenge and the money. There was no money in the pockets of the dead man's jeans."

"Could be…" Her voice trailed off, then strengthened again. "But you don't believe it was a busted drug deal, do you?"

"You've been around me too long. You and my wife see right through me." He put his hands behind his head. "No, Coop, I don't believe it. Murder offends me. I can't stand the thought of anyone getting away with it. The rules for getting along in this world are very simple. Thou shalt not kill, thou shalt not steal—seems reasonable to me. Oh, sure, there are times when I could brain my wife and vice versa—but I don't and she doesn't. I count to ten, sometimes I count to twenty. If I can act with a little restraint I figure others can too."

"Yes, but I think murder has to do with something deeper. Something infantile. Underneath it all a killer is saying 'I want my way.' Simple as that. They don't, they can't, even conceive that other people have legitimate needs that might be different and in conflict with their own. It's all me, me, me. Oh, they might dress it up and look mature, concerned, or whatever, but underneath they're infants in a violent, quivering rage."

Rick ran his hands over his receding hairline. "You been reading psychology books on me, Coop?"

"Nah."

The phone rang. Outside Rick's office an officer picked it up, then called out, "Cynthia, Motor Vehicles in California. Want to take it in Rick's office?"

"Sure." She reached over and punched a button. "Deputy Cooper here." She paused, listening. "I'd appreciate that." She gave the station's fax number. "Thank you very much." She hung up the phone. "Mike Huckstep. They're faxing his registration papers and driver's license to us. At least we'll have a physical description."

He grunted. "Who in the hell *is* Mike Huckstep?"

13

Valet parking set the tone for Mim's party. On the invitations she had written that it was a western theme party, complete with square dancing and barbecue. The valet parkers, Susan Tucker's son, Danny, and his high school friends, were dressed in plaid shirts with pointed yokes, jeans, and cowboy boots.

Mim sported beautiful ostrich cowboy boots the color of peanut brittle. Her white leather jeans had been custom made for her, fitting like a glove. She wore a white shirt with a turquoise yoke. Her scarf was Hermès and her Stetson was a 20X beaver. The hat alone must have cost more than $300, since most cowboy hats are only 2X or 4X at most, X being the grade of beaver. The hat, of course, was pure white.

Her husband had donned an old pair of jeans, well-worn boots, and a nicely pressed Wrangler brushpopper shirt. His belt buckle hinted at the family pocketbook. It was a large, beautifully worked silver oval with gold initials in the center.

All of Crozet attended the hoedown, as it was billed.

Harry borrowed a deerskin shirt with fringe on the yoke, front and back, as well as long fringe on the sleeves. She wore her one pair of Tony Lama boots that Susan had given her for her birthday three years ago. Blair looked like a younger, more handsome Marlboro man, right down to the chaps. Fair fried when he beheld his competition. Not that Fair was bad-looking, he wasn't, but somehow he could never quite synchronize his clothes. Cowboy attire suited his tall frame though, so he looked better than usual.

Mrs. Hogendobber, dangling loads of costume jewelry, swayed in a big red skirt and a Mexican blouse. Her blue cowboy hat hung on her back, the little silken thread like a necklace setting off her throat.

Reverend Jones dug out an old cavalry uniform. He wouldn't tell anyone where he found it. He could have ridden in from 1880.

The music, the food, the ever-flowing liquor, put the group in a wonderful mood.

Kerry McCray arrived early and alone. She said her date, the singer from the Light Opera series, would join them after his show at Ash Lawn. This didn't prevent her from sashaying over to Norman Cramer while Aysha jumped around the dance floor with another partner.

"Norman."

He turned at the sound of the familiar and once-beloved voice. "Kerry."

"Let me ask you something."

"Sure." His tone was hesitant.

"Are you happy?"

A long, long pause followed. He locked his long-lashed blue eyes into hers. "There are days when I think I am and there are days when I think I've made the biggest mistake of my life. What about you?"

"No. I'm not happy at all." She half smiled. "If nothing else, Norman, we can still be honest with one another."

An agonized expression crossed his features, and then he glanced over Kerry's shoulder, since the music had stopped. "Christ, here comes Aysha." He whispered, "I'll see you at work. Maybe we can have lunch—somewhere, you know."

She watched as he scurried to take his wife by the elbow and hustle her back out onto the dance floor. Tears sprang into Kerry's eyes. Little Marilyn had observed the exchange, although she'd not heard it. She came over.

"He's not worth it."

Kerry sniffed and fought back more tears. "It's not a question of worth, Marilyn. You either love a man or you don't."

Marilyn put her arm around Kerry's waist, walking her away from the dance floor.

Fair and Susan Tucker swung one another around on the floor while the voluptuous widow BoomBoom Craycroft, fabulously dressed, ensnared Blair. He didn't seem to mind. Harry danced with Reverend Jones. She dearly loved the rev and barely noticed the dramas around her. In fact, Harry often shut out those tempests of emotion. Sometimes that was a great idea. Sometimes it wasn't.

After the song ended, the band took a break. The stampede for the bar left the women at the tables as the men jostled for drinks to carry back to "the girls."

Both Blair and Fair arrived at Harry and Susan's table. Mrs. Hogendobber sat at the next table with Herbie and Bob and Sally Taylor, friends from church. Ned was off politicking with the other lawyers.

"Coca-Cola, darling." Fair placed a glass in front of Harry.

Before she could respond, Blair smacked down a gin and tonic. "Harry, you need a real drink."

"She doesn't drink." Fair smiled, baring his fangs.

"She does now." Blair bared his fangs in return.

"Are you trying to get Harry drunk? Pretty crude, Blair."

"Get over it. You divorced her, buddy. I happen to think she's a fascinating woman. Your loss is my gain."

By now the whole party was pretending to be talking with one another, but every ear was cocked in the direction of this exchange.

"She's not a raffle ticket. I haven't lost her and you haven't gained her." Fair squared his massive shoulders.

Blair turned around to sit down. "Cut the crap."

That fast Fair pulled Blair's chair out from under him. Blair sprawled on the ground with a thud.

Blair sprang up. "You stupid redneck."

Fair swung and missed. Blair was quick on his feet.

Within seconds the two strong men were pounding at one another. Blair sent the vet crashing into the table, which collapsed.

"Will you two grow up!" Harry shouted. She was preparing to haul off and sock whoever came closest to her, when a hand closed around her wrist like a steel vise.

"No, you come with me." Reverend Jones yanked her right out of there.

Susan and Mrs. Hogendobber cleared away as the punching and counterpunching increased. As each fist found its target, a *thunk* resounded over the party. The band hurried back to the bandstand and picked up a tune. Jim Sanburne moved toward the combatants, as did Reverend Jones once he deposited Harry with her hostess.

Harry, red-faced, mumbled, "Mim, I'm so sorry."

"Why apologize for them? You haven't done a thing. Anyway, ever since those drunken swans ruined my *Town & Country* party I just take it as it comes."

Mim's famed *Town & Country* party was one she gave years before, filled with stars and business leaders from all over the country. She imported swans for the pool turned lily pond. She drugged the swans for the occasion, but the drugs wore off and the swans invaded the party, got into the liquor and food, becoming pugnacious. Clips of her party made the nightly news on every station in the country. The presidential candidate for whom this extravaganza was planned was shown running from a swan whose wings were outstretched as well as its neck, beak aiming for that large presidential bottom.

"The swans behaved better than these two."

"Harry, I told you both of them are in love with you. You won't listen to me."

"I'm listening now."

Mim slugged back a refreshing gin rickey. "You can't just be friends with men. It doesn't work that way. And don't be mad at them because they can't be friends the way women can. If a man comes around, he wants more than friendship. You know that."

Harry watched as Jim Sanburne and Herbie finally separated the two men she thought of as her friends. Fair had a bloody nose and Blair's lip was split wide open. BoomBoom Craycroft rushed to minister to Blair, who shrugged her off. "I know it. And I hate it."

"Might as well hate men, then."

"You know I don't."

"Then you have to choose between these two or tell them how you feel about them." She paused. "How do you feel about them?"

Harry faltered. "I don't know. I used to love Fair heart and soul, nothing held back. I still love him, but I don't know if I can love him again in that way."

"Maybe *trust* is the operative word."

"Yeah." She rubbed her right hand over her eyes. Why was life so complicated?

"Blair?"

"He's a tender man. Very sensitive, and I'm drawn to him—but I'm afraid. Oh, Mim, I just don't know if I can go through loving anyone again."

"Whoever you love will hurt you. You'll hurt him. If you learn to forgive, to go on—you'll have something real." She fingered her Hermès scarf. "I wish I could explain it better than I am. You know that Jim used to cheat on me like there was no tomorrow."

"Uh—" Harry swallowed.

"No need to be polite. He did. The whole town knew it. But

Jim was a big, handsome, wild poor boy when I met him and I used my wealth to control him. Running through women was his revenge. I came so close to divorcing him, but, well, I couldn't. When I discovered I had breast cancer, I guess I rediscovered Jim. We opened up and talked to one another. After decades of marriage we finally just *talked* and we forgave one another and—here we are. Now, if a rich bitch like me can take a chance on life and love, I don't see why you can't."

Harry sat quietly for a long time. "I take your point."

"You decide between those two men."

"Blair hasn't exactly declared himself, you know."

"I'm not worried about his feelings right now. I'm worried about yours. Make up your mind."

14

Jangled by the previous night's events, Harry awoke early to a steady rain. As it was desperately needed, she didn't resent the gray one bit. She threw on her ancient Smith College T-shirt, a pair of cutoffs, and sneakers, and dashed to the barn.

After she fed the horses, she hung a bridle on a tack hook in the center aisle, grabbed a bar of saddle soap, a small bucket of water, a sponge, and a cloth to begin cleaning. Rhythmic tasks helped her sort out whatever was going on in her life.

Mrs. Murphy climbed into the hayloft to visit Simon. Being nocturnal, he was sound asleep, so she jumped on a stall door and then to an old but well-cared-for tack trunk. Sitting on four cinder blocks, the wooden trunk was painted blue and gold with M.C.M., Harry's initials, in the middle. Mary Charlotte Minor.

Once divorced, she had kept Haristeen. It was such a bother to lose your surname in the first place, and then to take it back was too confusing for everyone. That's what she said, but Susan Tucker declared she retained her married name because she wasn't yet done with Fair. Everyone had an opinion on Harry's emotional state and no one minded cramming it down her throat.

She'd had enough emotion and probing questions the night before. She wanted to be left alone. Fat chance.

Blair pulled up the drive to the barn. She had the lights on in the barn, so he knew where she was. Dodging the raindrops, he carried a wicker basket into the aisle.

"This is by way of an apology." He flipped open the wicker lid. Delicious scones, Fortnum and Mason jams and jellies, bitesize ham biscuits, a fragrant Stilton cheese, a small jar of exquisite French mustard, and a large batch of peanut butter cookies were crowded inside. There were even water crackers and tins of pâté stuck in the corners. Before she could reply or thank him, he hurried into the tack room carrying a bag of expensive coffee.

"Blair, I've got only a hotpot down here. I don't have anything for you to make fancy coffee with." She was going to apologize for ending her sentence with a preposition, but then thought, Oh, the hell with it. Grammar and speech were ever diverging currents in the English language.

He silently walked back to his truck, returning with a black Krups coffeemaker, an electric grinder, and a small device for frothing milk for cappuccino.

"You do now." He pointed to the espresso machine. "This will have to go in the kitchen. Now you've got everything you need."

"Blair"—her jaw dropped—"this is so, so, uh, I don't know what to say—thank you."

"I was an ass. I'm sorry. If you'll accept my apology, I'll brew whatever your heart desires. How about a strong cup of Colombian to start? Then we can dig in the basket and follow with espresso or cappuccino, whatever you wish."

"Sounds great to me." Harry vigorously rubbed a rein. "And I do accept your apology."

Mrs. Murphy, tail curled around her, swayed on the tack trunk.

She appeared to be sleeping while sitting upright. Humans fell for this trick every time. It was the perfect eavesdropping posture.

Tucker, rarely as subtle, hovered over the basket.

Blair spread a small tablecloth on the rickety table in the tack room. He spied an old coffee tin on a shelf that Harry used as a grain measure. He filled it with water, then dashed outside through the raindrops to pick black-eyed Susans. The coffee was brewed by the time he returned.

"You're soaked."

"Feels good." His hazel eyes were alight.

She put her hands on her hips and looked at the table. "I admire people who are artistic. I couldn't make anything that pretty out of odds and ends."

"You have other talents."

"Name one." Harry laughed.

"Fishing for compliments," Tucker murmured.

"You make people feel good. You have an infectious laugh, and I believe you know more about farming than anyone I've ever met."

"Blair," she laughed, "you didn't grow up on a farm. Anyone who has would seem smart."

"I see other farmers in the county. Their pastures aren't as rich, their fence lines aren't in as good repair, and their use of space and terrain isn't as logical. You're the best."

"Thanks." She bit into a ham biscuit drenched with the mustard. "I didn't know how hungry I was."

They ate, chatted, and ended their meal with spectacular cappuccino.

Blair inhaled the rich smell of leather, saddle soap, pine shavings, the distinct and warm aroma of the horses.

"This barn exudes peace and happiness."

"Dad and Mom poured a lot of love into this place. Dad's family migrated from the Tidewater immediately before the Revolutionary War, but we didn't find this piece of land until the 1840s. The rich Hepworths, that was Mom's family, stayed in the Tidewater. The Minors, hardscrabble farmers, took what they could. The Depression hurt Papaw and Mamaw, so by the time Dad came along and was old enough to pitch in, there was a lot to do. He realized there wasn't a living in farming anymore, so he worked outside and brought home money. Little by little he put things back in order, apples, hay, a small corn crop. Mom worked in the library. Early in the morning, late at night, they'd do the farm chores. I miss them, you know, but I look around and see the love they left."

"They left a lot of love in you too."

Tucker put her head on Harry's knee. *"Say something nice, Mom."*

"Thanks."

"I came over today to apologize and to, well, to tell you I like you a lot. I'm not on my feet...I mean, I am financially but I'm not emotionally. I really like you, Harry, and I haven't, oh—" He paused, as this was harder than he had anticipated. "I haven't been fair to you. I know now that our spending time together has had much greater significance to people here than if we lived in New York. I don't mean to be leading you on."

"I don't feel like you are at all. I'm happy with our friendship."

"That's good of you to say. I'm happy, too, but I vacillate. Sometimes I want more, but when I think about what it would mean here, I pull back. If we lived in New York, I'd know what to do. Here, uh, there's more responsibility involved. I love it when I'm here, but I love being on the road, too, and I guess my ego needs it, the attention. I hate to admit that but—"

"Your ego is what makes you good at what you do."

A sheepish smile and blush followed that remark. "Yeah, but there's something silly about standing around in clothes, being photographed. It's just—if I had any balls, Harry, I'd take acting classes, but I think deep down I know I don't have a scrap of talent. I'm just a pretty face." He laughed at his use of an expression generally used to describe women.

"You're more than that. It's up to you and hey, what does it cost to take acting classes—in money and in time? No one is going to throw tomatoes at you in a classroom. If you're any good at it, you'll know. Nothing ventured, nothing gained." She thought a moment. "The University of Virginia has a good drama department."

"You're okay." He reached across the table for her hand but the phone rang.

"Sorry." She stood up and reached for the wall phone. "Hi. Barn."

The deep timbre on the other line, Fair, said, "Will you still speak to me?"

"I'm speaking to you now."

"Very funny. I'm in the truck, had a call over at Mim's, so I'm on my way."

"Not now."

"What do you mean, not now?"

"I have company and—"

"Blair? Is that son of a bitch there?"

"Yes, he came to apologize."

"Goddammit!" Fair switched off his mobile phone.

Harry sat down again.

"Fair?"

"In an emotional tumult, as my mother would have said."

The phone rang again. "I bet that's him. I'm sorry, Blair." She picked up. It wasn't Fair, it was Susan Tucker. "Susan, I'm glad it's you."

"Of course you're glad it's me. I'm your best friend. Scoop."

"I'm ready." Harry mouthed the name Susan to Blair.

"Ned and Rick Shaw had a meeting today about the fundraiser for the department, and by the bye Rick said the corpse *is* Mike Huckstep, same fellow that owned the motorcycle. It will be in the papers tomorrow."

"I guess it's not a surprise. I mean, it's what we all figured anyway—that the cycle's owner was the dead man."

"Yeah, I guess that's the end of that. Got a minute?"

"Actually, I don't. Blair's here."

"Ah, that was what I wanted to talk to you about. He came to apologize, I hope."

"Yes."

"We can catch up later, but here it is in a nutshell: Little Marilyn has the hots for Blair."

"A nutshell is where that best belongs." Harry felt that every female under ninety must be swooning over Blair.

"Ah-ha, getting proprietary, are we?"

"No," Harry lied.

"Sure. Okay, I'll call you later for girl talk."

"Spare me. I can't bear one more emotional revelation. Mine or yours or anyone else's. Talk to you later. Bye."

Blair's face clouded over. "Did I just, uh, say too much?"

"Oh, no, no, I don't mean that, but, Blair, all my friends are so busy psychoanalyzing me, you, Fair. I'm sick of it. I'm beginning to think I'm a free movie for everyone."

"I think a single man offends them and a single woman is an object of pity." He held up his hand before she could protest. "It's sexist, but that's the world we live in."

She ran her forefinger over the smooth surface of the high-tech coffeemaker. "Do you want to get married? Wait, I don't mean to me, it's not that kind of question, but in theory, do you want to get married?"

"No. Right now, at this time in my life, the thought scares the hell out of me." He was as honest as a bone. "What about you?"

"Ditto. I mean, I've been married and I thought I was doing a pretty good job at it. Events proved otherwise."

"That was his stupidity, not yours."

"Maybe, but I'm very self-sufficient and I think Fair, and maybe most men, say they admire that quality but in reality they don't. Fair wanted me to be more, well, more conventional, more dependent, and, Blair, that just ain't me."

"Ever notice how people say they love you and then they try to change you?"

She felt so relieved. He said what she felt. "Yeah, I never thought of it that way, but yeah. I am who I am. I'm not perfect and I'm sure not a movie star, but I get along. I don't want to be any other way than the way I am."

"What about sex?"

She gulped. "I beg your pardon?"

He tipped back his head and roared. "Harry, I'm not that forward. What about people's attitudes about sex? If you have an affair, are you a slut in these parts?"

"No, I think that honor belongs to BoomBoom."

"Oooh." He whistled. "But if you sleep with someone, doesn't it imply a commitment? You can't get away with it. Everyone seems to know everything."

She cocked her head to one side. "True. That's why one has to look before one leaps. You can get away with it much more easily than I can. The double standard."

"That double standard you just applied to BoomBoom?"

"Ahhh—no. BoomBoom will have engraved on her tombstone 'At Last She Sleeps Alone.' She overdoes it. But I'd feel the same way about a man. You never met him, but BoomBoom's deceased husband was a real animal. He was fun and all, but if you were a woman, you knew never to trust him."

"Animal! I take offense." Tucker whined, got mad, and padded out to the aisle. She saw Mrs. Murphy and walked over to her friend. She touched her with her nose. *"Wake up."*

"I'm not asleep."

"You always say that. You're missing some good stuff."

"No, I'm not."

"Well, you think they'll go to bed?"

"I don't know. Not tonight anyway."

Back in the tack room Blair and Harry cleaned up. She packed the uneaten items back in the basket.

"Basket's yours too."

"You're being awfully good to me."

"I like you."

"I like you too."

He pulled her to him and kissed her on the cheek. "I don't know what will happen between us, but one thing you can count on, I'll be your friend."

Harry kissed him back, hugged him, and then let go. "That's a deal."

The Crozet National Bank, a squat brick building erected in 1910, sat on the corner of Railroad Avenue in a row of buildings that included the old Rexall's drugstore. The woodwork was white, the effect unadorned and businesslike, which suited its purpose.

Thanks to the frugality of a succession of good presidents over the decades, little money had been squandered on the interior. The same old hanging lights swayed overhead. Green-shaded bankers' lamps sat in the middle of heavy wooden desks. The tellers worked at a marble counter behind bronze bars. The austerity lent substance to the bank. The only intrusions of modernity were the computer terminals at each teller station and on each administrative desk.

The office of the bank president, Hogan Freely, was on the second floor. Mrs. Murphy, accompanying Harry, wandered up the back stairs. She thought she would generously distribute her personality. However, when she strolled into Norman Cramer's office at the far end of the small second story, she decided to hide behind the curtain. Hogan was pitching a major hissy.

"You're telling me you don't know? What in the goddamned hell am I paying you for, Norman?"

"Mr. Freely, please, the situation is highly abnormal."

"Abnormal, it's probably criminal! I'm calling Rick Shaw."

"Let's take this a step at a time." Norman, not the most masculine of men, sounded more masterful than Mrs. Murphy had ever heard him. "If you call in the authorities before I can run a skintight audit, you risk bad publicity, you risk outside auditors being called in. The abnormality in funds may be a glitch in the system. Then we'd be crying wolf. We'd look foolish. Crozet National has built its reputation on conservative investment, protecting our customers' assets and good old common sense. I will work day and night if I have to, but give me some time to comb through our records."

Hogan tapped the floor with his right foot. Mrs. Murphy could see his wing tips as she peered from under the curtain. "How many people do you need and how long?" He paused. "And don't ask Kerry to work on this. The tension between you two is disruptive to everyone."

"Give me the whole accounting department and the tellers as well," Norman replied, his ears red from embarrassment.

"How long?"

"Two days and nights, and we'll have to order in food, lots of food."

A long silence followed, then a forceful reply. "All right. You've got until Wednesday closing time or I'm calling the sheriff. I've got to know why the screen comes up blank when I ask for our assets. And I'm bringing in computer specialists. You work on the books. They'll work on the terminals."

As he started for the door, Norman called to him, "Mr. Freely, I'm head of this department. The buck stops here. If I can't locate the funds or if the technical experts can't find the computer malfunction, which I really believe this to be, then I will face the press. This is my responsibility."

"Norman, I'm sorry I blew up at you. I know you'll do your best—I'm jangled. What if the Threadneedle virus did hit us? I have no way of knowing how much money we have. I can't even keep track of simple daily transactions! How can I cover losses if we've had them? The future of this bank depends on your work. We'll be sitting ducks for a takeover." His voice cracked. "And how can I face my board of directors?"

"Mim Sanburne most particularly," Norman drawled. "We'll find it. Put it out of your mind if you can."

"Out of my mind—?" Hogan left before finishing his sentence.

Mrs. Murphy waited, then slipped out the door, jumping the stairs two at a time. She glided over to Harry, who was withdrawing one hundred and fifty dollars. The truck needed a new battery and she hadn't bought groceries in over two weeks.

"Mom, take it all out," the cat advised.

Harry felt a familiar rub on her legs. "Visiting done? Let's go back to work."

"Mom, this bank is in deep doo-doo. You'd better pay attention to me."

Of course, Harry didn't. She walked back to the post office, Mrs. Murphy glumly following at her heels.

Pewter waited for them outside the market. *"Murphy, is it true that the boys got into a fight over Harry?"*

"Yes." Mrs. Murphy evidenced no interest in the subject.

"Who won?"

"Nobody."

"You're a sourpuss." Pewter fell in alongside her friend.

"Pewts, I was upstairs at the bank and I heard Hogan Freely say that they can't get the computers to report transactions or the amount of money in the bank."

"Humans put too much faith in money."

"*Maybe so . . . I tried to tell Mom, but you know how that goes. She ought to get her money out of there.*"

"*Money. You can't eat it, it doesn't keep you warm. It's pieces of paper. Weird, when you think about it. I believe in the barter system myself.*"

Mrs. Murphy, lost in thought, missed her friend's comment. "*What'd you say?*"

"*Money's just paper. Not even good enough to shred for a dirt box. But I want to know about the fight.*"

"*I wasn't there.*"

"*Did she say anything about it?*"

"*No, but Blair came over to apologize.*"

"*Was he horribly contrite?*" Pewter wanted the details.

"*He bought her an expensive coffeemaking machine. And he brought a big wicker basket full of fancy food.*"

"*What kind of food?*" Pewter's mouth watered.

"*Uh—liver pâté, crackers, jellies, scones. Stuff.*"

"*Oh, I wish I'd been there. Liver pâté. My favorite.*"

"*Any food is your favorite.*"

"*Strawberries. I hate strawberries,*" Pewter contradicted her.

"*You know, Mom was on the phone with Susan over the weekend, and then this morning she talked to Mrs. Hogendobber about Fair and Blair, in particular; men, in general. She likes them both, but she's . . .*" Mrs. Murphy shrugged.

"*Burned her fingers. What's that expression? Fool me once, shame on you. Fool me twice, shame on me. Guess it haunts her.*"

"*Here comes Coop. She already picked up her mail.*"

Cooper pulled into the lot and saw the cats. "Hot outside, girls. Let's go in."

"*Okay.*" The two cats scooted inside when she opened the door.

Miranda glanced up. "Forget something?"

"No. Just a question for you and Harry."

Harry walked up to the counter. "Shoot."

"Oh, Harry, don't say that." Cynthia grinned. "What I want to know is did you notice anyone paying special attention to the bike when it was parked here?"

"Every man that walked by except for Larry Johnson." Larry was the old doctor in town. He hardly ever used his car. He hated machines, walked everywhere, did his own wood chopping and other chores, and enjoyed robust health.

"Names."

"Gee, Cynthia, *everyone*. Rob Collier, Ned Tucker, Jim Sanburne. Hogan Freely, Fair, Market, Blair—Danny Tucker about died over it and, uh, did I forget anyone?"

Miranda piped up. "Herbie and, let's see, oh, yes, Norman Cramer."

Cynthia furiously scribbled away. "Women?"

"Barely a glance except for me, of course." Harry added, "Why are you asking?"

"I went over that machine with a fine-toothed comb. Then I decided to go over the saddlebags. I was so busy worrying about what was in them—nothing—that I didn't scrutinize the outsides. Couldn't see much anyway since they're black, but I sent them to our little lab, just in case."

Tucker and Mrs. Murphy pricked their ears. Pewter was playing with a cricket in the corner.

"There was a small quantity of blood on one of the bags."

"I told you!" the cat yowled.

"Mrs. Murphy, get a grip," Harry chided her.

"Considering how the man was shot," Mrs. Hogendobber said, "wouldn't blood have splattered everywhere?"

"We know how he was killed, Miranda, but we don't really know where he was killed. We only know where the body was found. And the blood isn't his. The tests came back on the corpse. He had a rare type, AB negative. The blood on the bag was O positive."

"You mean—" Harry didn't finish her sentence.

"There might be another body." Miranda finished it for her.

"Don't jump to conclusions," Cynthia warned. "We've got a team up in Sugar Hollow. If there's anything there, they'll find it. Especially if it's . . ." She delicately left off.

"Flesh and blood," Tucker barked.

16

Harry, Miranda, and Susan combed the forest in the early evening light, the pale golden shafts illuminating spots here and there, the scent of moss and fallen leaves rising around them.

Although Cynthia had told them to keep out of it, they'd do more harm than good, once the sheriff's team left Sugar Hollow, the three women zipped in.

Mrs. Murphy somersaulted as she tried to catch a grasshopper. *"Spit, spit tobacco juice and then I'll let you go."*

"Gotta catch him first." Tucker thought grasshoppers beneath her attention.

"I will, O ye of little faith, and when I do I'll say, 'Spit, spit tobacco juice and then I'll let you go.'"

"Grasshoppers don't understand English." Tucker put her nose to the ground again. She wanted to assist the humans, but any trace of scent other than the smell of rot still hanging on the ground was gone. The humans could no longer smell the decay. *"There's*

nothing here. We've been walking in circles for an hour and I don't know why they want to stick their noses in it anyway," growled Tucker, who stuck her nose in everything.

"A dull summer. Besides, when has Mother ever been able to sit still?"

"I sure can." And with that Tucker plopped down.

The grasshopper or a close relative flipped by Murphy again, and she shot straight up in the air, came down with the insect between her paws, and rolled on the ground.

"Gotcha!"

However, she opened one paw slightly for a close look at her quarry and the grasshopper pushed off with its hind legs, squirting free. Murphy pounced, but the grasshopper jumped high and opened its wings to freedom. In a rage Murphy clawed at the leaves on the ground.

"Ha-ha," Tucker tormented her.

"Oh, shut up, stumpy." She batted the leaves once more in disgust. *"Tucker—"*

"What now?"

"Look."

The corgi reluctantly rose and walked over to the cat's side. She looked at the small clearing Mrs. Murphy made. *"A ring."*

"More than that. A wedding ring." Murphy touched it with one claw. *"There's an inscription inside. You stay here. I'll get Mom."*

"Good luck."

"I'm going straight for the leg. No meowing and brushing by."

"Like I said, good luck."

The leaves crunched underfoot, a fallen tree trunk emanating a dry and powdery aroma blocked her path. The cat soared right over it. She blasted into the middle of the humans.

"Busy bee." Mrs. Hogendobber noticed Murphy's antics.

" 'You ain't seen nothing yet.' " Mrs. Murphy parodied Al Jolson's line. She fixed her gaze on Harry, then turned, ran straight for her leg, and bit it.

"Ouch! What's the matter with you?" Harry swatted at her. Murphy expertly avoided the clumsy hand and bit the other leg.

"Rabies! That cat has rabies." Mrs. Hogendobber stepped backward into a vine and fell right on her large behind.

"Miranda, are you all right?" Susan hurried over to help up the older lady.

"Fortunately, yes. I have ample padding," she grumbled as she brushed off her bottom.

"Come on." Mrs. Murphy ran around in a tight circle, then sat still in front of Harry. *"Okay, Tucker, how about the National Anthem?"*

"'O say can you see—'" Tucker warbled.

"What an awful racket." Miranda held her hands over her ears. Susan laughed. "She doesn't think so."

"Come on. Follow me. Come on. You'll get it. Watch the pussycat." Mrs. Murphy backed up a few steps.

"She's yakking away as well." Susan watched Murphy.

"Might as well see what it is." Harry got the message. "For all I know, Tucker has her foot caught in a root or something. I never know what these two will get into."

"As long as it's not a skunk." Mrs. Hogendobber wrinkled her nose.

"We'd know by now." Susan crawled over the rotted trunk, which Murphy again cleared in one bound.

Mrs. Hogendobber negotiated the obstacle at a slower pace. By the time she was over, Harry had reached Tucker, who didn't budge.

"'—at twilight's last gleaming, whose broad stripes and—'"

"Tucker," Mrs. Murphy interrupted this outburst of patriotism, *"you can stop now."*

"I was just warming up."

"I know." The cat reached down and touched the ring. *"How long do you give them?"*

"A minute. There's three of them, and unless one of them steps on it, someone will see it."

Harry knelt down to pat Tucker. "You okay, girl?"

"Will you look here!" Mrs. Murphy fussed.

Susan did. "Jeez O Pete. Look."

Miranda bent over. "A wedding ring." She reached for it, then withdrew her hand. "Better not."

Harry snapped off a twig from a low branch, slipped it through the ring, and brought it up to her eyes. "M & M 6/12/86."

17

Coop decided not to gripe at Harry, Susan, and Miranda. After all, they did find the wedding ring, about fifty yards from where the body was found. She'd sent it out for prints, although she figured that was hopeless.

It wasn't even noon, but the day was getting away from her. Two accidents during rush hour and both on Route 29, which snarled up traffic. She'd sent out one officer, but with summer vacations depleting the staff, she covered the other one herself.

As soon as Cynthia had received the information from the Department of Motor Vehicles in California, she called the Los Angeles Police Department. She wondered if Huckstep had a criminal record. Sure enough, the answer came back positive for offenses in San Francisco.

The San Francisco Police Department told her Mike Huckstep had a record for minor offenses: assault and battery, traffic violations, and one charge of indecent exposure. The officer on duty suggested she call Frank Kenton, the owner of the Anvil, a San Francisco bar where Huckstep had worked. When Cynthia asked why, the officer said that they always believed Huckstep was involved in more than minor crime, but they could never nail him.

Cynthia picked up the phone. It would be eight in the morning in San Francisco. She'd gotten the phone number of the Anvil as well as the owner's name and number.

"Hello, Mr. Kenton, this is Deputy Cynthia Cooper of the Albemarle County Sheriff's Department."

A sleepy, gruff voice said, "Who?"

"Deputy Cooper, Albemarle County Sheriff's Department—"

"Where in the hell is Albemarle County?"

"In central Virginia. Around Charlottesville."

"Well, what in the hell do you want with me? It's early in the morning, lady, and I work till late at night."

"I know. I'm sorry. You are the owner of the Anvil, are you not?"

"If you know that, then you should have known not to call me until after one my time."

"I regret disturbing you, but we're investigating a murder and I think you can help us."

"Huh?" A note of interest crept into the heavy voice.

"We found a body which we've finally identified as Michael Huckstep."

"Good!"

"I beg your pardon."

"Good, I'm glad somebody killed that son of a bitch. I've wanted to do it myself. How'd he get it?" Frank Kenton, wide awake now, was eager for details.

"Three shots at close range to the chest with a .357 Magnum."

"Ha, he must have looked like a blown tire."

"Actually, he looked worse than that. He'd been out in the woods in the July heat for at least three days. Anything you can tell me, anything at all, might help us apprehend the killer."

"Shit, lady, I think you should give the killer a medal."

"Mr. Kenton, I've got a job to do. Maybe he deserved this, maybe he didn't. That's not mine to judge."

"He deserved it all right. I'll tell you why. He used to bartend for me. Mike had that look. Big broad shoulders, narrow waist, tight little buns. Good strong face and he'd let his beard go a few days. He was perfect for the Anvil. Think of him as gorgeous rough trade."

Cynthia knew that "rough trade" was a term originated by homosexuals that had passed into heterosexual parlance. It meant someone out of the class system, someone with the whiff of an outlaw, like a Hell's Angel. The term had devolved to mean anyone with whom one slept who was of a lower class than oneself. However, Cynthia assumed that Mike Huckstep was the real deal.

"Is the Anvil a straight or gay bar?"

"Gay."

"Was Mike gay?"

"No. I didn't know that, or I wouldn't have hired him. At first I didn't notice anything. He was good at his job, good with people. He flirted with the customers, made a haul in tips."

"You mean you didn't notice that he wasn't gay?"

"Lady, it was worse than that. He brought in his girlfriend, this flat-chested chick named Malibu. Where in the hell he found her, I'll never know. Anyway, he convinced me to let her help out here. Now, I'll never put a chick behind the bar. That's where we need action. But she fit in, worked hard, so I put her at the door. She could screen customers and handle admission."

"You charge for the bar?"

"On weekends. Always have a live band on weekends."

"Did they steal from you?"

"Not a penny. No, what they did was this. Mike would pick out someone rich. Actually, I think Malibu did the grunt work. Nobody took her seriously. Just another fruit fly, you know what I mean?"

Cynthia understood the term for a woman who hung around gay men. "I know."

"So she'd ask questions, cruise by people's houses if she could track down an address or if they gave it to Mike. Then Mike would trick with the rich guy and Malibu would take pictures."

"Like a threesome?"

"No," he bellowed, "she hid and took pictures and then they'd shake the poor sucker down."

"I thought San Francisco was a mecca for gay America."

"If you work in the financial district, it's not any more of a mecca than Des Moines. And some of the older men—well, they have a different outlook. They have a lot of fear, even here."

"So what happened?"

"One of my regulars, a good man, old San Francisco family, member of the Bohemian Club, wife, kids, the whole nine yards, Mike and Malibu nailed him. He shot himself in the head. A couple of friends told me they suspected maybe Mike was behind it. I finally put the pieces together. He got wind of it, or she did. He never came back to work. I haven't seen him since the day after George Jarvis killed himself, January 28, 1989."

"What about her?"

"Haven't seen her either."

"Were they married?"

"I don't know. They certainly deserved each other."

"One other question, Mr. Kenton, and I can't thank you enough for your help. Did they deal?"

Frank paused to light a cigarette. "Deputy Cooper, back in the seventies and eighties everyone dealt. Your own mother dealt drugs." He laughed. "Okay, maybe not your mother."

"I see."

"Now, can I ask you a favor?"

"You can try."

"If you've got a photograph of that rotten scumbag, you send it out here to me. I know a lot of people who will want to see Mike dead."

"It's pretty gruesome, Mr. Kenton."

"So was what he did. Send me the pictures."

"Well. . . . Thank you again, Mr. Kenton."

"Next time call after one." He hung up the phone.

Cynthia drummed her fingers on the tabletop. There was no shortage of people who wanted to kill Mike Huckstep. But would they follow him here after years had elapsed? What did Huckstep do between 1989 and now? Was Malibu with him? Where was she?

She called the San Francisco Police Department and spoke to the officer in charge of community liaison. He promised to co-operate. He knew the Anvil, knew Kenton. He'd put someone on the case to ask questions of anyone who might remember Huckstep. It wouldn't be his first priority, but he wouldn't forget.

Then she called the LAPD again. She had asked them to go over to Huckstep's apartment. Yolanda Delgreco was the officer in charge.

"Find anything?" Coop asked when Yolanda picked up the line.

"Funny you should call. I just got back. It's been crazy here. Anyway, I'm sorry I'm late. Place was cleaned out. Even the refrigerator was cleaned out. He wasn't planning on coming back."

"Did the landlord or neighbors know anything about him?"

"His landlord said he didn't work. Had a girlfriend. She dumped him. Huckstep told him he lived off his investments, so I ran a check through the banks. No bank account. No credit cards. Whatever he did was cash and carry."

"Or he had the money laundered."

"Yeah, I thought of that too. When my money's laundered it's because I forgot to clean out my pockets before putting my stuff in the washing machine." Yolanda laughed.

"Hey, thanks a lot. If you ever come to Virginia, stop by. We've got some good women in the department. It will take a while longer here than there probably, but we're working on it."

"Thanks. If I do find myself in Virginia, I'll visit. You have many murders there?"

Cynthia said, "No, it's pretty quiet that way."

"If anything turns up on Mike Huckstep, I'll buzz."

Cynthia hung up the phone. Most of her job on a case like this was footwork, research, asking a lot of questions. Over time and with a bit of luck a pattern usually emerged. So far, no pattern.

18

At seven-thirty in the morning the mercury hovered at a refreshing 63 degrees. Harry intended to jog to work, which took twenty minutes and gave Mrs. Murphy and Tucker exercise too. But she fell behind in her farm chores and hopped in the truck instead. The animals climbed in with her.

"Ready, steady, go." She cut on the ignition. The Superman-blue truck chugged a moment, coughed, and then turned over. "Better let it run a minute or two."

Mrs. Murphy's golden, intelligent eyes were merry. *"Mother, it's not the battery that's the problem. This truck is tired."*

"Yeah, we need reliable transportation," Tucker carped.

Harry hummed, then pushed in the clutch, popped it in first, and rolled down the driveway. She reached for the knob on the radio. A country music station blared.

"I hate that stuff." The cat slapped at the knob, making the reception fuzzy.

"Three points." Tucker encouraged her.

The tiger's paw shot out again and she moved the dial even more.

"Bless our nation's leaders in this time of moral peril, give them the courage to root out the evil of Satanism masquerading as liberalism, and lest we—"

"Gross." Murphy blasted the radio. *"Humans are weird beyond belief."*

The strains of a popular tune greeted her kitty ears.

"Better." Tucker's pink tongue hung out. *"Wrinkle music, you know."*

"What do you mean, wrinkle music?" The cat cocked her head at the soothing music.

"For old people. Haven't you noticed that no one wants to admit they're old? So radio stations advertise that they play hits from the fifties, sixties, seventies up to today. That's bunk. It's wrinkle music, but the listener can pretend he's hip or whatever word they used when they were young."

"I never thought of that." Mrs. Murphy admired her friend's insight. *"So how come we don't hear Benny Goodman?"*

"The Big Band generation is so old, they're going deaf."

"Savage, Tucker. Wait until you get old and I make fun of you." The cat laughed.

"You'll be old right along with me."

"Cats don't age like dogs do."

"Oh, bull!"

The news crackled over the radio. Harry leaned forward to turn up the sound. "Pipe down, you two. I want to hear the news and thank you, Mrs. Murphy, for manning the stations. Catting the radio? Doesn't sound right."

"You're welcome." Mrs. Murphy put her paws on the dash so she could see through the windshield.

"The state's largest banks are reporting computer breakdowns. For the last week technicians have been working to restore full function to the computer systems of Richmond Norfolk United,

Blue Ridge Bank, and Federated Investments, all of which are reporting the same problem. Smaller banks are also experiencing problems. Roland Gibson, president of United Trust in Roanoke, counsels people to have patience. He believes this is fallout from the Threadneedle virus, which hit businesses and banks on August first but caused no serious damage, so it was believed. Don't withdraw your money—"

"What do you think of that?" Harry whistled.

"I think I'd call my banker." Murphy arched a silky eyebrow.

"Yeah, me too," the dog echoed.

Harry pulled up behind the post office. When she opened the door the tantalizing aroma of orange-glazed muffins greeted her. Miranda, in a house-cleaning mood, put a checkered tablecloth on the little table. She was measuring the chairs for seat-cover fabric.

"Morning."

Harry's nostrils flared to better capture the scent. "Been reading *House and Garden* again?"

"Threadbare." She pointed to the chair seats. "Couldn't stand another minute of it. Have an orange muffin. My latest."

Harry shoved the muffin in her mouth and said thank you after she ate it. "I sure hope you took some of these next door. These are the best. The best ever." She gulped. "Threadbare. Threadneedle."

"What?" Miranda's lipstick was pearly pink.

A knock on the door diverted Harry's attention from her musing. Susan pushed through the back door. "Where's Rob?"

"Late. Why, are you offering to sort the mail?"

"No." Susan sniffed. "What is that divine smell?"

Harry pointed to the plate of muffins.

Mrs. Hogendobber nodded and Susan's hand darted into the pile. "Oh, oh—" was all she could manage. Swallowing, Susan licked her lips. "I have never tasted anything so delicious in my entire life."

"Now, now, base flattery. You know what the Good Book says about flatterers."

Susan held up her hand for stop. "I don't know what the Good

Book says, but I am not flattering you. These are absolutely out of this world!"

"*Well, I want one!*" Tucker yelped.

Mrs. Hogendobber gave the dog a morsel.

"What's up, Susan? It must be pretty good if you're here this early."

"I get up early." She brushed crumbs off her magenta T-shirt. "However, the buzz is that Mim is fit to be tied—in a total, complete, and obliterating rage."

"Why?"

"She owns a large, as in thirty-seven percent, chunk of Crozet National."

"So?" Harry reached for another orange delight.

"Two million dollars is missing from the bank."

"What!" Miranda shouted.

"Two million smackers." Susan ran her fingers through her blond curls. "Ned's on the board and Hogan called him last night to tell him that he has given Norman Cramer until Wednesday night to finish his audit. He's also called in computer whizzes, since that's where the mess seems to have started, but he believes the money is gone. He wants to prepare everyone before he gives a press statement Friday morning. He's not one hundred percent sure about the sum, but that's what the computer types are telling him as they piece the system back together."

"Good Lord." Mrs. Hogendobber shook her head. "What is—"

"It's the Threadneedle virus. Oops, sorry, Miranda, I interrupted you."

Mrs. Hogendobber waved her hand, no matter.

"*I changed the station. That's how she found out,*" the cat bragged.

"But Crozet National?" Susan continued. "It's small beer compared to United Trust. Of course, they aren't reporting missing funds—yet."

"The Soviets." Miranda smacked the table and scared Tucker, who barked.

"There aren't any more Soviets," Harry reminded her.

"Wrong." Miranda's chin jutted out. "There is no longer a USSR, but there are still Soviets. They're bad losers and they'd love to throw a clinker into capitalist enterprise."

"At Crozet National?" Harry had to fight not to laugh.

"Banks are symbols of the West."

"That's neither here nor there. I want to make sure my money is safe. So I called Hogan myself. Ned could have killed me. Hogan assured me that our money is safe, and even though two million is a terrible loss for the bank, it can absorb it. And the money may yet be found."

"Is Norman Cramer up to the job? I know he's head accountant over there, but—"

"Harry, what does he have to do but punch numbers into a computer? An audit's an audit. It's time consuming, but it doesn't take a lot of gray matter." Miranda, a good bookkeeper, still thought an adding machine could do the job.

The back door swung open. A depressed Mim came in, then brightened. "What is that marvelous—" She spied the muffins. "May I?"

"Indeed." Miranda held out her hand as if bestowing an orange muffin on her old acquaintance.

"Mmm." Mim brushed off her fingers after making short work of the delicious treat. "Susan tell you?"

"Uh—" Harry stalled.

"Yes."

"We can't do much until tomorrow afternoon, when the audit is complete. Worrying won't help." She poured herself a cup of coffee. "Anyone?"

"Any more caffeine and I'll be—"

"A bitch." Tucker finished her mother's sentence.

"Hello!" Pewter arrived through the animal door. *"What a beautiful day."*

"Hello, gray kitty." Susan stroked Pewter's round head. "What do you know that's good?"

"I just saw Kerry McCray tell Aysha Cramer to go to bloody hell."

"What?" the cat and dog asked.

"Isn't she cute?" Mrs. Hogendobber pinched off some muffin for the cat.

Rob Collier tossed the mail bag in the front door as Market Shiflett hustled in the back. Everyone yelled hi at everyone else.

"What a goddamned morning!" Market cursed. "I'm sorry, ladies. Even my cat had to get out of the store."

"What's going on?"

"Cynthia Cooper drove in the minute I opened. She was joking, her usual self, bought coffee and an orange muffin, ah, you brought some here too, Miranda. I'm sold out and it's not even eight. Anyway, Aysha zipped in, and as luck would have it, Kerry followed. They avoided each other just as you'd expect, but they both came to the counter at the same time. Cynthia was leaning against the counter, facing the door. I don't know what kicked it off, but Kerry told Aysha to move her fat butt. Aysha refused to move and called Kerry a cretin. The insults escalated. I never knew women could talk like that—"

"Like what?" Mim's eyes widened.

"Kerry called Aysha a slut. Aysha told Kerry if she'd kept Norman happy he'd have never left her. Well, Kerry said she wasn't a cocksucker, that she would leave that work to Aysha. Before I knew it, Aysha slapped Kerry and Kerry kicked Aysha in the shins. Doughnuts were flying and Cynthia put her coffee on the cake display and separated the two, who were by that point screaming. I just—" He shook his head.

"What despicable language!" Miranda picked up Pewter and held her hand over the cat's ears, realized what she'd done, and quickly removed her hand.

"Kerry told Aysha she was a fake. She doesn't come from an old family." Pewter relished the gossip.

Mrs. Hogendobber stroked the cat, oblivious of the details.

"It's true." Mrs. Murphy sat down and curled her tail around her. *"The Gills are no more first family of Virginia than Blair Bainbridge. The great thing about Blair is he couldn't care less."*

Market caught his breath. "Aysha scratched Cynthia, by mistake she said. I rushed over to pull Kerry back, since Cynthia was trapped between them, keeping them apart—I was sure they were gonna wreck my store. As we pulled them away from each other, Kerry noticed a wedding ring on the floor. She scooped down to pick it up, I had only one arm on her, you know, and she threw it in Aysha's face. 'You lost your wedding ring. That's bad luck, and I wish you a ton of it.' Aysha checked her left hand. She still had her ring on. But she picked up the ring and said, 'This isn't mine.' She held up her ring finger and that set Kerry off again. She lunged for Aysha. I thought I would never get Kerry out of the store. She apologized profusely once I did and then she burst into tears." He threw up his hands. "I feel bad for her.

"The ring had fallen out of Cynthia's pocket when she jumped into action, so to speak. Actually, I shouldn't make light of it. They were out of control and someone could have been hurt. Aysha handed the ring back to Cynthia. 'Married?' she asked. Cynthia said no, she had no secret life. The ring was found near the corpse in Sugar Hollow. She was a little sheepish about it, but she said if she carried it around, now that it was back from the lab, she was hoping it would give off a vibration and give her an idea."

He shook his head again. "Crazy morning. Oh, and Laura Freely came in just looking like death. What's the matter with her? Hogan running around or something?"

"Hogan doesn't run around," Mim said frostily.

"Kerry's got to get over Norman," Susan jumped in.

"Either that or kill Aysha," Market said.

19

Dark circles under Norman Cramer's eyes made him look like a raccoon. He stood before Hogan Freely, whose office was adorned with golf mementos.

"—the staff was great, but we couldn't find what does appear to be a two-million-dollar deficit. We keep coming up short, but we can't find the location of the loss, so to speak. We've gone over everything and I feel responsible for this—"

Hogan interrupted him. "Don't blame yourself."

"I was hoping this was an isolated accounting error."

"This must be what the Threadneedle virus was really about."

"I don't know, sir. Other banks aren't reporting losses. They're reporting downed computers."

"Norman, go home and get some sleep. I'll face the music."

"I should be there with you. This isn't your fault."

"I appreciate that, but the duty is mine to break the news to our investors and customers. Why don't you just go home and sleep? You look like you need it. I appreciate how hard you've worked on this."

"Well"—Norman folded his hands behind his back—"there has to be an answer."

"Yeah"—Hogan smiled weakly—"I just hope I live long enough to find it. Some slick investigator will figure this out. I spoke to an old college buddy down in Virginia Beach at Atlantic Savings and he said the bank has already retained the services of Lorton & Rabinowitz."

"The experts on corporate sabotage." Norman's pupils widened.

Hogan stood up. "Go on, get some sleep."

Wednesdays Fair worked the western end of Albemarle County. That was his excuse to show up at Harry's farm. He found her repairing fences on the back line of her property.

"In the neighborhood."

"So I see," Harry replied.

"I was wrong. That guy pisses me off, but I was wrong."

"How about an apology for hanging up on me."

"That too. If you'd waited a minute, I would have gotten to that. I'm sorry I swore at you and hung up." He jammed his hands in his pockets.

"Apology accepted."

"Need a hand?"

"Sure."

They worked side by side as they had done for the years of their marriage. The light faded, the mosquitoes appeared, but they pressed on until it was too dark. They knew one another so well, they could work in silence without worrying about it.

20

The hot, hazy, humid days of August fled before a mass of cool, sparkling air from Canada, the second in the last ten days. The clear skies and rejuvenating seventy-degree temperatures delighted everyone's senses except perhaps those of Hogan Freely, Norman Cramer, and Mim Sanburne. Not that people clapped their hands when they heard over the morning radio and local television that money was missing from the bank, but in the relief from summer's swelter it didn't seem so immediately important. Also, they believed Hogan when he declared their funds were secure.

Mrs. Hogendobber drove over to Waynesboro Nursery. She wanted a pin oak for the northern corner of her property, a half-acre lot right behind the post office on the other side of the alleyway.

Mrs. Murphy slept in the mail cart. Tucker stretched out under the table in the back. Harry boiled water for tea to counteract her midmorning slump.

The door opened. Aysha glanced around before stepping inside. "Morning."

"Morning, Aysha. No one's here."

"As long as Kerry's not around." Aysha slipped the key in her mailbox, opened the heavy little door, and scooped out her mail. "I suppose you heard what happened yesterday. I guess everyone has."

"Market said you and Kerry got into it." Harry shrugged. "It'll blow over."

Aysha placed her mail on the counter. "She's mental. How can it blow over when she's obsessed with Norman and likewise obsessed with me—negatively, of course. If he had been in love with her, if it had been the right combination, he would have stayed, right?"

"I guess." Harry was never comfortable when people veered toward analyzing one another. She figured psychology was another set of rules with which to restrain people. Instead of invoking the wrath of God, one now invoked self-esteem, lack of fulfillment, being out of touch with one's emotions. The list could go on and on. She tuned out.

"What am I supposed to do?" Aysha wondered. "Hide? Not appear at any social function where Kerry might be present lest I bruise her fragile emotions? Everybody wants to be loved by everybody. That's her real problem, it's not just Norman. She has to be the center of attention. This sure is one way to get it. Why...I even worry about going into the bank. If she had any decency, she'd transfer to another branch. Norman says he avoids her like the plague."

Harry thought Kerry a bit emotional, but the Kerry she knew didn't fit Aysha's description. "Right now neither one of you can be expected to feel good about the other. Ignore her if you can."

"Ignore someone who would have killed me if she could?"

"It wasn't that bad."

"You weren't there. She would have killed me if Cynthia hadn't separated us. Thank God she was there. I'm telling you, Harry, the girl is disturbed."

"Love does strange things to people."

Susan and Mim, one by the front door the other by the back, entered at the same time.

"How's Norman?" Mim asked.

"Stressed out. He can't sleep. He's frantic over the missing money." She knitted her eyebrows. "And this episode with Kerry preys on his mind. He insisted on going to work today, on being there when Hogan made his press statement. I keep telling him, 'Honey, no one blames you,' but he blames himself. He needs a vacation, something."

Mim changed the subject. "Marilyn will take your place at Ash Lawn tomorrow. I know she called and left a message on your machine, but since I'm here, I thought I'd tell you."

"Bless her heart." Aysha's face relaxed. "I can spend tomorrow with Norman. Maybe I can slip a tranquilizer into his coffee or something. Poor baby."

Susan, in her tennis blouse and skirt, checked the old railroad clock. "Harry, I'm late for my game. You gonna be around tonight?"

"Uh-huh. I'm on the back fence line."

"Okay. Ned's going to Richmond, so I'll bring a cold supper."

"Great."

Susan left, Aysha swept out, and Mim stayed. She flipped up the divider and walked behind the counter. As Harry's tea water was boiling, she poured Harry's cup of tea and one for herself too. "New seat covers."

"Miranda couldn't stand the old ones. She's so good at stuff like this."

"Harry, will you do me a favor?"

"If I can."

"When you sort the mail, if you see an unusual number of registered letters or large packages from brokerage houses"—she paused—"I guess you can't tell me, but call Rick Shaw immediately."

Harry gratefully sipped the hot beverage. "I can do that."

"I think the money has to go somewhere. Buying large quantities of stock would be one place, although not the safest. I considered that." Her large gold bangle bracelets clanged together when she reached for her cup. "But a person could say the money was inherited or they could even be in collusion with a broker. But the culprit could be anywhere, and two million dollars doesn't disappear."

Harry, not knowing much about high finance, said, "Is it difficult to get one of those numbered accounts in Switzerland?"

"Not really."

"I would think the temptation to spend the money would be overwhelming. I'd buy a new tractor and truck today."

"Whoever did this is patient and highly skilled at deceit, but then, I suppose we all are to one extent or another."

"Patient or deceitful?" Harry laughed.

"Deceitful. We learn early to mask our feelings, to be polite."

"Who would be smart enough to pull this off?"

"Someone with a more rapacious appetite than the rest of us ever realized."

Just then Reverend Jones stepped into the post office.

Mrs. Murphy looked up at her mother just as Mim did. Mim and Harry looked at the portly reverend and said, "Never."

"What are you girls talking about?"

"Appetites," Harry answered.

Kerry McCray nibbled at carrot sticks and celery. She wasn't hungry and she'd cried so much, she felt nauseated. Reverend Jones, just back from the post office, shepherded her to the slate patio in the back of his house, scrounged in the refrigerator for something to eat, and made some iced tea.

"I don't know what to do." She teared up again, her upturned nose sniffing.

"Everyone loses his or her temper. I wouldn't worry too much about that."

"I know, I know, but I love him and I don't think she does. Oh, she fawns all over him for show, but she doesn't really love him. How could she? All she thinks about is herself. She hasn't changed much since grade school except she's better-looking. The boob job helped."

Herb blushed. "I wouldn't know about that."

"How can you miss it?"

"Now, Kerry, if you dwell on Aysha and Norman, you'll worry yourself to a shadow. You've lost weight. You've lost your sparkle."

"Reverend Jones, I pray. I ask for help. I think God's put me on call-waiting."

He smiled. "That's my Kerry. You haven't lost your sense of humor. We are each tested in this life, although I don't know why. I could quote you Scripture. I could even give you a sermon, but I don't really know why we have to suffer as we do. War. Disease. Betrayal. Death. Some of us suffer greater hardships than others, but still, we all suffer. The richest and the poorest alike know heartache. Maybe it's the only way we can learn not to be selfish."

"Then Aysha needs to suffer."

"I've felt that way about a few people I don't much like, too, but you know, leave them to heaven. Trust me."

"I do, Reverend Jones, but I'd like to see her suffer. I don't feel like waiting until I'm forty. In fact, I'd like to kill her." Kerry's lower lip trembled. "And that's what scares me. I've never hated anyone like I hate her."

"It'll pass, honey. Try to think about other things. Take up a new hobby or a vacation, something to jolt you out of your routine. You'll feel better, I promise."

As Reverend Jones counseled Kerry with his mixture of warmth and good sense, Susan and Harry finished up the fence repairs.

Mrs. Murphy chased a mouse. *"Gotcha!"* She grabbed at the

mouse, but the little devil squirmed from under her paw to scoot under a pile of branches that Harry had made when she pruned the trees in the back.

Tucker, also in on the chase, whined, *"Come on out, coward."*

"They never do." Murphy checked the back of the woodpile just in case.

"Locust posts are hard to find." Harry admired the posts her father put in twenty years earlier. "The boards last maybe fifteen years, but these posts will probably outlast me."

"You'll live a long time. You'll replace them once before you go." Susan picked up her hammer. "I should do this more often. No wonder you never gain an ounce."

"You say that, but you look the same as when we were in high school."

"Ha."

"Don't accept the compliment, then." Harry grinned, checked the ground for nails, and stood up. "Wish we had a little more light. We could take a trail ride."

"Me too. Let's go over the weekend."

"Did I tell you what Mim said to me at her party? She said that men and women couldn't really be friends. Do you believe that?"

"No, but I think her generation does. I've got scads of male friends and Ned has women friends."

"But you still have to settle the issue of sex."

Susan swung her hammer to and fro. "If a man doesn't mention it, I sure don't. I think it's their worry not ours. Think about it. If they don't make a pass at a lady, have they insulted her? I suppose it's more complicated than that, but it seems to me they're damned if they do and damned if they don't. If they take the cue from us that it's okay to forget about it, then I think most of them do. Anyway, after a certain age a man figures out that the first three months sleeping with a new woman will be as thrilling as always. After that it's the same old same old."

"Are we getting cynical?"

"No. Realistic. Everyone you meet in life has problems. If you dump one person and pick up another, you've picked up a new set of problems. It might be that person number two's problems are easier for you to handle, that's all."

"I'm between person number one and person number two and I'm sick of problems. I'm considering being a hermit."

"Everyone says that. Fair's person number one and—"

"It galls me that he thinks he can waltz back into my life."

"Yeah, that would get me too, sometimes, but hey, give him credit for knowing you're the right person and he screwed up."

"Screwed *around*."

"Mother, give him a break," Tucker said.

"Nonetheless, my point stands. As for Blair—"

"Blair hasn't declared himself, so I'm not taking him as seriously as everyone else is."

"But you like him—I mean, *like* him?" Susan's voice was expectant.

"Yeah—I like him."

"You can be maddeningly diffident. I'm glad I'm not in love with you." Susan punched her.

"Don't be ugly."

They trudged toward the barn in the distance. Mrs. Murphy raced ahead, sat down, and as soon as they drew near her, she'd race off again. Tucker plodded along with the humans.

As they put away the tools, Harry blurted out, "Susan, when did the money disappear from the bank?"

"Last week, why?"

"No one has pinpointed an exact time, have they?"

"Not that I recall."

"There's got to be a way to find out." Harry grabbed the phone in the tack room and dialed Norman Cramer. She peppered the tired man with questions, then hung up. "He said he doesn't know for certain the exact time, but yes, it could have started on August first."

Susan rolled the big red toolbox against the corner of the tack room. "The damn virus did work, but doesn't it seem weird to you that other banks aren't reporting missing funds?"

"Yeah, it does. Come on into the house."

Once inside, Harry sat cross-legged on the floor of the library just as she did when she was a child. Books surrounded her. She paged through an *Oxford English Dictionary*. Susan, in Daddy Minor's chair, propped her feet up on the hassock, leafing through a book on the timetables of history.

Mrs. Murphy prowled the bookshelves as Tucker wedged her body next to Harry's.

"They've got all the books they need."

The cat announced, *"There's a mouse in the walls. I don't care about the books."*

"You won't get her out. You haven't been having much luck with mice lately."

"You don't know."

"Say, where's Paddy?" Tucker wondered where Mrs. Murphy's ex, a handsome black and white tom with the charm and wit of the Irish, was living these days.

"Nantucket. His people decided the island would be dull without him, so I guess he's up there chasing seagulls and eating lots of fish."

Harry flipped to "thread." It covered two pages of the unabridged version of the *O.E.D.*

She found "threadbare," which was first used in writing in 1362. The gap between when a word is used and when it is written down can be decades, not that it mattered in this case.

Her eyes swept down the thin, fine grade of paper. "Ah-ha."

"Ah-ha what?"

"Listen! 'Threadneedle' first appeared in writing in 1751. It's a children's game where all join hands. The players at one end of this human string pass between the last two at the other end and then all pass through."

"I can't see that that has anything to do with the problem."

"Me neither."

"Are there other meanings?"

"Yeah. As a verb phrase, 'thread the needle.' It was written in 1844. It refers to a dancing movement when a lady passes under her partner's arm, their hands being joined." Harry glanced up from the dictionary. "I never knew that."

"Me neither. Anything else?"

"It can also mean to fire a rifle ball through an augur hole barely large enough to allow the ball to pass without enlarging the hole." Harry closed the big volume, making a thick, slapping sound. "What have you found?"

"On August 1, 1137, King Louis VI of France died. So did Queen Anne of Britain in 1714." She read some more. "And Germany declared war on Russia in 1914. Well, that certainly changed the world."

"Let's try another book. There has to be something we're missing."

"It could be a red herring, you know."

"Yeah, I do know, but there's something about this that smells of superiority. Whoever is fooling around—"

"Stealing."

"Right, whoever is stealing money is going to rub our noses in how dumb we are."

"Here." Mrs. Murphy, with her paw, pulled out another book listing events in history. The book fell to the floor.

"Murphy." Harry shook her finger at the cat. "You can break a book's spine doing that."

"Don't be such a pill."

"Back talk." Susan laughed. "It sounds exactly the same whether it's your animals or your children."

"I never talk back," Tucker stated.

"Liar," came the cat's swift reply. She jumped down from the bookshelf to sit next to Harry. Susan left her chair and sat on the floor on the other side of Harry.

"Okay. August first. Slavery was abolished in the British Empire in 1834."

"That reminds me, Mim was talking to Kate Bittner about the Civil War series on PBS. Mim said, 'If I'd known it was going to cause this much fuss, I would have picked the cotton myself.'"

Harry leaned back, hands on knees. "Jeez, what did Kate do?" As Kate was of African descent, this was not an idle question.

"Roared. Just roared."

"Good for her. Think she'll be voted president of the Democratic Party in the county?"

"Yes, although Ottoline Gill and—"

"Ottoline's a Republican."

"Not anymore. She had a fight with Jake Berryhill. Bolted from the party."

"What a tempest in a teapot. Let's see what else. In the Middle Ages, August first was considered an Egyptian Day which was supposed to be unlucky."

"Give me that." Susan took the book from Harry. "You're too slow." Her eyes scanned the dense print. "Harry, here's something." She pointed to the item halfway down the page.

They read aloud, "In 1732, the foundation stone was laid for the Bank of England's building on Threadneedle Street in the City of London."

Harry leapt up and grabbed the phone in the kitchen. "Hey, Coop. Listen to this."

Susan, on her feet now, held the book for Harry to read.

When she finished reading, Harry said, "Susan and I—huh?"

Coop interrupted her, "Keep it right there. Between you and Susan."

Offended, Harry replied, "We aren't going to take out an ad in the paper with this."

"I know, but in your enthusiasm you might spill the beans." Coop apologized. "I'm sorry if I snapped at you. We're understaffed. People rotating off for summer vacation. I'm stressed out and I'm taking it out on you."

"I understand."

"You've done good work. Threadneedle means something . . . I guess. It's about banks. You know, this whole thing is screwy. The Threadneedle virus seemed to be a prank. Then two million dollars cannot be accounted for at Crozet National. There's a rash of car wrecks on 29 and a very dead Mike Huckstep, about whom we know little, is on a slab in the morgue. Everything happens at once."

"Sure seems to." Harry had held the earpiece for Susan, who heard everything.

"Hang in there, Coop," Susan encouraged.

"I will. I'm just blowing off steam," she said. "Listen, thanks for your help. I'll see you soon."

"Sure. Bye."

"Bye."

Harry hung up the phone. "Poor Coop."

"This too shall pass."

"I know that. She knows that, but I don't want my money to pass with it. My money is in Crozet National. It may not be so much, but it's all I have."

"Me too." Susan cupped her hand under her chin, deep in thought. In a moment she asked, "You're getting pretty good on the computer, aren't you?"

Harry nodded.

Susan continued. "I'm not so bad myself. I had to learn in self-defense because Danny and Brookie use the thing constantly. At first I didn't know what they were talking about. It really is great that they learn this stuff at school. To them it's just business as usual."

"Want to raid Crozet National's computer?"

"You read my mind," Susan said, grinning. "We could never get in there though. Hogan might be willing, but Norman Cramer would die if anyone touched his babies. I guess his staff wouldn't be too thrilled about it either. What if we screwed it up?"

"Somebody's done that for us," Harry said. " 'Course, we could sneak in."

"Harry, you're nuts. The building has an alarm system."

"I could sneak in," Mrs. Murphy bragged, her ears pricked forward, her eyes flashing.

"She could. Let her do it," Tucker agreed.

"You guys must be hungry again." Harry patted Tucker's head and rubbed her long ears.

"Every time we say anything, she thinks we want to go out or we want to eat." Mrs. Murphy sighed. *"Tucker, we can go into the bank ourselves."*

"When do you want to do it?"

"Tomorrow night."

21

A heavy mist enshrouded the buildings. Downtown Crozet seemed magical in the dim, soft night. Mrs. Murphy and Tucker left the house at one-thirty A.M. with Harry sound asleep. Moving at a steady trot, they arrived at the bank by two.

"You stay outside and bark if you need me."

"What if you need me?" Tucker sensibly asked.

"I'll be all right. I wonder if Pewter is awake? She could help."

"If she's asleep, it will take too long to get her up and going." Tucker knew the gray cat only too well.

"You're right." The tiger sniffed the heavy air. A perfumed scent lingered. "Smell that?"

"Yeah."

"Why here?"

"I don't know."

"Hmm, well, I'm going inside." Her tail straight up, the cat moved to the back door with its old wooden steps. Bricks in the foundation had loosened over the years, and a hole big enough for a cat, a possum, or a bold raccoon, accommodated Mrs. Murphy. She swept her whiskers forward, listened intently, then dropped down into the basement. She quickly ran up the stairs to the first floor. She smelled that perfume again. Much stronger now. She jumped on the cool marble counter in front of the teller windows. She trotted down the counter to the end. The carpeted stairway leading to the second floor was nearby. She followed her nose to the stairs, silently leaping two at a time. The only noise was that of her claws in the carpet as she grabbed for a foothold.

As she neared the top of the stairs, she heard human voices, low, urgent. She flattened herself and slunk along the hallway. She arrived at Hogan's office, where sitting on the floor in the dark were Norman Cramer and Kerry McCray. She froze.

"—to do." Norman's voice was ragged.

"Get a divorce."

"She'll never allow it."

"Norman, what's she going to do—kill you?"

He laughed nervously. "She's violently in love with me, or so she says, but I don't think she really loves me. She loves the idea of a husband. When no one's around, she tells me what to do like I'm an idiot. And if she's not telling me what to do, Ottoline takes up the slack."

"Just tell her it isn't working for you. You're sorry."

He sighed. "Yeah, yeah, I can try. I don't know what happened to me. I don't know why I left you. But it was like I had malaria or something. A fever. I couldn't think straight."

Kerry didn't really want to hear this part. "You need to be real clear. Just 'I'm sorry, I want a divorce' is a good way to start. Okay, so she loses her temper and runs you down all over town. Everyone does that when they break up, or almost everyone."

"Yeah—yeah, I know. It's just that I'm under so much pressure now. This mess here at the bank. I don't know if I can handle two crises at the same time. I need to solve one before attacking the other. I'm not stringing you along. I love you, I know that now. I know I've always loved you and I want to spend the rest of my life with you, but can't you wait—until I get things straightened out here? Please, Kerry. Please, you won't regret it."

"I—" She began crying. "I'll try."

"I do love you." He put his arm around her and kissed her.

Mrs. Murphy, belly low, quietly backed away, then turned and tiptoed down the hall to the stairs. Once on the first floor, she raced across the polished parquet in that sanctuary of money, scooted back down into the cellar, and squeezed out the hole to freedom.

Tucker, relieved to see her friend, bounced up and down on her stubby legs.

"Kerry and Norman are in there crying and kissing. Damn." Mrs. Murphy sat and wrapped her tail around her, for the air was quite cool now.

"Where're their cars?" Tucker was curious. *"They had to have hidden them. Everyone knows everyone, right? Imagine if Reverend Jones or anybody, really, drove by and found their cars at the bank. I want to know where they've stashed their cars."*

"Me too." Mrs. Murphy inhaled the cool air. *"I hate love triangles. Someone always gets hurt."*

"Usually all three," the dog sagely noted. *"Come on. Let's check in the alleyway behind the post office."*

They hurried across the railroad tracks. No car rewarded their speedy efforts.

"If you were a human, where would you park your car?" the cat wondered. *"Under something or behind something unused or ignored in some way."*

They thought for a time.

"There are always cars behind Berryman's garage. Let's look."

They ran back out to Railroad Avenue and loped west, turning south at the railroad underpass onto Route 240. The little garage, freshly painted, was on the next corner.

Stuck behind the other cars waiting to be repaired was Norman's Audi.

"Score one!" Tucker yipped.

"We'd better head home. If we circle the town trying to find Kerry's car, we won't be home by daylight. Mom will be worried. We found one, that's good enough for now."

Footsteps in the distance alerted them. Norman Cramer was heading their way.

"Ssst, here." Mrs. Murphy pointed to a truck that was easy to crawl under.

They peered out but remained motionless. Norman, wiping his eyes, quietly opened the driver's door, got in, started the motor, and drove about half a block without lights before turning them on.

"He looks like Death eating a cracker," Tucker said.

They made it home by sunrise. When Harry fed them she noticed grease on Tucker's back. "Damn, Tucker, have you been playing under the truck again? Now I've got to give you a bath."

"Oh, no!" Tucker wailed to Murphy. *"See the trouble you got me into."*

22

"I'm not stupid." Aysha's lower lip stuck out when she pouted. "You weren't at work late last night."

"I was."

"Don't lie to me, Norman. I drove by the bank and your car wasn't parked there."

"I was there until ten-thirty." He devoutly prayed that she hadn't driven by before that, but as she had attended an Ash Lawn meeting, a special fund-raiser, he figured she wouldn't have gotten out until ten-thirty or eleven. "Then I dropped the papers off at Hogan Freely's and he wanted to talk. I couldn't very well give my boss the finger, could I?"

Red-faced, Aysha picked up the phone and dialed. "Laura, hello, Aysha Cramer. I'm calling for Norman. He thinks he left his Mark Cross pen over there from his meeting last night with Hogan. Have you found it?"

"No. Let me ask Hogan, he's right here." Laura returned to the phone. "No, he hasn't found anything either."

"I'm sorry to disturb you."

"No trouble at all. Tell Norman to rest."

"I will, and thank you. Good-bye." She hung up the phone carefully, then faced her husband. "I apologize. You were there."

"Honey, what's the matter with you? Everything is going to be fine. I'm not going to run off or keel over from a heart attack or whatever you're worried about. We're both under pressure. Let's try to relax."

"It's Kerry, I'm worried about Kerry! I know you can handle the job, but I don't know about—"

He put his arms around her waist and nuzzled her neck. "I married you, didn't I?"

23

"Never, never am I speaking to you again!" Mrs. Murphy hissed.

"One more," Dr. Parker cooed as she hit up the cat with her rabies booster. "There we go, all over."

Ears flat against her head, hunched up and livid, Mrs. Murphy shot off the examining table. She raced around the room.

"Murphy, calm down."

"You lied to get me here," Mrs. Murphy howled.

The doctor checked her needles. "She'll stop in a minute. She does this once a year and I expect she'll do it next year."

"I'll remember when the year rolls around. I won't get in the truck." Murphy, ears still flat back, sat with her back to the humans.

"Come on," Harry cajoled her.

The sleek tiger refused to budge or even turn her face to her friend. Humans give the cold shoulder. Cats give the cold body.

Scooping her up with one hand under her bottom and the

other around her chest, Harry said, "You were a brave girl. Let's go home."

As they rode back into town, Mrs. Murphy stared out the window, back still turned toward Harry.

"Now, look here, Murphy, I hate it when you get in one of your snits. These shots are for your own good. After what you and Tucker did last year, I can't dream of hauling you in to Dr. Parker together. It cost me $123 to replace the curtains in her waiting room. Do you know how long I have to work to make $123? I—"

"Oh, shut up. I don't want to hear how poor you are. My rear end hurts."

"What a yowl. Murphy—Murphy, look at me."

The cat hopped down and crouched on the floor.

Harry's voice rose. "Don't you dare pee in this truck. I mean it." She quickly pulled to the side of the road, got out, and opened the passenger door. She walked into a field, Murphy in her arms. "If you have to go, go here."

"I'm not doing anything you ask me to do." She hunched down amid the daisies.

By the time Harry rolled into Crozet, both cat and human were frazzled. Harry pulled into the market. When she opened the door, Mrs. Murphy nimbly squeezed past her and rushed to the door.

"Open up, Pewter, open up. She's torturing me!"

Harry pushed open the glass door and the cat ran between her legs. Pewter, having heard the complaint, hurried out to touch her nose and have a consoling sniff.

"What happened?"

"Dr. Parker."

"Oh." Pewter licked Mrs. Murphy's ears in sympathy. "I am sorry. I'm sick for a day after those nasty shots."

"Once, just once, I want to go to the doctor with Harry and watch her get the needle." Murphy fluffed her tail.

"Arm or rear?"

"Both! Let her suffer. She won't be able to sit down, and let's see her *pick up a hay bale."* Murphy licked her lips. *"When she opens the door, let's run over to Miranda's. I want to hear her holler."*

"Where's Tucker?"

"Susan's."

"There she goes." Murphy trailed Harry's sneaker, and when the door opened, she shot out, followed by Pewter, less speedy. *"Follow me."*

Harry thought Mrs. Murphy would go to the truck. When the cat zigzagged to the left, she knew this was going to be one of those days. She placed the lettuce and English muffins in the seat of the truck and walked after them. If she ran, then Murphy would run faster. The culprits ambled behind the post office.

"Murphy!" Harry called when she reached the alleyway. She could see a tiger tail protruding from under a blue hydrangea near the alley. Every time she'd call Murphy's name, the cat's tail would twitch.

From opposite ends of the alley drove Kerry McCray in one car and Aysha and Norman Cramer in another. Kerry pulled in behind Market's store and immediately behind her came Hogan Freely, who pulled in next to her. Norman, driving, paused for a moment. Too late to hurry away. Aysha steamed as Harry came up to the window.

"Hi, Harry." Norman called loudly to those behind her, "Hello, Hogan. Hi, Kerry."

They nodded and entered the market.

"If you roll on down the alleyway, go slow. Mrs. Murphy and Pewter are on the rampage."

"I'll pull up behind the post office." He smiled. Aysha did not. "Anyway, we're out of paper towels."

"Norman."

"Just a second, honey. I'll be right back."

Wordlessly, she opened her door and followed him. Damned if she'd let him go in there with Kerry alone.

Harry, torn between conflicting desires, was rooted to the spot. She wanted to catch Murphy. On the other hand, she was only human. What if Kerry and Aysha went ballistic again? Mrs. Hogendobber, in her apron, came out of her back door. Harry motioned her over, quickly explained, and the two tried not to run into the store.

"Do you believe those two?" Pewter giggled.

"I'm insulted. She's supposed to get down on her hands and knees and beg me to come back to the truck." Murphy pouted.

Inside the market everyone grabbed a few items off the shelves so as to not look too obvious. As luck would have it, Susan Tucker and Reverend Jones walked in.

"How's your golf game?" Herb asked Hogan.

"Driving's great. The short game..." Hogan turned down his thumb.

"I'm sorry to hear about the losses at the bank. I know how much that must weigh on you." The reverend's voice, deep and resonant, made the listener feel better already.

"I have turned that problem inside and out. Upside down. You name it. And still nothing."

Aysha and Norman joined them. Kerry hung back, but she wasn't leaving. Susan joined the circle and Harry stayed a step back with Kerry. Mrs. H. walked behind the counter with Market.

"It's in the computer," Susan blurted out.

"Susan, the computer techies checked our system." Norman grimaced. "Nothing."

"The Threadneedle virus." Susan beamed. "Harry and I—"

"No, wait a minute," Harry protested.

"All right, it was Harry's idea. She said that the moneys were noticed missing within a day or two of the Threadneedle scare—"

"We nipped that in the bud." Norman crossed his arms over his chest.

"That's just it," Harry offered. "Whatever the commands were, there must have been a rider, something to delay and then trigger a transfer of money."

"Like an override." Hogan rubbed his chin, a habit when his

mind raced. "Uh-huh. I wonder. Well, we know the problem's not in the machine, so if we can figure out the sequence, we'll know."

"It could be something as simple as, say, whenever you punch in the word *Threadneedle,* a command is given to take money," Susan hypothesized.

"Now, ladies, with all due respect, it isn't that easy. If it were, we would have found it." Norman smiled weakly.

Aysha, eye on Kerry, chimed in. "Let's go, honey, we'll be late for Mother's dinner."

"Oh, sure."

"I think I'll fiddle around tonight at the bank. I work best at night, when it's quiet. You've given me an idea, you two." Hogan glanced from Susan to Harry.

Norman rolled his eyes. Both Aysha and Kerry noticed. Keeping his voice steady, he said, "Now, boss, don't scramble my files." This was followed by an anemic laugh.

"Don't worry." Hogan grabbed his grocery bag. "Those pastries, Miranda—too much." He left.

Norman and Aysha followed.

Kerry, fighting back her urge to trash Aysha, smacked her carton of eggs on the counter so hard, she broke some of them. "Oh, no, look what I've done."

Susan opened the egg carton. "You sure have. Kerry, it's never as bad as you think it is."

"Thanks," came the wobbly reply.

"Where's Tucker?" Harry asked of Susan.

"Back at the house."

"I'm going out to get Murphy. She won't speak to me. Mrs. H.—"

"Yes."

"Vet day. If I can't convince that furry monster to go home with me, will you keep an eye on her? She'll go to the post office or your back door."

"I'll put her in the store with Pewter. Murphy can't resist a bite of sirloin," Market offered.

He was right. Both cats waltzed through the back door about an hour later.

Late that night with the lights out, Murphy told Pewter what she had heard at the bank. They sat in the big storefront window and watched the fog roll down.

"You've never spent a night in the store," Pewter observed. *"It's fun. I can go out if I want since Market put in a kitty door like yours, but mostly I like to sit in the window and watch everything."*

"It was nice of Market to let me stay. Nice of him to call Harry too. I suppose she thinks I'm learning a lesson. Fat chance. I'll remember the date."

"She fooled you. She took you to the vet on Sunday. Special trip."

Mrs. Murphy thought about that. *"She's smarter than I think. Wonder what she had to pay Dr. Parker to make a special trip to the office?"*

When Hogan pulled into the bank, his headlights were diffused in the thickening mist. The cats could just make him out as he unlocked the front door and entered. Within a minute the lights went on upstairs, in a fuzzy golden square.

"Diligent," Pewter said. She licked one paw and wiped it over an ear.

Lights turned off in other buildings as the hours passed. Finally only a few neon lights shone in store windows or over signs; the street lamps glowed. The cats dozed, then Mrs. Murphy opened her eyes.

"Pewter, wake up. I heard a car behind us."

"People use the alleyway."

A door slammed, they heard the crunch of human shoes. Then a figure appeared at the corner. Whoever it was had walked the length of the alleyway. They couldn't make out who it was or even what gender, as the fog was now dense. In a moment, swirling gray swallowed the person.

Inside his office Hogan kept blinking. His eyes, exhausted by the screen of the computer, burned. His brain burned too. He tried all manner of things. He punched in the word *Threadneedle*. He remembered the void commands. He finally decided he would review clients' accounts. Something might turn up that Norman had missed. An odd transfer or an offshore transfer. He could go through the accounts quickly since he knew these people and their small businesses. He was at the end of the H's by midnight. An unfamiliar yet familiar name snagged him.

"Huckstep," he said aloud. "Huckstep." He punched in the code to review the account. It had been opened July 30 in the name of Michael and Malibu Huckstep, a joint account. Of course—the murdered man. He must have intended to stick around, if he opened an account. That meant he had an account card with his signature and his wife's. He was going to go downstairs to check the card files, but first the buttons clicked as he checked the amount in the savings account: $4,218.64. Not a lot of money but enough. He rubbed his eyes and checked his wristwatch. Past twelve. Too late to call Rick Shaw. He'd call him first thing in the morning.

Meanwhile he'd go down and check those signature cards. He stood up, interlocked his fingers, and stretched his hands over his head. His knuckles cracked just as the bullet from a .357 tore into his shoulder. He opened his mouth to call out his assailant's name, but too late. The next one exploded his heart and he crashed down into his chair.

Back in the store, the cats heard the gunfire.

"*Hurry!*" Mrs. Murphy yelled as they both screeched out the kitty door. As they ran toward the bank, they heard through the dense fog footsteps running in the opposite direction, up at the corner.

"*Damn! Damn!*" The tiger cursed herself.

"*What's the matter?*"

"*Pewter, we should have gone around back to see the car.*"

"Too late now." The smallish but rotund gray cat barreled toward the bank.

Arriving at the front step only a couple of minutes after the gunfire, they stopped so fast at the door that they tumbled over one another and landed on a figure slumped in the doorway, a smoking .357 in her hand.

"Oh, NO!" Murphy cried.

$$\boxed{24}$$

Kerry McCray lay slumped across the front doorway of the bank. A small trickle of blood oozed from her head. The acrid odor of gunpowder filled the air. The pistol was securely grasped in her right hand.

"We've got to get Mrs. Hogendobber." Mrs. Murphy sniffed Kerry's wound.

"Maybe I should stay here with her." Pewter kept patting Kerry's face in a vain effort to revive her.

"If only Tucker were here." The tiger paced around the inert form. "She could guard Kerry. Look, Pewter, we'll have to risk that she'll be safe. It's going to take two of us to get Mrs. Hogendobber here."

That said, the two sped through the fog, running so low to the ground and so fast that the pads of their paws barely touched it. They pulled up under Miranda's bedroom window which was

wide open to catch the cooling night air. A screen covered the
window.

"Let's sing," Murphy commanded.

They hooted, hollered, and screeched. Those two cats could
have awakened the dead.

Miranda, in her nightdress, shoe in hand, came to the window.
She opened the screen and let fly. Mrs. Murphy and Pewter
dodged the missile with ease.

"Bad shot! Come on, Mrs. H., come on!"

"Pewter?" Miranda squinted into the fog.

The tubby kitty jumped up on the windowsill followed by
Mrs. Murphy before Miranda could close the screen.

*"Oh, please, Mrs. Hogendobber, please listen to us. There's terrible
trouble—"* Pewter said.

"Somebody's hurt!" Murphy bellowed.

"You two are getting on my nerves. Now, you get on out of
here." Miranda slid the screen up again.

"No!" they replied in unison.

"Follow me." Murphy ran to the door of the bedroom.

Miranda simply didn't get it even though Pewter kept telling
her to hurry, hurry.

"Watch out. She might swat," Murphy warned Pewter as she
snuck in low and bit Miranda's ankle.

"Ouch!" Outraged, Mrs. Hogendobber switched on the light
and picked up the phone. As she did, she noticed the cats circling
her and then going back and forth to the door. Their distress af-
fected her, but she wasn't sure what to do and she was mad at
Murphy. She dialed Harry.

A dull hello greeted her.

"Your cat has just bit me on the ankle and is acting crazy.
Rabies."

"Mrs. Hogendobber—" Harry was awake now.

"Pewter's here too. Screeching under my window like banshees
and I opened the window and they jumped in and—" She bent
down as Pewter rubbed her leg. She noticed a bit of blood on

Pewter's foreleg and paw where the cat had patted Kerry's head. "Pewter has blood on her paw. Oh, dear, Harry, I think you'd better come here and get these cats. I don't know what to do."

"Keep them inside, okay? I'll be right over, and I'm sorry Murphy bit you. Don't worry about rabies—she's had her shots, remember?" Harry hung up the phone, jumped into her jeans and an old workshirt. She hurried to the truck and cranked it up. As she blasted down the road, she stuck some gum in her mouth. She'd been in too big a rush to brush her teeth.

In seven minutes she was at Miranda's door. As Harry entered the living room Murphy said, *"Try again, Pewter. Mother's a little smarter than Miranda."*

They both hollered, *"Kerry McCray's hurt."*

"Something's wrong." Harry reached for Pewter's paw, but the cat eluded her and ran to the front door.

"Rabies." Miranda folded her arms across her bosom.

"No, it isn't."

"That tiger, that hellcat, bit me." She dangled her ankle out from under her nightdress. Two perfect fang marks, not deep but indenting the skin, were revealed.

"Come on," Murphy yowled at the top of her lungs. She scratched at the front door.

"These two want something. I'm going to see. Why don't you go back to bed. And I do apologize."

"I'm wide awake now." Miranda returned to her bedroom, threw on a robe and slippers, and reappeared. "I can't go back to sleep once I've been awakened. Might as well prove that I'm as crazy as you and these cats are." With that she sailed through the open door. "I can barely see my hand in front of my face. How'd you get here so quickly?"

"Drove too fast."

"Come on. Come on." Murphy trotted up ahead in the gray mists, then back. *"Follow my voice."*

"Harry, we're out on Main Street and they're headed for the railroad tracks."

"I know." The air felt clammy on her skin.

"Is this some cat trick?"

"Shut up and hurry!" Pewter's patience was wearing thin.

"Something definitely is agitating them and Murphy's a reasonable cat—usually."

"Cats are by definition unreasonable." Miranda stepped faster. The bank loomed in the mist, the upstairs light still burning.

The cats called to them through the fog. Harry saw Kerry first, lying facedown, right hand outstretched with the gun in it. Mrs. Murphy and Pewter sat beside her.

"Miranda!"

Mrs. Hogendobber moved faster, then she, too, saw what at first seemed like an apparition and then like a bad dream. "Good heavens."

Harry skidded up to Kerry. She knelt down and felt for a pulse. Miranda was now next to her.

"Is she all right?" Mrs. Murphy asked.

"Her pulse is regular."

Miranda watched Pewter touch Kerry's head. "We've got to get an ambulance. I'll go in the bank and call. The door's open. That's odd."

"I'll do it. I have a funny feeling something is really wrong in there. You stay here with her and don't touch anything, especially the gun."

Miranda realized as Harry disappeared into the bank that she'd been so distraught at the sight of the young woman, she hadn't noticed the gun.

Harry returned shortly. "Got Cynthia. Called Reverend Jones too."

"If this is as bad as I think it is, then I suppose Kerry needs a minister." Miranda's teeth were chattering although the night was mild.

Kerry opened her eyes. "Mrs. Murphy."

The cat purred. *"You'll be fine."*

"After the headache goes away," Pewter advised.

"Kerry—"

"Harry—" Kerry reached to touch her head as she rolled onto her side and realized a gun was in her right hand. She dropped it as if it were on fire and sat straight up. "Oh." She clasped her head with both hands.

"Honey, you'd better lie back down." Miranda sat beside her to ease her down.

"No, no—let me stay still." Kerry forced a weak smile.

A coughing motor announced Herb. He pulled alongside the bank and got out. He couldn't see them yet.

"Herbie, we're at the front door," Miranda called loudly to him.

His footsteps came closer. He appeared out of an envelope of thick gray fog. "What's going on?"

"We don't really know," Miranda answered.

Kerry replied, "I feel dizzy and a little sick to my stomach."

Herb noticed the bank door was wide open.

Harry said, "It was open. I used the phone inside, but I didn't look around. Something's wrong."

"Yes—" He felt it too. "I'm going in."

"Take the gun," Miranda advised.

"No. No need." He disappeared into the bank.

"Should we go with him?" Pewter wondered.

"No, I'm not leaving Mother." Murphy continued purring because she thought the soothing sound might calm the humans.

"What little friends you are." Kerry petted the cats, then stopped because even that made her stomach queasy.

"They found you and then they found us—well, it's a long story." Harry sat on the other side of Kerry.

"Herb, what's the matter?" Miranda was shocked when he reappeared. His face, drained of all color, gave him a frightful appearance. He looked as sick as Kerry.

"Hogan Freely's been murdered." He sat heavily on the pavement almost the way a tired child drops down. "I've known him all my life. What a good man—what a good man." Tears ran down his cheeks. "I've got to tell Laura."

"I'll go with you," Miranda offered. "We can go after the sheriff arrives."

"Kerry." Harry, shaking, pointed to the gun.

Kerry's voice wavered. "I didn't kill him. I don't even own a gun."

"Can you remember what happened?" Harry asked.

"Up to a point, I can." Kerry sucked in air, trying to drive out the pain. "I was over at Mother and Dad's. Dad's sick again, so I stayed late to help Mom. I didn't leave until a little past midnight, and I was crawling along because of the fog. I passed the corner and thought I saw a light in Hogan's office window. It was fuzzy but I was curious. I turned around and parked in the lot. I figured he was up there trying to find the money like he said he was going to do and I was going to surprise him, just kind of cheer him up. I walked up these steps and opened the door, and that's all I remember."

"What about sounds?" Harry asked.

"Or smells?" Pewter added. *"Murphy, let's go in and see if we can pick up a scent. Harry's all right. No one's around to hit her on the head and Kerry won't do anything crazy."*

"Okay."

The two cats left.

"I remember opening the door. I don't remember footsteps or anything like that, but somebody must have heard me. I didn't think I was making that much noise."

"Luck of the draw," Herb said. "You were going in as he was going out."

The sirens in the distance meant Cynthia was approaching.

The two cats lifted their noses and sniffed.

"Let's go upstairs." Mrs. Murphy led the way.

As they neared Hogan's office, Pewter said in a small voice, *"I don't think I want to see this."*

"Close your eyes and use your nose. And don't step in anything."

Murphy padded into the room. Hogan was sitting upright in his chair; his shoulder was torn away. Blood spattered the wall behind him. A small hole bore evidence to the bullet that killed him. Murphy could smell the blood seeping into the upholstery of the chair.

Pewter opened one eye and then shut it. *"I can't smell anything but blood and gunpowder."*

"Blood and gunpowder." Mrs. Murphy leapt onto his desk with a single bound. She tried not to look into Hogan's glassy stare. She liked him and didn't want to remember him like this.

His computer was turned off. His desk drawers were closed. There was no sign of struggle. She touched her nose to every article on his desk. Then she jumped back to the floor. She stopped by the front of his desk.

"Here."

Pewter placed her nose on the spot. *"Rubber. Rubber and wet."*

"From the misty night, I would think. Rubber won't leave much of a print and not in this carpet. Dammit! Rubber, blood, and gunsmoke. Whoever did this was no dummy."

"Maybe so, Murphy, but whoever did this was in a hurry. The computer is off but still warm." Pewter noticed Hogan's feet under the desk. *"Let's talk about this outside. This place gives me the creeps."*

"Okay." It bothered Murphy, too, but she didn't want to admit it.

As they walked back down the stairs, Pewter continued. *"If someone wanted to dispatch Hogan Freely, there are better ways to do it."*

"I agree. So, he was getting close to the missing money."

As the cats passed through the lobby, Rick Shaw entered. He saw them but didn't say anything.

The blue and red flashing lights of the squad car and the ambulance reflected off the fog.

Kerry, on a stretcher, was being carried to the back of the ambulance.

The cats stood next to Harry and Mrs. Hogendobber. Herb, with a slow tread, turned to enter the bank. Cynthia, pad out, was taking notes.

"Herb, I'll go with you."

"Good."

"We'll wait here." Harry pulled Miranda back as she was about to follow. "You'll have nightmares."

"You're right—but I feel so awful. I hate to think of him up there, alone and—"

"Don't think about it and don't let Laura think about it either when you go over there with Reverend Jones. It's too painful. She doesn't have to know all the details."

"You're right." Miranda lowered her eyes. "This is dreadful."

"Dreadful—" Mrs. Murphy whispered, *"and just beginning."*

25

The hospital smell bothered Harry, reminding her of her mother's last days on earth. She avoided visiting anyone in a hospital if she could, but invariably duty overcame aversion and she would venture down the impersonal corridors.

Kerry was being kept for twenty-four hours to make sure she suffered no further effects from her assault. The doctors treated any blow to the head as serious. Cynthia Cooper was sitting next to Kerry's bed when Harry entered the room.

"How you doing?"

"Okay—considering."

"Hi, Coop."

"Hi." Coop shifted in her seat. "Hell of a night."

Kerry fiddled with her hospital identification wristband. "Cynthia went with Rick and Herbie to Laura Freely's. Laura collapsed when they told her."

"Who's with her until Dudley and Thea can fly home?" Dudley and Thea were the Freelys' adult children.

"Miranda spent the night there. Mim's with Laura right now. The ladies will take turns even once the children return. There's so much to do and Laura is sedated. She can't make any of the decisions that need to be made. I think Ellie Wood Baxter, Port, and even BoomBoom will work out a schedule." Cynthia stretched her legs.

"Kerry, I dropped by to see if you needed anything from home, what with your dad being sick. I'm happy to pick up stuff for you."

"Thanks, but I'm okay."

"Cynthia—?" Harry's eyebrows pointed upward quizzically.

"I'm here to see she doesn't make a run for it. The .357 in her hand was the gun that killed Hogan. And it's registered to Kerry McCray."

"I don't own a gun." Kerry teared up.

"According to the records, you bought one at Hassett's in Waynesboro, July tenth."

"Are you arresting my friend here?" Harry tried to keep her voice light.

"No, not yet."

"Cynthia, you can't possibly believe that Kerry would kill anyone."

"I'm a police officer. I can't afford emotions."

"Bullshit," came Harry's swift retort.

"Thanks, Harry. We're not close friends, and here you are— thanks." Kerry flopped back on the pillows, then winced because she felt the throb in her head. "I never bought a gun. I've never been to Hassett's. On July tenth I worked all day as usual, handling new accounts."

Cynthia firmly said, "According to records, you showed your driver's license."

"I never set foot in that gun shop."

"What if Kerry is the one who masterminded the bank theft? Maybe Hogan is starting to figure out her m.o." Cynthia used the police shorthand for modus operandi. "She's getting nervous. She knew he was working late in that bank that night. Millions of dollars are at stake. She kills Hogan."

"And hits herself on the head hard enough to knock herself out—yet still keep the gun in her hand?" Harry was incredulous.

"That presents a problem." Cynthia nodded. "But Kerry could have an accomplice. He or she hits her on the head so she looks innocent."

"And I could fly to the moon." Harry sharply inhaled. "This summer is sure turning to crap."

"How elegantly put." Cynthia half smiled.

"Forget being an officer and be one of the girls just for a minute, Coop. Do you really think Kerry killed Hogan?"

Cynthia waited a long time. "I don't know, but I do know that the .357 is the same gun that killed Mike Huckstep."

"What?" Harry felt her throat constrict.

"Ballistics report came back at six this morning. Rick's lashing everyone on. Same gun. We'd like to keep that tidbit out of the papers, but I doubt the boss can. His job is so damned political."

"Huckstep and Hogan Freely." Harry frowned. "One's a Hell's Angel and the other's a bank president."

"Maybe Hogan had a secret life?" Kerry spoke up.

"Not that secret." Harry shook her head.

"You'd be amazed at what people can hide from one another," Cynthia replied.

"I know that, but at some point you've got to trust your instincts," Harry replied.

"Well then, what do your instincts tell you?" Cynthia challenged her.

"Hogan was getting close and that means the answer is in the bank."

"Think you're right."

Kerry moaned. "My goose is cooked, isn't it?"

Cynthia stared hard at her.

26

Because of federal regulations, the bank could not be closed on Monday. In fact, if Hogan had been shot during banking hours, the way the law reads he would have been left there and business would have continued while the sheriff worked. People would have had to step over the body. These stringent rules against closing a bank were born in the 1930s when banks bolted their doors or folded like houses of cards. As is customary when legislators cook up some ameliorative law, it never covers the human condition. The employees of Crozet National worked with black armbands around their left arms. A huge black wreath hung at the end of the lobby, a smaller one on the front door. Out front, the Virginia state flag flew at half mast. Mary Thigpen, the head teller for twenty-five years, kept bursting into tears. Many eyes were red-rimmed.

All the talk about Kerry so outraged Norman that he shouted, "She's innocent until proven guilty, so shut up!"

Rick Shaw had taken over the second floor, squeezing the accounting department, but they managed. The blood splattered on the wall of Hogan's office made Norman woozy. He wasn't the only one.

Mim Sanburne came by after her turn with Laura Freely to inform everyone that the funeral service would be held that Thursday at the Crozet Lutheran Church. The family would receive Wednesday night at home.

A subdued hush followed her announcement.

Over at the post office Harry asked Blair to help while Mrs. Hogendobber organized the food for Wednesday night. Dudley Freely proved incompetent due to shock. Thea, the older Freely child, was better at making some of the decisions forced upon her by the event. What kind of casket, or would it be cremation? What cemetery? Flowers or contributions to charity? She fielded these questions, but sometimes she would have to sit down, fatigued beyond endurance. She didn't realize a great emotional blow is physically exhausting. Mim and Miranda did. They took over. Ottoline Gill and Aysha handled the phone duties. Laura languished in bed. When she regained consciousness she would sob uncontrollably.

Rick and Cynthia tried to question her, but she couldn't get through even a gentle interrogation.

Rick pulled aside Mim outside the post office, as they had both driven in to get their mail. "Mrs. Sanburne, you knew Hogan all his life. Can you imagine him involved in some kind of scheme to defraud people—"

She cut him off. "Hogan Freely was the most honest and generous man I've ever known."

"Don't get huffy, Mrs. Sanburne, I've got two murders on my hands. I have to ask uncomfortable questions. He could have been involved in the theft and had his partner or partners turn on him. It's not an uncommon occurrence."

"I'm sorry, but you must understand. Hogan loved this town and he loved banking. If you knew the people he took chances on, the people he helped get started in business, well, he was about a lot more than money."

"I know. He helped me get my mortgage." Rick opened the door for Mim as they stepped into the post office.

Mrs. Murphy, crouched on the little ledge dividing the mailboxes, waited for Rick and Mim to open their boxes.

Rick opened his first and the tiger reached into his box, swatting his hand as he withdrew his mail.

"Murphy." He walked to the counter and looked around the corner of the boxes.

She looked back at him. *"I wanted to make you feel better."*

"That cat going to grab me?" Mim called.

Harry lifted her from the small counter, ideally suited for sorting into the rows of postboxes. "No, I've got her right here in my arms."

Tucker, head on her paws, said, *"Murphy, nothing is going to make people feel better right now."*

Rick chucked the tiger under the chin. "If only animals could talk. Who knows what she saw the night Hogan was murdered?"

"I didn't see anything because of the fog and I missed a chance to identify the killer's car. I wasn't so smart, sheriff."

"You did the right thing, Murphy, you found help," Tucker lauded her.

Rick left, Mim gave Harry and Blair the information about the family gathering and the funeral, and then she left too.

Harry moved with a heavy tread. "I feel awful."

Blair put his arm around her shoulders. "Everyone does."

$$\boxed{27}$$

"We're going to be late." Norman checked his watch as he paced.

"I'm almost ready. I ran into Kate Bittner at the 19th Hole, and you know how she can talk."

He bit his tongue. She was always late. Running into someone at the supermarket was just another excuse. A car turning into the driveway diverted his attention away from pushing Aysha on.

Ottoline, in full regalia, stepped out of her Volvo station wagon.

"Oh, no," he said under his breath.

Ottoline came in the front door without knocking.

"Norman, you look ashen."

"I'm very tired, Ottoline."

"Where's my angel?"

"In the bathroom, where else?"

She squinted at him, her pointy chin sticking out. "A woman must look her best. You men don't understand that these things take time. I have yet to meet the man who wants an ugly woman on his arm."

"Aysha could never be ugly."

"Quite." She click-clacked down the hallway. The bathroom door was open. "You need different earrings."

"But, Mummy, I like these."

"Too much color. We're going to pay our sympathies. This may be a gathering, but it's not a party."

"Well—"

"Wear the drop pearl earrings. Discreet, yet they make a statement."

"All right." Aysha marched into the bedroom, took off her enameled earrings, and plucked out the pendant pearls. "These?"

Exasperated, Norman joined them. "Aysha—please."

"All right, all right," she crossly replied. "I'm ready."

"I hope you'll be made president of the branch now." Ottoline inspected her son-in-law's attire. He passed muster.

"This isn't the time to think about that."

Her lips pursed. "Believe me, there are others not nearly so scrupulous. You need to go into Charlottesville and talk to Donald Petrus. You're young, but you're the obvious person for the job."

"I don't know if that's true."

"Just do as I say," she snapped.

"There are others with more seniority," he snapped back.

"Old women."

"Kerry McCray."

"Ha!" Aysha finally entered into the conversation. "She murdered Hogan Freely."

"Like hell she did. She'll be found innocent."

Ottoline tapped her foot on the floor. "Innocent or guilty . . . she's irrelevant. You must seize the day, Norman."

He looked from mother-in-law to wife and sighed.

28

Harry hated these dolorous social events, but she would attend. Sad as such events were, not to pay one's last respects meant just that, no respect.

She hurried home from the post office. Miranda had spent the day dashing back and forth between the mailboxes and her kitchen. Luckily, Blair had helped drive food over to the Freelys' and had run errands for Miranda, because the mail load, unusually heavy for a Wednesday, kept her pinned to the post office more than she had wished.

Once home, Harry hopped in the shower, applied some mascara and lipstick. Her short hair, naturally curly, needed only a quick run-through with her fingers while it was wet.

"What's she doing in there?" Tucker languidly rolled on the floor, ending up tummy in the air.

"Tarting herself up."

"Did she remember the blusher? She forgets half the time," Tucker noted.

"I'll go see." Mrs. Murphy quietly padded into the small bathroom. Harry had forgotten. The cat leapt onto the little sink and knocked the blusher into the sink. *"You need some rose in your cheeks."*

"Murphy." Harry reached down and picked up the square black container. "Guess this wouldn't hurt." She touched her cheek with the brush. "There. A raving beauty. I mean, men quiver at my approach. Women's eyes narrow to slits. Kingdoms are offered me for a kiss."

"Mice! Moles! Catnip, all at your feet." Mrs. Murphy enjoyed the dream.

"Who's there? Who's there?" Tucker barreled toward the back door.

Fair knocked, then stepped over the little dog, who immediately stopped barking.

"Hi, cute cakes." Fair smoothed his hand over Tucker's graceful ears, then he called, "It's me."

"I didn't know you were coming," Harry called from the bathroom.

"Uh, I should have called, but it's been one of those days. Had to put down Tommy Bolender's old mare. Twenty-six. He loved that mare and I told him to just go ahead and cry. He did, too, and then I got teary myself. Then that high-priced foal over at Dolan's crashed a fence. Big laceration on her chest. And Patty has thrush."

Patty, a sweet school horse at Sally and Bob Taylor's Mountain Hollow Farm, had taught two generations of people to ride.

Harry joined him. She wore a long skirt, sandals, and a crisp cotton blouse.

"I don't think I've seen you in a skirt since the day we were married."

"That long, huh?" She paused. "Now, Fair, you should have

called me because I'm supposed to go to the Freelys' with Blair and—"

Fair held up his hand in the stop position. "We'll both take you."

"He may not take kindly to that notion."

He held up his hand again. "Leave him out of the loop for a minute. Do you take kindly to it?"

"If you both behave."

"How about this." Tucker wagged her non-tail. *"Mom's being escorted by the two best-looking men in the county. The phone lines will burn tonight."*

"BoomBoom's will burn the brightest." Mrs. Murphy was now sitting next to Tucker.

"You'll be pleased to know that I called Blair on my way over, since I anticipated this."

"Why didn't you call me?"

"What if you'd said no? Then I'd lose a chance to see you, and in a skirt too."

Another vehicle came down the driveway. Tucker ran barking to the door. She stopped quickly. *"Blair, in the Mercedes."*

Harry kissed the cat and dog and walked outside with Fair. They both got into Blair's Mercedes and drove off.

"How do you like that?" Tucker watched the red taillights.

"I like it a lot. It proves that Fair and Blair can both learn to get along and put Harry's interests first. That's what I care about. I want someone in Mom's life who makes her life easier. Love shouldn't feel like a job."

29

Flowers, mostly pastels and whites, filled every room of the Freely house. Laura sat in the big wing chair by the living room fireplace. At moments she recognized people. Other times she lapsed into an anguished trance.

Dudley, subdued, greeted people at the door. He'd pulled himself together. A few people cold-shouldered Ned Tucker since they heard he'd taken Kerry McCray's case.

Thea, with the assistance of Mrs. Hogendobber, Mim, and Little Marilyn, accepted condolences, shared memories, made sure that people had something to eat and drink. Ottoline Gill, relishing her self-appointed position, led people to Laura and then quietly led them away toward the food table. Everything was well organized.

In the dining room, Market Shiflett kept replenishing the food supply at his own expense. Hogan had helped him secure his business loan. In the parlor, Aysha and Norman talked to people. From time to time Norman glanced at the front door. He looked miserable. Aysha looked appropriately sad.

Harry's arrival with the two men riveted people's attention until Kerry, released from the hospital that morning, arrived with Cynthia Cooper. At the door she greeted Dudley, who waved off Ottoline. He listened intently, then took Kerry directly to his mother. Ottoline was scandalized, and it showed. A hush fell over the room.

"Laura, I'm so terribly sorry."

Laura lifted her head in recognition. "Did you shoot my Hogan?"

"No. I know it looks bad, but I didn't. I admired and respected him. I would never have done anything so horrible. I'm here to offer my deepest sympathy."

You could have heard a pin drop.

Jim Sanburne took control of the situation. "Folks, we've got to reach out for the best in each other. We'll get through this, we'll celebrate Hogan's life by being more like him, and that's by helping other people."

"And by catching his killer!" Aysha glared directly at Kerry until Norman squeezed her upper arm—hard.

"Hear. Hear." Many in the room shared this sentiment.

As people gathered around Aysha, more people poured into the house. There was barely room to turn around. Norman slipped out. Kerry observed this and left, too, after saying good-bye to Laura. Cooper followed her at a discreet distance.

Norman was lighting a cigarette. He stood, forlorn, in the green expanse of the manicured lawn.

She slipped her arm through his, surprising him. "I *must* see you."

"Soon." He offered her a cigarette.

A car was heading toward them. He adroitly extricated them from the approaching light. "Maybe we'd better walk away from the house."

As they walked off to the side yard, Kerry pleaded, "I can't live this way, Norman. Are you going to tell her or not?"

"Tell her what?"

"That you're leaving her."

"Kerry, I told you I can't handle a crisis in my home life and at work at the same time. And right now you're looking down the barrel of a gun." He stopped. "Sorry, it's a figure of speech. Let me get through this thing at work and then I can attend to Aysha."

"Attend to Aysha first," she pleaded.

"It's not that easy. She's not that easy."

"I know that. She used to be my best friend, remember?"

"Kerry"—he flicked the cigarette into the grass—"maybe I should give my marriage a chance. Maybe the stress at work has blunted my, uh—kept me from feeling close to Aysha."

Kerry, shaking lightly, said, "Please don't do that. Don't jerk me around. Aysha cares only for Aysha."

"I don't want to jerk you around, but I'm in no condition to make a major decision, and neither are you. Monday I passed Hogan's office. Blood was splattered on the wall. It made me sick. Every time I went downstairs I passed the mess. If you'd seen the blood, you'd be shook too." He shuddered. "I can't take this."

"Time isn't going to make you love Aysha."

"I loved her once."

"You thought you did."

"But what if I do? I don't know what I feel."

Kerry threw her arms around him and kissed him hard. He kissed her back. "What do you feel now?"

"Confused. I still love you." He shrugged. "Oh, God, I don't know anything. I just want to get away for a while."

He reached out and kissed her again. They didn't hear the soft crunch moving toward them.

"Kerry, you *slut*." Aysha hauled off and belted her. "A murderer and a slut."

Norman grabbed his wife, pulling her away. "Don't hit her. Hit me. This is my fault."

"Shut up, Norman. I know this bitch inside and out. Whatever I have, she has to have it. She's competed with me since we were tiny. It just never stops, does it, Kerry?"

"I had him first!"

The shouting grew louder. Harry and Miranda walked out of the house because of the shouting just as Cynthia Cooper stepped out from behind a big oak. She moved toward the trio.

"You didn't want him. You were going to bed with Jake Berryhill at the same time."

Kerry's face was distorted in rage. "Liar."

"You told me yourself. You said you knew that Norman loved you and he was sweet but he was boring in bed." Aysha relished the moment.

Kerry screamed, "You bitch!"

Again Norman pulled them apart with the help of Cynthia. He was mortified to see her.

"For God's sake, keep your voices down. The Freelys don't deserve this!" Harry's lips tightened as she ran over.

"Norman, tell her you're leaving her."

"I can't." Norman seemed to shrink before everyone's eyes.

Kerry's sobs transformed into white-hot hate. "Then I hope you drop dead!"

She twisted away from Cynthia, who caught her. "Time for a ride home until you are formally charged." She pushed Kerry into the squad car.

Norman meekly addressed the little group. "I apologize."

"Go home," Harry said flatly.

Aysha turned and preceded Norman to their car as her mother pushed open the front door. Ottoline called out to her daughter and son-in-law, but they avoided her.

Miranda folded her arms across her chest and shook her head. "Norman Cramer?"

30

Re-inking the postage meter meant sticky red ink on her fingers, her shirt, and the counter too. No matter how hard she tried, Harry managed to spill some.

Mrs. Hogendobber brought over a towel and wiped up the droplets. "Looks like blood."

Harry snapped shut the top of the meter. "Gives me the willies—what with everything that's happened."

Little Marilyn came in with a brisk "Hello." She opened her mailbox with such force, the metal and glass door clacked into the adjoining box. She removed her mail, sorted it by the wastebin, then stopped at the counter. "A letter from Steve O'Grady in Africa. Don't you love looking at foreign stamps?"

"Yes. It's a miniature art form," Miranda replied.

"When Kerry and Aysha and I went to Europe after college, we stayed in Florence awhile, then split up. I had a Eurailpass, so I must have whisked through every country not behind the Iron

Curtain. I made a point of sending them postcards and letters more so they could have the stamps than read my scrawl. We were devoted letter writers."

Miranda offered Little Marilyn a piece of fresh banana cake. "You three were best friends for so long. What happened?"

"Nothing. Nothing in Europe anyway. We wanted to do different things, but no one was angry about it. Kerry came home first. She was in London and got homesick. Aysha lived in Paris and I ended up in Hamburg. Mom said either I was to get a job or marry the head of Porsche. I told her he was in Stuttgart, but she wasn't amused. You know, I still have the letters we sent to one another over that time. Aysha wrote long ones. Kerry was more to the point. It was this business with Norman that broke up the three musketeers. Even when I was married and they were single we stayed close. Then, when Kerry was dating Norman and I was divorcing the monster, we went out together."

"Maybe Norman has hidden talents," Harry mused.

"Very hidden," Mrs. Murphy called out from the bottom of the mail cart.

"Kerry thought so. They always had stuff to talk about." Marilyn laughed. "As for Aysha, she got panicky. All your friends are married and you're not—that kind of thing. Plus, Ottoline lashed her on."

"Panic? It must have been a grand mal seizure." Mrs. Murphy stuck her head out of the mail cart.

Pewter pushed through the animal door. *"It's me."*

"I know," Murphy called back. Pewter jumped in the mail cart with her.

"Isn't it a miracle the way those two cats found Kerry?" Marilyn watched the two felines roll around and bat at one another in the mail cart.

"The Lord moves in mysterious ways His wonders to perform," Mrs. H. said.

Mrs. Murphy and Pewter stopped.

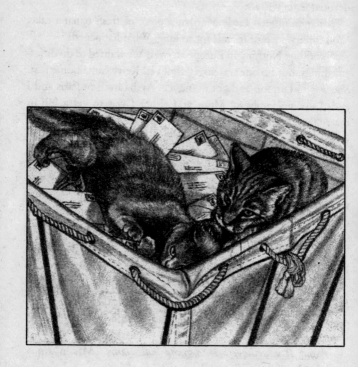

"You'd think they'd realize that the Almighty is a cat. Humans are lower down in the chain of beings."

"They'll never get it. Too egocentric." Pewter swatted Murphy's tail and renewed the combat.

"I ought to get out those old letters." Little Marilyn headed for the door. "Be interesting to see who we were then and who we are now."

"Bring them in someday so I can look at the stamps."

"Okay."

Miranda cut another piece of banana bread. "Marilyn, do you believe Kerry could kill someone?"

"Yes. I believe any of us could kill someone if we had to do it."

"But Hogan?"

She breathed deeply. "Mrs. H., I just don't know. It seems impossible, but..."

"Where did Kerry work in London—if she did?"

"At a bank. London branch of one of the big American banks. That's when she found her vocation, at least that's what she told me."

"I never heard that." Harry's mind raced.

"She's quiet. Then again, how many people are interested in banking, and you two are acquaintances at best. I mean, there's nothing shifty in her not telling you."

"Yeah," Harry weakly responded.

"Well, this is errand day." Marilyn pushed open the door and a blast of muggy air swept in.

So did Rick and Cynthia.

"May I?" Rick pointed to the low countertop door separating the lobby and mailbox area from the work area.

"How polite to ask." Mrs. Hogendobber flipped up the countertop.

Cynthia followed. She placed a folder on the table and opened it. "The owner of a bar in San Francisco where Huckstep worked sent me these." She handed newspaper articles about George Jarvis's suicide to Harry and Mrs. Hogendobber.

Harry finished hers first, then read over Miranda's shoulder.

"The real story is that this man Jarvis, a member of the Bohemian Club, pillar-of-the-community type, was homosexual. No one knew. He was being blackmailed by Mike Huckstep and his girlfriend or wife—we aren't sure if they were really married—Malibu. She must be a cold customer, because she would hide and photograph Mike cavorting with his victims and that's how the blackmailing would start."

"The wedding ring said M & M." Harry handed the clipping back to Cynthia.

"I'm not jumping to conclusions. We've checked marriage records in San Francisco for June 12, 1986. Nothing on Huckstep. It's like finding a needle in a haystack. Checked the surrounding counties too. Given enough time, we'll get through all the records in California."

"Those two could have stood before the ocean and pledged eternal troth." Rick was sarcastic. "Or gone to Reno."

"We've sent out a bulletin to every police department in the nation and to the court of records for every county. Nothing may come of it, but we're sloggin' away."

Cynthia pulled out an eight-by-ten glossy blow-up of a snapshot. "Mike."

"Looking better than when he roared up to Ash Lawn."

"No one has claimed the body," Rick informed them. "We buried him in the county plot. We've got dental records to prove it was really him. We had to get him in the ground, obviously."

"Here's another. This is all Frank Kenton found. He said he called everyone he could remember from those days when Mike tended bar."

A figure, blurred, her back turned, stood in the background of the photo. "Malibu?" Harry asked.

Mrs. Hogendobber put on her glasses. "All I can see is long hair."

"Frank knows little about her. She worked part-time at the Anvil, the bar he owns—caters to gay men. Malibu might as well have been wallpaper as far as the patrons were concerned, plus she seemed like the retiring type. Frank said he can't recall ever having a personal conversation with her."

"Did he know their scam?" Harry stared at the figure.

"Eventually. Huckstep and Malibu left in the nick of time. I suppose they left with a carload of money. They moved to L.A., where they probably continued their 'trade,' although no one seems to have caught them. Easy, I guess, in such a big city."

Rick jumped in when Cynthia finished. "We believe she was in the Charlottesville area when Mike arrived. We don't know if she's still around. Oh, one other sidelight. We've pieced together bits of Mike's. background. His social security number helped us there. Frank Kenton had the number in his records. Mike was raised in Fort Wayne, Indiana. Majored in computer science at Northwestern University, where he made straight A's."

"The Threadneedle virus!" Harry clapped her hands.

"That's a long shot, Harry," Rick admonished, then thought a minute. "Puts Kerry right in the perfect place to call in."

Harry folded a mail sack. "If she was smart enough to create their scam or to link up with the computer genius, she sure was dumb to get caught. Somehow it doesn't fit."

"The murder weapon sure fits." Cynthia took a piece of banana bread offered by Miranda.

"Now, you two"—Miranda's voice was laced with humor—"you're not here to show us a photograph of someone's back. I know you have two murders to solve. You'd put most of your effort into finding Hogan's killer, not the stranger's killer. So you must believe they are connected and you must need us in some fashion."

Rick's jaw froze in mid-chew. Mrs. Hogendobber was smarter than he gave her credit for being. "Well—"

"We're trustworthy." Miranda offered him another piece of banana bread.

He gulped. "No question of that. It's just—"

Cynthia interrupted. "We'd better tell them."

A silence followed.

"All right," Rick reluctantly agreed. "You tell them, I'll eat."

Cynthia grabbed a piece of bread before he could devour the whole loaf.

"We've had our people working on Crozet National's computers. It's frustrating, obviously, because the thief has covered his tracks. But we did find one interesting item. An account opened in the name of Mr. and Mrs. Michael Huckstep."

Harry whistled.

Miranda said, "Mr. and Mrs.?"

Cynthia continued. "We pulled the signature cards. But we can't really verify his signature or hers."

"Can't you match it to the signature on his driver's license?" Harry asked.

"Superficially, yes. They match. But to verify it we need a handwriting expert. We've got a lady coming down from Washington." She paused for breath. "As for Mrs. Huckstep's signature... it doesn't match, superficially again, anyone's handwriting in the bank."

"When did he or she open the account?" Harry asked.

"July thirtieth. He deposited $4,218.64 in cash." Rick wiped his mouth with a napkin supplied by Miranda. "The bank officer in charge of opening the account was Kerry McCray."

"Not so good." Harry exhaled.

"What if..." Mrs. Hogendobber pressed her fingers together. "Oh, forget it."

"No, go on," Rick encouraged her.

"What if Kerry did open the account? That doesn't mean she knew him."

"Kerry declares she never opened an account for Mr. and Mrs. Huckstep even though she was on the floor all of July thirtieth," Rick said heavily. "There's a number on each new account, an identifying employee number. Kerry's is on Huckstep's."

"Is the missing money in his account?" Harry queried.

"No," both answered.

Cynthia spoke. "We can't find a nickel."

"Well, I hate to even ask this. Was it in Hogan Freely's account?" Harry winced under Miranda's scornful reaction.

"No," Rick replied.

"For all we know, the money that disappeared on August first or second could be sitting in an account whose code we can't crack, to be called out at some later, safer date," Cynthia added.

"Maybe the money is in another bank or even another country," Miranda said.

"If two million or more dollars showed up in a personal account, we'd know it by now."

"Rick, what about a corporate account?"

"Harry, that's a bit more difficult because the big companies routinely shift around substantial sums. Sooner or later I think we'd catch it, but the thief and most likely the murderer, one and the same, would have to have someone on the inside of one or more Fortune 500 firms," Rick explained.

"Or someone inside another bank." Harry couldn't figure this out. She didn't even have a hunch.

"Possible." Cynthia cracked her knuckles. "Sorry."

"What can we do?" Miranda wanted to help.

"Everybody tromps through here. Keep your eyes and ears open," Rick requested.

"We do that anyway." Harry laughed. "You know, Big Marilyn asked us to watch for registered letters. Could be stock certificates. Nothing."

"Thank you for the information about Threadneedle." Rick stood up. "I don't think Kerry could pull this off alone."

Miranda swallowed.

As if reading her thoughts, Harry whispered, "Norman?"

"We're keeping an eye on him." Rick shrugged. "We've got nothing on him at all. But we're scrutinizing everyone in that bank down to the janitor."

"Keep your eyes open." Rick flipped up the Dutch door countertop and Cooper followed.

"If people will kill for a thousand bucks, think what they'll do for two million." Cynthia patted Harry on the back. "Remember, we said watch. We didn't say get involved."

As they left, both Miranda and Harry started talking at once.

"Telling those two to stay out of it is like telling a dog not to wag her tail," Mrs. Murphy said to Pewter.

" 'Cept for Tucker," Pewter teased.

Tucker replied from her spot under the table, *"I resent that."*

31

"Where does this stuff come from?" Dismayed, Harry surveyed her junk room.

Calling it the junk room wasn't fair to the room, a board-and-batten, half-screened back porch complete with Shaker pegs upon which to hang coats, a heavy wrought iron boot scraper, and big standing bootjack and a long, massive oak table. Dark green and ochre painted squares of equal size brightened the floor. The last line at catching the mud was a heavy welcome mat at the door into the kitchen.

Twice a year the mood would strike Harry and she'd organize the porch. The tools were easy to hang on the walls or take back out to the barn depending on their original home. The boxes of magazines, letters, and old clothes demanded sorting.

Mrs. Murphy scratched in the magazine box. The sound of claws over shiny, expensive paper delighted her. Tucker contented herself with nosing through the old clothes. If Harry tossed a sweatshirt or a pair of jeans in a carton, they really were old. She was raised in the use-it-up wear-it-out make-it-do-or-do-without school. The clothes would be cut into square pieces of cloth for barn rags. Whatever remained afterward, Harry would toss out, although she swore one day she would learn to make hooked rugs so she could utilize the scraps.

"Find anything?" Tucker asked Mrs. Murphy.

"Lot of old New Yorker *magazines. She sees an article she wants to read, doesn't have time to read it then, and saves the magazine. Now, I'll bet you a Milk-Bone she'll sit on the floor, go through these magazines, and tear out the articles she wants to save so she'll still have a pile of stuff to read but not as huge a one as if she'd saved the magazines intact. If she didn't work in the post office, Gossip Central, she'd work in the library like her mother did."*

"My bet is the broken bridle will get her attention first. She needs to replace the headstall. She's going to pick it up, mumble, then put it in the trunk to take to Sam Kimball."

"Maybe so. At least that will go quickly. Once she buries her nose in a book or magazine, she takes forever.*"*

"Think she'll forget supper?"

"Tucker, you're as bad as Pewter."

"She fooled us both," the dog exclaimed.

Harry, armed with a pair of scissors, began cutting up the old clothes. "Mrs. Murphy, don't rip apart the magazines. I need to go through them first."

"Give me some catnip. I can be bought off." Mrs. Murphy scratched and tore with increased vigor.

Harry stopped snipping and picked up the magazine box. It was heavier than she anticipated, so she put it back down. "I was going to shake you up."

"Catnip." Murphy's eyes enlarged, she performed a somersault in the box.

"Aren't you the acrobat?" Harry put the box on the oak table. She looked at the hanging herbs placed inside to dry. A large clutch of catnip, leaves down, emitted a sweet, enticing odor.

Murphy shot out of the box, straight up, and swatted the tip of the catnip. A little higher and she could have had a slam dunk.

"Catnip!"

"Druggie." Harry smiled and snapped off a sprig.

"Yahoo." Mrs. Murphy snatched the catnip from Harry's hands, threw it on the table, chewed it a little, rolled on it, tossed it up in the air, caught it, rolled some more. Her antics escalated.

"Nuts. You're a loony tunes, out there, Blue Angels."

"Mother, she's always that way. The catnip brings it out more. Now, me, I'm a sane and sober dog. Reliable. Protective. I can herd and fetch and follow at your heels. Even with a bone, which I would enjoy right now, I would never descend to such raucous behavior."

"Bugger off," Mrs. Murphy hissed at Tucker. The weed made her aggressive.

"Fair is fair." Harry walked into the kitchen and brought out a bone for Tucker before returning to her task.

As the animals busied themselves, Harry finished off the box of clothing. She reached into the magazine box and flipped through the table of contents. "Umm, better save this article." She clipped out a long piece on the Amazon rain forests.

"Someone's coming," Tucker barked.

"Shut up." Murphy lolled her head. *"You're hurting my ears."*

"Friend or foe?" the corgi challenged as the car pulled into the driveway.

"Do you really think a foe would drive up to the back door?"

"Shut up, yourself. I'm doing my job, and besides, this is the South. All one's foes act like friends."

"Got that right," the cat agreed, rousing herself from her catnip torpor. *"It's Little Marilyn. What the heck is she doing here at seven in the evening?"*

"Come on in," Harry called. "I'm doing my spring cleaning, in August."

Marilyn opened the porch door. "At least you're doing it. I've got a ton of my stuff to sort through. I'll never get to it."

"How about an iced tea or coffee? I can make a good pot of hot coffee too."

"Thank you, no."

"If you don't need the iced tea, I do." Harry put down her scissors.

The two humans repaired to the kitchen. Harry's kitchen, scrupulously clean, smelled like nutmeg and cinnamon. She prided herself on her sense of order. She had to pride herself on something in the kitchen, since she couldn't cook worth a damn.

"Milk or lemon?" Harry wouldn't take no for an answer.

"Oh, thank you. Lemon. I'm going to keep you from your chores." Marilyn fidgeted.

"They'll wait. I've been on my feet all day anyway, so it's good to have a sit-down."

"Harry, we aren't the best of friends, so I hope you don't mind my barging in on you like this."

"It's fine."

She cast her eyes about the kitchen, then settled down. "I don't know what to do. Two weeks ago Kerry asked me for a loan. I refused her. I hated to do it, but, well, she wanted three thousand dollars."

"What for?"

"She said she knew her father's cancer was getting worse. If she could invest the money, she could help defray what his insurance won't cover. She said she'd split the profit with me and return the principal in a year's time."

"Kerry's a lot sharper than I thought."

"Yes." Little Marilyn sat stock-still.

"Have you told Rick Shaw or Cynthia?"

"No. I came to you first. It's been preying on my mind. I mean, she's in so much trouble as it is."

"Yeah, I know, but"—Harry held up her hands—"you've got to tell them."

Mrs. Murphy, sitting on the kitchen counter, said, *"What do you really think, Marilyn?"*

"She's hungry." Harry got up to open two cans of food for Mrs. Murphy and Tucker. Tucker gobbled her food while Mrs. Murphy daintily ate hers.

"Thanks for hearing me out. We were all such good friends once. I feel like a traitor."

"You're not. And horrendous as the process is, that's what the courts are for—if Kerry is innocent, she'll be spared. At least, I hope so."

"Don't you know that old proverb? 'Better to fall into the hands of the Devil than into the hands of the lawyers.'"

"You think she's sunk, don't you?"

"Uh-huh." Little Marilyn nodded in the affirmative, tears in her eyes.

32

Every spare moment she had, Kerry punched into the computer in a back office. Cynthia told her she could go to work. She'd be formally arraigned tomorrow. Rick told the acting president, Norman Cramer, to allow Kerry to work. He had a few words with the staff which amounted to "innocent until proven guilty." What he hoped for was a slip on Kerry's part or the part of her accomplice.

The thick carpeting in the officer branch of the bank muffled the footsteps behind her as she frantically pulled up records on the computer. Norman Cramer tapped her shoulder.

"What are you doing?"

"Fooling around. Kind of like you, Norman." Kerry's face burned.

"Kerry, this is none of your business. You'll interfere with Rick Shaw's investigation."

What neither of them knew was that Rick was monitoring

Kerry's computer. An officer down in the basement saw everything she called up.

"Hogan Freely's murder is everybody's business. And I'd rather be chewed out by you than not try and come up with some clue, any clue."

His sallow complexion darkened. "Listen to me. Forget it."

"Why don't you and I go outside and talk?"

"And risk another scene? No."

"I knew you were a coward. I hoped it wasn't true. I really believed you when you told me you'd leave Aysha—"

He sharply reprimanded her. "It's not appropriate to discuss personal matters at work."

"You won't discuss them at any other time."

"I can't. Maybe I know things you don't and maybe you should forget about me for a while. You shouldn't have come in today. It upsets everyone." He spun on his heel and walked away.

Steam wasn't hotter than Kerry McCray. She followed him. "You sorry son of a bitch."

He grabbed her arm so hard he hurt her as he half pushed, half dragged her down the narrow corridor to the back door. He practically threw her down the steps into the parking lot. "Take the day off! I don't care if Rick Shaw thinks it's okay for you to be here. I don't. Now, get out and chill out!" He slammed the door.

Kerry sobbed in the middle of the parking lot. She walked over to her car, opened the door, and got inside. Then she put her head on the steering wheel and sobbed some more.

Mrs. Hogendobber passed on her way from the bank. She hesitated but then walked over.

"Kerry, can I help?" she asked through the rolled-down window.

Kerry looked up. "Mrs. Hogendobber, I wish you could."

Mrs. Hogendobber patted her on the back. "'Love your enemies, bless them that curse you, do good to them that hate you . . . For if ye love them which love you, what reward have ye? Do not even the publicans the same?'"

Kerry recovered enough to remark, "Make that Republicans."

"There, there, I knew you'd perk up. I find the Bible always helps me in time of need."

"I think it was you as much as your quote. I wish I could be as wise and as calm as you are, Mrs. Hogendobber." She opened her glove compartment for a tissue. "Do you believe I killed Hogan Freely?"

Miranda said, "No." She waited for Kerry to finish blowing her nose. "You just don't seem like the type to me. I can imagine you killing Norman in a lover's rage, but not Hogan." She paused. "If you live long enough, honey, you see everything. You're still seeing many things for the first time, including a two-timing ex-boyfriend. After a while you know what's worth getting het up over and what just to let go. He married Aysha. Let him go. Reading the Good Book and praying to the Lord never hurt anyone. You'll find solace there and sooner or later the right man will come into your life." She inhaled. "It's so hot. You'll fry in that car. Come on over to the P.O. and I'll make you some iced tea. I have some chocolate chip cookies, macadamia nut ones too."

"Thank you. I'm wrung out. I think I'll go home and maybe I'll take your advice and read the Bible." She wiped her eyes. "Thank you."

"Don't give it a second thought." Miranda smiled, then turned for the post office.

Kerry drove off.

Mrs. Hogendobber waited until there was no one else in the building to tell Harry about the episode. Crozet, being a town of only 1,733 people, didn't miss much. A few noticed Kerry's pursuit of Norman down the corridor. BoomBoom Craycroft saw him push her out of the building and fifteen people coming and going saw Mrs. Hogendobber consoling Kerry in the parking lot. Variations of the events made the rounds. Each telling exaggerated Kerry's unhappiness and surmised guilt until she was suicidal. Norman's handling of her seemed tinged by heroism to many.

By the time Little Marilyn drove up to Ash Lawn to relieve

Aysha, the tale was worthy of a soap opera, but then, maybe daily life is a soap opera.

Everyone at Ash Lawn was working double duty since Laura Freely would not be returning for the remainder of the year. Trying to schedule and work in Ottoline, who substituted for Laura, frazzled Little Marilyn, in charge of the docents.

Marilyn combed her hair and straightened up as Aysha finished a tour for a group of sightseers. More were coming, but Marilyn had about ten minutes before she would gather up a new group to commence the tour.

Aysha related her version of the Norman-Kerry episode. Her gloating offended Marilyn Sanburne, Jr.

"She's the loser. You're the winner. Be gracious enough to ignore her."

Aysha threw her shoulders back and squared her chin, prelude to some pronouncement of emotional significance tinged with her imagined superiority. "Who are you to dictate manners to me?"

"I used to be your best friend. Now I wonder."

"You're on her side. I knew it. Oh, don't women just love a victim and Kerry paints herself as a real martyr to love—she's a murderer, for chrissakes!"

"You don't know that and you don't have to wallow in it."

"I'm not."

"You look like you're gloating to me," Marilyn shot back. "Just drop it."

Aysha's voice lowered, a signal that what she was about to impart was really, truly, terribly important and that she'd been keeping it in only because she was such a lady. "She kissed my husband at Hogan Freely's wake."

Since neither Harry nor Cynthia had ever mentioned it, Marilyn didn't know about the kissing part of the incident. As the two rivals had yelled and screamed at the top of their lungs, she certainly knew about the rest of it. She heard every word, as did most of the other mourners. "Look, I'd have been upset. I understand that. I wouldn't want anyone kissing my husband, especially a former lover. But, Aysha, get over it. Every time you react to her, she gets what she wants. She's the center of your attention, Norman isn't, and she's the center of Norman's attention and you're not. Rise above it."

"Easy for you to say. I remember in school how devious she was—so nice to your face, so vicious when you were out of sight—"

"I don't want to hear that stuff." Marilyn advanced toward Aysha a step, realized what she was doing, and stopped. "Keep this up, Aysha, and you'll be as big a bitch as your mother."

"You think you're better than the rest of us because you'll inherit your mother's fortune. If Big Marilyn were my mother, I'd be worried. Every woman turns into her mother. Mine is small potatoes compared to yours."

"I don't care about the money."

"Those who have it never care about it. That's the point! Someday I hope I have as much as you do so I can rub your nose in it."

"Your time is up. I'll take over now." Marilyn quietly walked into the front room to greet the visitors to Monroe's home.

33

Air-conditioning was a luxury Harry couldn't afford. Her house at the foot of Yellow Mountain stayed cool except on the worst of those sultry summer nights. This was one of those nights. Every window was open to catch the breezes that weren't there. Harry tossed and turned, sweated, and finally cursed.

"I don't know how you can sleep through this," she grumbled as she stepped over Tucker and headed toward the bathroom.

As Harry brushed her teeth Mrs. Murphy alighted nimbly on the sink. *"Hotter than Tophet."*

Harry, mouth full of toothpaste, didn't reply to Murphy's observation. After rinsing, she petted the cat, who purred with appreciation.

Walking through the house provided no relief. She wandered into the library, shadowed by Murphy.

"Mother, this is the hottest room in the house. Why don't you put ice cubes on your head and a baseball cap over them? That will help."

"I'm hot too, sweetheart." Harry glanced at the old books her mother gleaned from the library sales she used to administer. "Here's the plan. Let's go into the barn, move the little table from the tack room out into the aisle, and think. The barn's the coolest place right now."

"Worth a try." Murphy raced to the screened-porch door and pushed it open. The hook dangled uselessly because the screw eye was long gone.

As they walked into the barn, the big owl swooshed overhead. *"You two idiots will spoil a good night of hunting."*

"Tough." Mrs. Murphy's fur fluffed out.

When Harry switched on the lights, the opossum popped his head out of a plastic feed bucket. *"Hey."*

"Simon, don't worry. She doesn't care. We're going to do some research."

"Here?"

"Too hot inside."

"Feels like being wrapped in a big wet towel out here. Must be even worse in the house," Simon concurred.

Harry, having no idea of the lively conversation taking place between her cat and the possum, carried the small table to the aisle, set up a fan, grabbed a pencil and yellow tablet, sat down, and started making notes. Every now and then Harry would slap her arm or the back of her neck.

"How come the skeeters bite me and leave you alone?" she asked the tiger, who batted at the moving pencil.

"Can't get through the fur. You humans lack most protective equipment. You keep telling the rest of us it's because you're so highly evolved. Not true. An eagle's eyes are much more developed than yours. So are mine, for that matter. Put on mosquito repellent."

"I wish you could talk."

"I can talk. You just can't understand what I say."

"Murphy, I love it when you trill at me. Wish you could read too."

"What makes you think I can't? Trouble is, you mostly write about"

yourselves and not other animals, so I find few books that hold my interest. Tucker says she can read, but she's pretty shaky. Simon, can you read?"

"No." Simon had moved to another feed bucket, where he picked through the sweet feed. He especially liked the little bits of corn.

Harry listed each of the events as she remembered them, starting with Mike Huckstep's appearance at Ash Lawn.

She listed times, weather, and any other people who happened to be around.

Starting with the Ash Lawn incident, she noted it was hot. It was five of five. Laura Freely was in charge of the docents: Marilyn Sanburne, Jr., Aysha Cramer, Kerry McCray. Susan Tucker ran the gift shop. Danny Tucker was working in the yard to the left of the house. She and Blair were in the living room.

She tried to remember every detail of every incident up to and including Little Marilyn's visit to her concerning Kerry's request for a loan.

"Murphy, I give up. It's still a jumble."

The cat put her paw on the pencil, stopping its progress. *"Listen. Whoever is behind this can't be that much smarter than you are. If they came up with this, then you'll figure it out. The question is, if you do figure it out, will you be safe?"*

Harry absentmindedly petted Murphy as the cat tried to talk sense to her.

"You know, I've sat up half the night making lists. The so-called facts are leading me nowhere. Sitting here with you, Murphy, no chores, totally quiet, I can think. Time to trust my instincts. Mike Huckstep knew his killer. He walked deep into the woods with him. Hogan Freely may or may not have known his killer, but the murderer certainly knew Hogan, knew he was working that night, and had the good fortune to walk into an unlocked bank, or he or she had a key. Any one of us in Market Shiflett's store knew Hogan would be in the bank. He told us. Laura knew, but I think we can let her off the hook. I wonder if he told anyone else?"

"The thick fog gave the killer a real bonus." Mrs. Murphy remembered the night vividly.

Harry tapped the pencil on the table. "Was it planned or was it impulse?"

Harry wrote out her thoughts and waited for the sunrise. At six, since Mrs. H. was up and baking by then, she phoned her friend. She asked her to cover for her for half an hour. She needed to drop something off at the sheriff's office.

At seven she was at Rick Shaw's office, where she left her notes with Ed Wright, who was ending his night shift. By eight Rick called. He'd read the notes and he thanked her.

She sorted the mail with Miranda while telling her what she wrote down for Sheriff Shaw. On those rare occasions when she was up all night she usually got very sleepy about three in the afternoon. She figured she'd nod out and she warned Mrs. Hogendobber not to be too angry with her. However, the events of the day would keep her wide awake.

34

At the beginning of the day Harry blamed the bizarre chain of events on the fact that it was cloudy. That, however, couldn't explain how the day ended.

At ten-thirty Blair Bainbridge pulled into the front parking lot of the post office on a brand-new, gorgeous Harley-Davidson. It appeared to be black, especially under the clouds, but in the bright sunlight the color would sparkle a deep plum.

"What do you think?" Blair asked.

Harry walked outside to admire the machine. "What got into you?"

"Grabbing at summer." He grinned. "And you know, when I saw Mike Huckstep's Harley, I was flooded with memories. Who says I have to be mature and responsible twenty-four hours a day? How about twenty hours a day, and for four hours I can be wild again?"

"Sounds good to me."

Miranda opened the front door. "You'll get killed on that thing."

"I hope not. Is there a Bible quote for excessive speed?"

"Off the top of my head, I can't think of one. I'll put my mind to it." She closed the door.

"Oh, Blair, she'll worry herself to a nub. She'll call her buddies in Bible study class. She won't rest until she finds an appropriate citation."

"Should I take her for a ride?"

"I doubt it. If it's not her Ford Falcon, she doesn't want to get in it or on it."

"Bet you five dollars." With that he hopped up the steps into the post office.

Harry closed the door behind her as Mrs. Murphy and Tucker greeted Blair.

"Mrs. Hogendobber, I just happen to have two helmets and I want to take you for a ride. We can float across the countryside."

"Now, isn't that nice?" But she shook her head no.

Before he could warm up to his subject, the front door flew open and a glowering Norman Cramer stormed in.

"How can you? This is in such bad taste!"

"What are you talking about?" Blair replied since the hostility was directed at him.

"That, that's what I'm talking about!" Norman gesticulated in the direction of the beautiful bike.

"You don't like Harleys? Okay, you're a BMW man." Blair shrugged.

"Everything was all right around here until the day that motorcycle appeared. How can you ride around on it? How can you even touch it! What'd you do, slip Rick Shaw money under the table? I thought unclaimed property was to go to public auction held by the Sheriff's Department."

"Wait a minute." Blair relaxed. "That isn't the murdered guy's Harley. It's not even black. Go out and take another look. I just bought this bike."

"Huh?"

"Go look." Blair opened the door for Norman.

The two men circled the bike as the humans and animals observed from inside.

"Norman's losing it." One side of Harry's mouth turned up.

"If you were caught between Kerry and Aysha, I expect you'd unravel too. Scylla and Charybdis."

"Steam was coming out of his ears. And how could he say something like that about Rick Shaw? Jesus, the crap that goes through people's minds."

"Don't take the name of Our Savior in vain."

"Sorry. Hey, here comes Herbie."

The reverend stopped to chat with the men, then entered the building. "Cheap transportation. Those things must get fifty miles to the gallon. If gas taxes continue to rise, then I might get one myself. How about a motorcycle with a sidecar?"

"You going to paint a cross on it? A little sign to hang on the handlebars, 'Clergy'?"

"Mary Minor Haristeen, do I detect a whiff of sarcasm in your tone? Haven't you read of the journeys of St. Paul? Imagine if he'd had a motorcycle. Why, he could have created congregations throughout the Mediterranean, Gaul even. Sped along the process of Christianization."

"On a Harley. I like that image."

"You two. What will you come up with next?" Miranda sauntered over to the counter.

"Imagine if Jesus had a car. What would he drive?" Herbie loved to torment Miranda, and since he was an ordained minister he knew she would have to pay attention to him.

"The best car in the world," Miranda said, "my Ford Falcon."

"Might as well go back to sandals." Harry joined in the game. "I bet he'd drive a Subaru station wagon because the car goes forever, rarely needs to be serviced, and he could squeeze the twelve disciples inside."

"Now, that's a thought." Herb reached down to pat Tucker, who walked out from under the countertop.

Blair rejoined them. Norman too.

"I'm sorry. I'm a little edgy." Norman cast down his eyes.

"Norman, you've got one woman too many in your life, and that's not including Ottoline." Mrs. Hogendobber was forthright.

He blushed, then nodded.

Blair lightheartedly said, "All those men out there looking for a woman, and you've got them to spare. How do you do it?"

"By being stupid." Norman valiantly tried to smile, then left.

"Well, what do you think of that?" Miranda exclaimed.

"I think he's about to check into Heartbreak Hotel," Harry replied.

"Depressed." Blair opened his mailbox.

"Now, now, if he loves Aysha, he'll work it out." Herb believed in the sacrament of marriage. After all, he'd married half the town.

"But what if he doesn't love her?" Harry questioned.

"Then I don't know." Herb folded his arms across his chest. "All marriage is a compromise. Maybe he can find the middle ground. Maybe Aysha can too. Her social climbing tries even my patience."

As Herb left, Cynthia Cooper arrived. "Thanks for your notes."

"Couldn't sleep. Had to do something."

"I was up all night too," Blair added. "If I'd known that, I would have come over."

"You devil." Cynthia would have died to hear him say that to her. "Well, we checked out the signature card handwriting with the signature on Mike Huckstep's income tax statements and driver's license application with the graphologist from Washington. They are authentic. And Mrs. Huckstep's signature is not his handwriting. He didn't forge a signature. It's not Kerry's signature either. Two people signed the card."

"How'd you find out so fast?"

"Wasn't that fast. Try getting the IRS to listen to a tiny sheriff's department in central Virginia. Rick finally called up our congressman and then things started to move. The DMV part was easy."

"Did Mike actually go into the bank and sign cards?"

"Well, no one at the bank remembers seeing a man of his description. Or won't admit to it."

"Coop, how did he sign?" Blair asked.

"At gunpoint?"

"Have you been able to question Laura yet?" Mrs. H. inquired. "She might remember something."

"She's cooperated to the max. Once the shock wore off, she's helped as much as she can because she wants to catch Hogan's murderer. Dudley and Thea are doing all they can too. Unfortunately, Laura says she's never seen anyone matching Huckstep's description. Hogan would occasionally discuss bank problems with Laura, but usually they were people problems. The tension between Norman Cramer and Kerry McCray disturbed him. Other than that, she said everything seemed normal."

"And there's nothing peculiar in anyone's background at Crozet National?" Mrs. Hogendobber played with her bangle bracelets.

"No. No criminal records."

"We're still at a dead end." Harry sighed.

"You know, Harry, you're the only person who has seen the killer," Cooper replied.

"I've wondered about that."

"What do you mean?" Blair and Miranda talked over each other but basically they said the same thing.

"Whoever was riding that motorcycle when it almost sideswiped Harry at Sugar Hollow was most likely our man. Unless Huckstep rode out and rode back later."

"And all I saw was a black helmet with a black visor and someone all in black leather. A real Hell's Angel."

"Why didn't you say anything?" Miranda wanted to know.

"I did. I told Rick and Cynthia. I've racked my brain for anything, a hint, an attitude, but it happened so fast."

After Blair left to go riding around the countryside, Cynthia stayed on for a little bit. People came in and out as always, and at five the friends closed the post office to go home.

Susan Tucker drove over with Danny and Brookie. They left Harry's house about eight. Then Fair called. The night cooled off a bit, so Harry gratefully drifted off to sleep early.

The jangle of the phone irritated her. The big, old-fashioned alarm clock read four-thirty. She reached over and picked it up.

"Hello."

"Harry. It's Fair. I'm coming over."

"It's four-thirty in the morning."

"Norman Cramer's been strangled."

"What?" Harry sat bolt upright.

"I'll tell you everything when I get there. Stay put."

35

Cinnamon-flavored coffee perfectly perked awakened Harry's senses. She'd brought the Krups machine into the kitchen from the barn. It was so fancy, she thought it was too nice to keep in the stable. Mrs. Murphy and Tucker ate an early breakfast with her. The owl, again furious at the invasion of privacy, swept low over Fair's head as he trudged to the back door.

"What happened?" she asked as she poured him a cup and set out muffins on the table.

His face parchment white, he sat down heavily. "Bad case of torsion colic. Steve Alton's big Hanoverian. He brought her over to the clinic and I operated. I didn't finish up until three, three-thirty. Steve wanted to stay with her, but I sent him home to get some sleep. I came in through town and turned left on Railroad Avenue. Not a soul in sight. Then I passed the old Del Monte plant and I saw Norman Cramer sitting in his car. The lights were on, and the motor too. He was just kind of staring into space and his tongue was hanging out kind of funny. I stopped and got out of the truck, and as I drew closer I saw bad bruises around his neck. I opened the door and he keeled over out onto the macadam. Called Rick. He arrived in less than ten minutes—he must have gone a hundred miles an hour. Cynthia made it in twenty minutes. All I'd done was put my fingerprints on the door handle. I didn't touch the body. Anyway, I told them what I knew, stayed around, and then Rick sent me home."

"Fair, I'm sorry." Harry's hands trembled. "If you'd been earlier, the murderer might have gone after you."

"I'll see those dead eyes staring out at me for a long, long time. Rick said the body was still warm." He reached for her hand.

"If I make up the bed in the guest room, do you think you can sleep?"

"No. Let me take a catnap on the sofa. I've got to get back to the clinic by seven-thirty."

She brought out some pillows and a light blanket for the sofa. Fair kicked off his shoes and stretched out. He wistfully looked at Harry as she reached to turn off the light. "I love being in this house."

"It's good to have you here. I'll wake you at six-thirty."

"Are you going back to sleep?"

"No. I've got some thinking to do." He fell asleep before she finished her sentence.

36

Harry used the tack room as an office. She pulled out her trusty yellow legal pad and wrote down everything Fair had just told her. Then she described what she knew about the killer of Mike Huckstep and Hogan Freely. Whether or not the same person or persons killed Norman was up for grabs, but he was head of the accounting department at Crozet National. Her guess was the three murders were tied together.

She wrote:

1. Knows how to operate a computer.
2. Knows the habits of the victims.
3. Knows the habits of the rest of us, although nearly caught after killing Hogan Freely.
4. Kills under pressure. A quick thinker. Knocked out Kerry before Kerry could see him, then set her up as

the killer...unless killer is Kerry's accomplice. A
real possibility.
5.   Works in the bank or knows banking routines perhaps
from another job. Might have key.
6.   Possibly knows Malibu. May use her as bait. Perhaps
Malibu is the killer or the killer's partner.
7.   Feels superior to the rest of us. Fed media
disinformation about the Threadneedle virus and then
watched us eat it up.
8.   Can ride a motorcycle.

At six Harry picked up the old black wall phone and called Susan
Tucker. Murphy sat on the legal pad. The cat couldn't think of
anything to add unless it was "armed and dangerous."

"Susan, I'm sorry to wake you."

"Harry, are you okay?"

"Yes. Fair's asleep on the couch. He found Norman Cramer
strangled early this morning."

"What? Wait a minute. Ned—*Ned*, wake up." Susan shook her
husband.

Harry could hear him mumble in the background, a pair of
feet hitting the floor, then the extension picked up.

"Harry."

"Sorry to wake you, Ned, but I think this might help Kerry
since you're her lawyer. Fair found Norman Cramer strangled in
his car in front of the Del Monte plant. About three-thirty this
morning. He didn't know he was dead. He opened the door and
Norman keeled over onto the pavement. Fair said huge bruises
around his throat and the condition of his face pointed to stran-
gulation."

"My God." Ned spoke slowly. "You were right to call us."

"Is everyone crazy? Is the murderer going to pick us off one by
one?" Susan exploded.

"If any of us interfere or get too close, I'd say we're next." Harry
wasn't reassuring.

"I'm going to call Mrs. H. and Mim. Then I've got to wake up Fair. How about we all meet for breakfast at the café—seven-thirty? Umm, maybe I'd better phone Blair too. What do you think?"

"Yes, to both," Susan answered.

"Good enough. We'll see you there." Ned paused. "And thank you again."

Harry called Mrs. Hogendobber, who was shocked; Big Marilyn, who was both shocked and angry that this could happen in her town; and Blair, awakened from a heavy sleep, was in a daze.

She fed the horses, Mrs. Murphy, and Tucker. Then she woke Fair. They freshened up.

"Mrs. Murphy and Tucker, this is going to be a difficult day. You two stay home." She left the kitchen door open so the animals could go onto the porch. She left each of them a large bowl of crunchies.

"Take me with you," Tucker whined.

"Forget it," Mrs. Murphy said impassively. *"As soon as she's down the drive, I've got a plan."*

"Tell me now."

"No, the humans are standing right here."

"They don't understand what you're saying."

"Better safe than sorry."

Harry kissed both pets, then hopped in the old truck while Fair climbed into his big Chevy truck. They headed for the downtown café. He had called the clinic. The horse was doing fine, so he decided to join the group for breakfast.

"Follow me," Murphy commanded once the truck motors could not longer be heard.

"I don't mind doing what you ask, but I hate taking orders," Tucker grumbled.

"Dogs are obedient. Cats are independent."

"You're full of it."

Nonetheless, Tucker followed as Mrs. Murphy scampered through the front meadows and the line of big sycamores along the creek that divided the pastures.

"Where are we going?"

"To Kerry McCray's. The fastest way is to head south. We can avoid the road that way too, but we'll have to cross the creek."

"You get your paws wet?"

"If I have to" was the cat's determined reply.

Moving at a sustained trot, the two animals covered ground rapidly. When they reached the big creek, Murphy stopped.

"It's high. How can it be high with no rain?"

Tucker walked to a bend along the bank. *"Here's your answer. A great big beaver dam."*

Mrs. Murphy joined her low-slung friend. *"I don't want to tangle with a beaver."*

"Me neither. But they're probably asleep. We could run over the dam. By the time they woke up, we'd probably be across. It's either that or find a place to ford downstream, where it's low."

"That will take too long." She inhaled deeply. *"Okay, let's run like blazes. Want me to go first?"*

"Sure. I'll be right behind."

With that, Mrs. Murphy shot off, all fours in the air, but running across a beaver dam proved difficult. She had to stop here and there, since heavy branches and stout twigs provided a snaggy surface. Murphy could hear movement inside the beaver lodge. She picked her way through the timber as fast as she could.

"Whatever happens, Murphy, don't hit the water. They'll pull you under. Better to fight it out on top of the dam."

"I know, I know, but there are more of them than us and they're stronger than we are." She slipped, her right front leg pushing into the lodge. She pulled it out as if it were on fire.

Slipping and sliding, Murphy made it to the other side. Tucker, heavier, was struggling. A beaver head popped up in the water at the other end of the dam.

"Hurry!" the cat shouted.

Tucker, without looking back, moved as rapidly as she could. The beaver swam alongside the dam. He was closing in on Tucker.

"*Leave her alone. She's trying to cross the creek. We mean no harm,*" the pretty tiger pleaded.

"*That's what they all say, and the next thing that happens is that men show up with guns, wreck the dam, and kill us. Dogs are the enemy.*"

"*No, man is the enemy.*" Mrs. Murphy was desperate. "*We don't belong to a person like that.*"

"*You may be right, but if I make a mistake, my whole family could be dead.*" The beaver was now alongside Tucker, who was almost to the creek bank. He reached up to grab Tucker's hind leg.

The dog whirled around and snarled. The beaver drew back for an instant. Tucker scrambled off the dam as the large animal advanced on her again. On terra firma both Tucker and Mrs. Murphy could outrun the beaver. They scorched the earth getting out of there.

At the edge of the woods they stopped to catch their breath.

"*How are we going to get back?*" Mrs. Murphy wondered aloud. "*I don't want to travel along the road. People drive like lunatics.*"

"*We'll have to find a place to ford far enough downstream so the beaver can't hear us. We can't swim it now. The lodge will be on alert.*"

"*It's going to take us over an hour to get home, but we'll worry about it later. We can be at Kerry McCray's in another ten minutes if we run.*"

"*I've got my wind back. Let's boogie.*"

They dashed through the fields of Queen Anne's lace, butterfly weed, and tall goldenrod. A small brick rancher came into view. Two squad cars were parked behind Kerry's Toyota. Its trunk lid was up.

"*I hope we're not too late.*" Murphy put on the turbocharger.

Tucker, a speed demon when she needed to be, raced next to her.

They made it to the cars as Kerry was being led out of her

house by Sheriff Shaw. Cynthia Cooper carried a woven silk drapery cord with tasseled ends in a plastic bag.

"Damn!" Murphy snarled.

"Too late?" Tucker, having lived with Mrs. Murphy all her life, figured that the cat had wanted to explore before the cops arrived.

"There's still a chance. You jump on Cynthia when she reaches to pet you and grab the plastic bag. I'll shred it as quickly as I can. Stick your nose in there and tell me if Kerry's scent is on the rope."

Without answering, Tucker charged Cynthia, who smiled at the sight of the little dog.

"Tucker, how did you get over here?" Tucker clamped her powerful jaws on the clear plastic bag, catching Officer Cooper by surprise. "Hey!"

Yanking it out of Cooper's hand, Tucker raced back to Mrs. Murphy, who was crouched back in the field, where Cynthia couldn't see her.

The minute Tucker dropped the bag under Murphy's nose, she unleashed her claws and tore for all she was worth. Cooper advanced on them, although she didn't know Murphy was there.

Tucker stuck her nose in the bag. *"It's not Kerry's scent."*

"Whose scent, then?"

"Rubber gloves. No scent other than Norman's cologne."

"Mrs. Murphy, you're as big a troublemaker as Tucker." Cooper disgustedly picked up the shredded bag.

"If you had a brain in your head, you'd realize we're trying to help." Murphy backed away from Cynthia. *"Tucker, just to be sure, go sniff Kerry."*

Tucker eluded Cynthia's grasp and ran over to Kerry, who was standing by the squad car.

"Tucker Haristeen." Kerry's eyes filled with tears. "At least I've got one friend."

Tucker licked her hand. *"I'm sorry."*

Rick moved toward Tucker, and the dog spurted out of his reach. "Tucker, come on back here. Come on, girl."

"No way." The dog barked as she rejoined Mrs. Murphy, lying flat on her belly in the orchard grass.

"Let's head back before they take us to the pound for punishment."

"They wouldn't do that." Tucker glanced back at the humans.

"Coop might." Murphy giggled.

"Kerry's scent isn't on the cord. After checking, I'm doubly positive."

As they leisurely walked back toward their farm, the two animals commiserated over Kerry's fate. The killer planted the murder weapon in the trunk of her car. Given Kerry's threats to kill Norman, which every human and animal in Crozet knew about by now, she had as much chance of being found innocent as a snowball in hell. Even if there was doubt about her shooting Hogan Freely, there would be no doubt about Norman.

By the time they reached the creek, they both felt down.

"Think we're far enough away from the beaver?"

"Murphy, it's not that deep downstream. If we fool around and try to find a fording place you can clear with one leap, we'll be here all day. Just get your paws wet and be done with it."

"Easy for you to say. You like water."

"Close your eyes and run if it's that bad."

Tucker splashed across the creek. Murphy, after ferocious complaining, followed. Once on the other side, Tucker had to wait for her to elaborately shake each paw, then lick it.

"Do that when we get home."

Mrs. Murphy, sitting on her rear end, had her right hind leg straight up in the air. *"I'm not walking around with this creek smell on me."*

Tucker sat down since she couldn't budge Mrs. Murphy from her toilette. *"Think Norman was in on it?"*

"That's obvious."

"Only to us." Tucker stretched her head upward.

"The humans will accept that Kerry killed him. A few might think that he was getting too close to the killer in the bank—or that he was her accomplice and he wimped out."

"Kerry could have killed him and used rubber gloves. It's possible that we're wrong."

"Doesn't everything come down to character?"

"Yes, it does."

"Tucker, if Norman wasn't the person behind the computer virus, do you think he was the type to track the killer? To keep on the case?"

"He wasn't a total coward. He could have unearthed something. Since he works in the bank, he'd tell someone. Word would get around—"

Mrs. Murphy finished her ablutions, stood up, and shook. "True enough. But we've got to trust our instincts. There men have been killed with no sign of struggle. I could kick myself from here to Sunday for not running into the alleyway to see the car. I heard the killer's car the night Hogan was shot. Both Pewter and I did."

"I've told you before, Murphy, you did the right thing." Tucker started walking again. "I don't think the murderer will strike again unless it's another bank worker."

"Who knows?"

37

Harry, Fair, Mrs. Hogendobber, Susan, Ned, Blair, Big Marilyn, and Little Marilyn watched out the café window as Cynthia Cooper drove by in the squad car. Kerry McCray sat in the back seat behind the cage. No sooner had the dolorous spectacle passed than Aysha Cramer, pedal to the metal, roared past the café in her dark green car. Fair stood up, and as he opened the door, a crash could be heard. Within seconds Rick Shaw screeched by, a cloud of dust fanning out behind him. He hit the brakes hard, fishtailing as he stopped.

By now the remainder of the group hurried outside to join Fair, who was running at top speed toward the site of the wreck. Aysha had deliberately sideswiped Cynthia Cooper's squad car, forcing the deputy off the road. Cynthia, ever alert, stayed inside the car and locked the doors. She was talking on the radio.

"I'll kill her! Unlock this door! Goddammit, Cynthia, how can you protect her? She killed my husband!"

Rick pulled in behind Cooper. He leapt out of the car and hurried over to Aysha.

"Aysha, that's enough."

"You're protecting her. Let me at her! An eye for an eye, a tooth for a tooth."

As Rick and Fair struggled with Aysha, who would not release the door handle, Mrs. Hogendobber quoted under her breath, "'Vengeance is mine, I will repay, says the Lord'—"

From inside the car Kerry screamed, "I did not kill him. You killed him. You drove him to his death!"

Aysha went berserk. She twisted away from the two men, strengthened by blind rage. She picked up a rock and smashed the back window of the car. Fair grabbed her from behind, slipping his powerful arms inside hers. She kicked backward and hit his shin, but he perservered and, with Rick, Ned, and Blair, pulled her away from the car. She collapsed in a heap by the side of the road. Aysha curled up in a ball, rocking back and forth and sobbing.

Cynthia prudently used the moment to pull away.

Rick motioned for the men to help him put Aysha in his car. Fair picked her up and carried her. He placed her in the back seat. She fell over and continued weeping.

Big Marilyn walked around to the other side of the car. Ned stepped in. "Mim, I'll go. If she loses it again, you may not be able to restrain her."

"I'll get in the front with Sheriff Shaw. We'd better get her to Larry." Larry Johnson, the old town doctor, and his partner, Hayden McIntire, treated most of the residents of Crozet.

"That's fine," the sheriff agreed. "I've had to tell many people terrible news, but I've never been through one like this. She ran right over me and jumped into her car."

"Takes everyone differently, I guess." Harry felt awful. "Better call her mother."

As if on cue, Ottoline sped down the road, slammed on the brakes, and fishtailed in behind her daughter's car. She got out, leaving her door open.

"This doesn't bring him back." Ottoline slid into the back seat of Rick's car.

"I hate her!" Aysha sobbed. "She's alive and Norman's dead." She scrambled out of the other side of the back seat. Ottoline grabbed for her, but too late. Aysha stood by Deputy Cooper's car, screaming, "Why didn't you put her in jail after she shot Hogan Freely? You left a killer out among us, and now..." She collapsed in tears.

Ottoline, by now out of Rick's cruiser, helped her to her feet.

Rick hung his head. "There were extenuating circumstances."

"Like what?" Ottoline snarled.

"Like the fact that Kerry McCray had a goose egg on her head and was knocked out cold," Cynthia answered.

"And she had the gun that killed Hogan in her hand!" Aysha lurched away from her mother. She faced Rick. "You're responsible. Norman is dead because of you."

"Come on, honey, let me take you home." Ottoline tugged at Aysha.

"Aysha," Harry said coolly, "did Norman have a close friend in the bank?"

Aysha turned a bloodshot eye on Harry. "What?"

"Did he have a buddy at Crozet National?"

"Everyone. Everyone loved him," Aysha sobbed.

"Come on now. You're going to make yourself sick. Come on." Ottoline pushed her toward her car, the driver's side door still hanging open. She imparted a shot to Harry. "Your sense of timing is deplorable."

"Sorry, Ottoline. I'm trying to help."

"Harry, stick to postcards." Ottoline's tone was withering.

Harry had to bite her lip.

As Ottoline with Aysha, and Cynthia with Kerry, drove away, the remaining friends stood in the middle of the street, bewildered. Market and Pewter were running toward them along with Reverend Jones. Harry cast her eyes up and down the street. She could see faces in every window. It was eerie.

Fair brushed himself off. "Folks, I've got to get back to the clinic. If you need me, call." He slowly walked to his truck, parked in front of the café.

"Excuse me." Blair trotted to catch up to Fair.

"Oh, my, we forgot to pay," Little Marilyn remembered.

"Let's all go back and settle up." Harry turned for the café and wondered what the two men were talking about.

38

A dejected Cynthia Cooper returned to her desk after depositing Kerry, in a state of shock, at the county jail. Fortunately, there were no other women in custody, so she wouldn't be hounded by drug addicts, drunks, or the occasional hooker.

Cynthia was plenty disturbed. The phones rang off the hook. Reporters called from newspapers throughout the state and the local TV crew was setting up right outside the department building.

That would put Rick in a foul mood. And if Rick wasn't happy, nobody was happy.

She sat down, then stood up, then down, up, down, up. Finally she walked through the corridors to the vending machines and bought a pack of unfiltered Lucky Strikes. She stared at the bull's-eye in the middle of the pack. She'd better damn well get lucky. She peeled off the thin cellophane cord, slipped off the top, tore a small square in the end, and turned the pack upside down. The aroma of fresh tobacco wafted to her nostrils. Right now that sweet scent smelled better than her favorite perfume. She tapped the base of the pack and three white cigarettes slid down. She plucked one, turned the pack right side up, and slipped it in her front shirt pocket. Matches came down the chute with the pack. She struck one and lit up. Leaning against the corridor wall, she didn't know when a cigarette had tasted this good.

The back door opened, and she heard the garble of reporters. Rick slammed the door behind him, walked past her, grabbed the cigarette out of her mouth, and stuck it in his own.

"Unfiltered," she called out to him.

"Good. Another nail in my coffin." He spun on his heel and returned to her. She had already lit another cigarette. "I should have arrested Kerry right away. I used her for bait and it didn't work."

"I think it did. Even if she killed Norman. He was her accomplice. Cool. Very cool. He married Aysha to throw us off."

"So you don't buy that Kerry McCray took the wind out of Norman's sails?" Rick gave her a sour look.

Cynthia continued. "It was perfect."

"And Hogan?"

"Got too close or—too greedy."

Rick took a long, long drag as he considered her thoughts. "A real cigarette, not some low-tar, low-nicotine crap. If I'm gonna smoke, then I might as well go back to what made me smoke in the first place."

"What was it for you?"

"Camels."

"My dad smoked those. Then he switched to Pall Mall."

"How about you?"

"Oh, Marlboro. At sixteen I couldn't resist the cowboy in the ads."

"I would have thought you'd have gone for one of those brands like Viceroy or Virginia Slims."

"The murder weapon was on the seat of Kerry's Toyota,"

Cynthia said. "As for Virginia Slims, too nelly...know what I mean?"

"Yeah, I do. As to the cord...it'll come back no prints. I'll bet you a carton of these babies."

"I'm not taking that bet, but, boss, no prints doesn't mean Kerry wasn't smart enough to wear gloves. She's been threatening to kill Norman for days."

"That's just it, Coop. Smart. If she was smart enough to team up with Norman, to invent the Threadneedle virus, she wouldn't be dumb enough to get caught with a .357 in her hand or that cord in her possession." Rick nearly shouted. "And there's the unfortunate problem of Mike Huckstep."

"Yeah." She thought a minute. "Think she'll get out on bail?"

"I hope not." A blue, curling line of smoke twirled out of his mouth. "She's safer in there and I can keep the reporters happy with the news she's booked for murder."

"Safer?"

"Hell, what if Aysha goes after her?"

"Or she goes after Aysha?"

"More likely. This way we can keep everyone out of our hair for a little bit."

"You're up to something." Coop had observed Rick's shrewdness too many times not to know he was springing a trap.

"You're going to talk Frank Kenton into flying out here from San Francisco."

"Fat chance!"

"We'll pay his way." He held up his hand. "Just leave the wrangling about money to me. Don't worry about it."

"You think he can identify Malibu?"

"He can take a good look at Kerry. That's a start."

"But Kerry never lived in San Francisco."

"How do we know? We'll question her and cross-examine her and it's possible, just possible, that something will slip. I think if she sees him, it will scare the devil out of her."

"Or someone else." Cynthia stubbed out her cigarette in the standing ashtray filled with sand.

"That too. That too. So, topgirl, get on it."

"What's this topgirl stuff?"

"Dunno, just popped into my head."

39

BoomBoom Craycroft dashed into the post office. The place had been a madhouse all day as people hurried in and hurried out, each one with a theory. Pewter curled up in the mail cart. She missed her friends, but she was glad to catch the human gossip.

"Guess you heard I was pushed off the road by Aysha. How was I to know Norman had been killed and she was chasing Kerry?"

"None of us knew, and you look none the worse for wear. The Jag seems okay too." Harry's tone was even.

"My guardian angel was working overtime." BoomBoom opened her mailbox. "These bills. Have you ever noticed they come right on time but the checks never do? Then again, the stock market being what it is, who knows from quarter to quarter how much money they have? I hate that. I hate not knowing how much money I've got *coming in*. Which reminds me. Did you know the bank found $250,000 in Kerry's account?"

"Oh?" Mrs. Hogendobber came over to the counter.

"I just came from there. The place is a beehive—$250,000! She certainly didn't make that much at Crozet National. And it wasn't in her account yesterday. If she'd been patient, she could have had it all, unless, of course, she's a small fry and this is a payoff."

"BoomBoom, who told you? I'd think the bank or at least the Sheriff's Department would want to control this information."

"Control information? You were born and bred in Crozet. You know better than that," BoomBoom hooted.

"How'd you find out?" Mrs. Hogendobber was pleasant.

"Flirted with Dick Williams." She mentioned a handsome bank officer who was always solicitous of the ladies but most especially of his wife, Bea. BoomBoom added, "Well, actually it was Jim Craig who told me and Dick, politely, mind you, told him to hold his cards close to his chest for a while. So I batted my eyes at both of them and swore I'd never tell. Who cares? It will be on Channel 29 tonight."

And with that she breezed out the door.

"What an airhead."

"You don't like her because she took up with Fair after your divorce."

"You don't like her either."

"That's true," Miranda confessed.

Pewter popped her head up over the mail cart. *She's a fake, but half the people you meet are fakes. What's one more?*

"Do you want to come home with me tonight?"

"Harry, I would love to come home with you." Pewter hopped out and vigorously rubbed Harry's legs.

"Lavish with her affections," Mrs. Hogendobber observed. The older woman sat down. "I feel so tired. I shouldn't be. I got enough sleep, but I can't keep my head up."

"Emotions. They're exhausting. We're all ragged out. I know I am."

Before Harry could sit down with Miranda, Susan opened the back door and stuck in her head. "Me."

"Come in," Mrs. Hogendobber invited her. "You usually do."

Susan dropped into the seat opposite Miranda. "Poor Ned. People are calling up, outraged that he's defending Kerry McCray. The fact that every citizen has the right to a trial before their peers escapes them."

"Trial by gossip." Mrs. Hogendobber shook her head.

"If people want to be ugly, there's not a lot you or Ned can do about it. If I were in trouble, I'd sure want Ned as my attorney."

Susan smiled. "I should count my blessings. After all, my husband wasn't killed, and what are a few hate calls?"

"I bet Kerry doesn't even have a toothbrush," Miranda thought out loud. "Girls, we should go over to her house and pack some clothes for her. This is the United States of America. Innocent until proven guilty. Makes no matter what public opinion is, she's innocent under the law until proven guilty. So we shouldn't shun her."

The other two sat quietly.

Finally, Susan replied, "Miranda, you always bring us back to the moral issue. Of course we'll go over there after work."

40

"This place is pin tidy." Mrs. Hogendobber put her hands on her hips. "I had no idea Kerry was such a good housekeeper."

"Remind me never to invite you to my place." Cynthia Cooper carefully packed some toiletries.

Harry, Mrs. Hogendobber, and Susan called Cynthia before going over to Kerry's. The Sheriff's Department scoured the place, so Rick Shaw said okay to the ladies' visit as long as Cynthia accompanied them.

He didn't know that Mrs. Murphy, Pewter, and Tee Tucker accompanied them also.

While Susan and Harry threw underclothes, T-shirts, and jeans as well as a good dress into a carryall bag, the animals went prowling.

"There've been so many people in here, so many scents." Tucker shook her head.

Mrs. Murphy spied the trapdoor to the attic. Pewter craned her neck at the door.

"Think we could get up there?" Pewter asked.

"I'll yodel. Mom hates that worst of all." Tucker laughed, threw her head back, and produced her canine yodel which could awaken the dead.

"My God, Harry, what's wrong with your dog?" Cynthia called from the bathroom.

Harry walked into the hallway to the bedrooms and beheld Tucker yowling in the key of awful. Mrs. Murphy circled around her legs. Pewter was frozen under the attic trapdoor.

"If I go any faster, I'll make myself dizzy." The cat slowed down.

"You three are pests. I should have left you home."

"Oh, yeah?" Murphy reached up with her claws on Harry's jeans, wiggled her rear end, and climbed up Harry so quickly that the young woman barely had time to complain about the claws.

"Ouch" was all she could say as Mrs. Murphy reached her shoulders, then stood on her hind legs and batted at the attic door.

"If she doesn't get it, she's comatose," Pewter wryly noted.

Susan stuck her head out in the hallway. "A human scratching post. What a good idea. What does she see up there?" Susan noticed Murphy's antics.

"A trapdoor, stupid," Tucker yapped.

"Hey. Hey, Cynthia," Pewter called, as did Susan.

Cynthia and Mrs. H. walked out as Susan called. Susan pointed to the trapdoor. Harry cocked her head to one side to see it and then Mrs. Murphy jumped off.

"Did I tell you that your animals were here when we arrested Kerry? Tucker ran off with the plastic bag in which we had the cord, the suspected murder weapon, all sealed up. She dropped it in the field. Mrs. Murphy used her claws like a chainsaw. What a mess. Fortunately, I retrieved it before she damaged the evidence. This place has to be five miles from your house."

"I'm going to start locking you two up. You hear?"

"We hear but we aren't listening," Murphy sassed.

Pewter was impressed. *"Did you really do that?"*

"Piece of cake," Mrs. Murphy bragged.

"You couldn't have done it without me." Tucker was jealous.

Susan brought a chair in from the kitchen, stood on it, and opened the trapdoor. A little whiff of scorching-hot air blasted her in the face.

After searching around, they found a ladder in the basement. Cynthia went up first, with a flashlight from her squad car. "Good. There's a switch here."

Mrs. Murphy, who loved climbing ladders, hurried up as soon as Cynthia crawled into the attic. Tucker, irritably, waited down below. Harry climbed up. Pewter followed.

"Even the attic is neat," Cynthia noted. "You know, I don't think our boys were up here. Don't repeat that. It makes the department look sloppy, and guess what, they were sloppy."

"It's easy to miss what's over your head."

"Harry, we're paid not to miss evidence," Cynthia firmly told her.

"I'm coming up too," Susan called up.

"Well, don't knock down the ladder when you get up here, Susan, or we'll be swinging from the trapdoor."

"Thanks for the vote of confidence." Susan appeared in the attic. "How can you breathe?"

"With difficulty." Harry grimaced.

"What's up there?" Miranda called from below.

"Not much. Two big trunks. An old pair of skis," Harry informed her.

"A large wasps' nest in the eave." Mrs. Murphy fought the urge to chase wasps. The buzz so attracted her. The consequences did not. *"Let's open the trunk."*

Cynthia pulled a handkerchief out of her pocket and gingerly opened the old steamer trunk. "A wedding dress. Old."

Harry and Susan, on their knees, looked in as Mrs. Murphy gracefully put a paw onto the satin. Cynthia smacked her paw. "Don't even think about it."

"Lift up the dress." The cat held her temper.

"Bet this was Kerry's grandmother's. It's about that vintage." Susan admired the lace.

"Harry, take that end and I'll lift this one," Cynthia directed.

They lifted up the beautiful old dress. Underneath were old family photo albums and some letters from overseas.

Harry picked up a pile neatly tied in a ribbon. The postmark of the top letter was Roanoke, Virginia, 1952. The pile under that was from overseas from the mid-1980s. They were addressed to Kerry's mother. "I think this is her mother's stuff. She probably brought the trunk over here after Barbara McCray died. Do you need to go through it, you know, read the letters and stuff?"

Cynthia rooted through the rest of the trunk, then carefully replaced everything. "I don't know. If Rick wants me to do it, I can, but I'll ask first. Right now we've got a lot on her."

"It's circumstantial," Susan quietly reminded her.

"That $250,000 is a lot of circumstance." Cynthia sighed and closed the lid of the trunk.

Pewter, squatting on the second trunk, directed them. *"Hurry up and open this one. It's hot up here."*

"Go downstairs, then," Mrs. Murphy told her.

"No, I might miss something."

Cynthia gently lifted Pewter off the trunk. "Heavy little bugger."

Mrs. Murphy laughed while Pewter fumed.

Cynthia lifted the lid. "Oh, boy."

Harry and Susan looked into the trunk. Mrs. Murphy and Pewter, on their hind legs, front paws resting on the trunk, saw it too.

"Her goose is cooked!" Mrs. Murphy exclaimed.

A black motorcycle jacket, black leather pants, and a black helmet were neatly placed in the trunk.

"You know, I had hoped it wasn't her." Cynthia softly closed the trunk lid.

"Me too." Susan sadly agreed.

"It looks bad, but—" Harry lost her voice in the heat, then regained it. "But she'll get a fair trial. We can't convict her over a motorcycle helmet."

"I can tell you, the Commonwealth's Attorney will sure try," Cynthia said.

Susan patted Harry's shoulder. "It's hard to accept."

They climbed down the ladder, Mrs. Murphy first, and filled in the expectant Mrs. Hogendobber.

"Well?" Tucker inquired.

"Motorcycle gear in the trunk." The cat, dejected, licked Tucker's ear. Grooming Tucker or even Harry made her feel useful if not better.

"Oh, dear" was all Mrs. Hogendobber could say.

Pewter clambered down to join them. *"Kerry's going to be stamping out license plates."*

41

Norman Cramer's funeral was as subdued as Hogan Freely's was grand. Aysha, disconsolate, had to be propped up by her mother, immaculate in black linen. Ottoline couldn't bear Aysha's grief, but as she and her daughter were the center of attention, she appeared as noble as she knew how. Although part of it was an act, part of it wasn't, for Ottoline lived for and through her daughter.

The residents of Crozet, stunned at this last murder, sat motionless in the pews. Laura Freely wasn't there, which was proper, as she was in deep mourning. Reverend Jones spared everyone the fluff about how death releases one to the kingdom of glory. Right now no one wanted to hear that. They wanted Kerry McCray tried and sentenced. If hanging were still in the penal code, they'd have demanded to see her swing. Even those who at first gave her the benefit of the doubt were swayed by the money in her account, and the motorcycle gear in her attic.

Mrs. Hogendobber constantly told people the courts decide,

not public opinion. No one listened. Susan, as Ned's wife, was particularly circumspect. Harry said little. She couldn't shake the feeling that the other shoe hadn't yet dropped.

She sat in the fourth pew in the front right side of the church, the pews being assigned on the basis of when your family had arrived in Albemarle County. The Minors settled here over two centuries ago. In fact, one of the Minors founded Crozet's Lutheran church and was buried in the old graveyard behind it. The Hepworths, her mother's family, were Church of England, and they held down their own front-line pew in the Tidewater.

She sat there even when the service ended and the congregation filed out. She scrutinized their faces in an unobtrusive way. Harry scanned for answers. Anyone could be in on this. She imagined each person killing the biker, then Hogan, and finally Norman. What kind of person could do that? Then she imagined Kerry's face. Could she kill?

Probably anyone could kill to defend oneself or one's family or friends, but premeditated murder, cold-blooded murder? No. She could so easily picture Kerry bursting into fury and killing Norman or Aysha, but she couldn't imagine her tracking him down or hiding in the back seat of his car, popping up, asking him to pull over, and then choking the life out of him with a rope. It didn't fit.

She walked outside. The overcast sky promised rain but had yet to deliver. Blair and Fair were waiting for her.

"You two a team or something?"

"We thought we might go to the cemetery together. It will keep us from squabbling, now, won't it?" Fair shrugged his shoulders.

"Are you two up to something?"

"What a distrustful thing to say," Blair mildly replied. "Yes, we're up to being gentlemen. I think we both are ashamed of how we acted at Mim's. We've decided to present a united front in public and spare you further embarrassment."

"Remarkable." Harry dully got in the car.

42

Labor Day marked the end of summer. The usual round of barbecues, parties, tubing down the James River, golf tournaments, and last-minute school shopping crammed the weekend.

Over two weeks had passed since Norman was strangled. Kerry McCray, her defense in the hands of Ned Tucker, was freed on $100,000 bail, raised by her much older brother, Kyle, who lived in Colorado Springs. He was shocked when informed of events, but he stuck by his sister. Kerry, ordered by Ned to keep her mouth shut, did just that. Kyle took a leave of absence from his job to stay with her. He feared Kerry would be badly treated. He swore on a month of Sundays that the motorcycle gear was his. When it came back from the lab, no blood or powder burns had been found on it. Most people said he was lying to save his sister's skin, ignoring the fact that in the early seventies he'd had a motorcycle.

The sun set earlier each day, and Harry, much as she loved the soft light of fall and winter, found the shorter days hectic. So often she woke up in the dark and came home in the dark. She had to do her farm chores no matter what.

Fair and Blair took polite turns asking her out. Sometimes it was too much attention. Mrs. Hogendobber told her to enjoy every minute of it.

Cynthia Cooper and Rick Shaw relaxed a little bit. Cynthia hinted that as soon as schedules could be coordinated, they had a person who could sink Kerry's ship.

Mrs. Murphy, Tucker, and even Pewter racked their brains to think if there was a missing link, but no one could find it. Even if the humans could have understood the truth about scent, which never falters—one's scent is one's scent—and even if they could have understood that Kerry's scent was not on the murder weapon, chances were they would have discounted it. Humans tend to validate only those senses *they* perceive. They ignore any other species' reality, and, worse, they blot out any conflicting evidence. Humans need to feel safe. The two cats and dog were far wiser on that score. No one is ever safe. So why not live as much as you can?

The avalanche of mail at the post office on Tuesday following the holiday astonished Harry and Mrs. Hogendobber.

"Fall catalogues," Harry moaned. "After a while they get heavy."

Little Marilyn walked through the front door and up to the counter. "You must hate holidays."

"Nah." Harry shook her head. "It's these catalogues."

"You know what I've been doing?" She put her purse on the counter. "I've been rereading the letters Kerry and Aysha and I sent to one another when we were abroad and the letters Aysha sent to me when I returned home. I can't find anything unbalanced in Kerry's letters. It's what you would expect of two young women right out of college. We wrote about where we went, what we read, who we met, and who we were dating. I guess I've been searching for some kind of answer to how someone I've known so long could be a murderer." She rested her head on her hand. "No answers. Of course, I still have a shoebox left. Maybe there will be something in there."

"Would you mind if I read them too?"

"Harry, that's private correspondence." Miranda frowned.

"That's why I'm asking. Marilyn can always say no."

"I'd be happy for you to read them. Maybe you'll catch something I've missed. You know how the keys you're looking for are always the ones right under your nose. You wanted to see the stamps anyway."

"In that case, would you mind if I joined you?" Mrs. Hogendobber invited herself, and, naturally, Little Marilyn said she wouldn't mind at all.

Two cups of coffee and a slice each of Mrs. Hogendobber's cherry pie later, the ladies sat in Little Marilyn's living room surrounded by shoeboxes. Mrs. Murphy squeezed herself into one where she slept. Tucker, head on her paws, dozed on the cool slate hearth.

"See, nothing special."

"Except that everyone expresses themselves well."

Harry added, "My favorite was the letter where Aysha said you should lend her a thousand dollars because you have it to lend."

Little Marilyn waved her hand. "She got over it. Well, I've finished the last. Might as well put these back in order."

Big Marilyn knocked on the door. Her daughter lived on a dependency on her mother's estate. Dependency, although the correct word, hardly described the lovely frame house, a chaste Federal with a tin roof and green-black shutters. "Hello, girls. Find anything?"

"No, Mother. We were just putting the letters back in place."

"You tried, that's the important thing." She breathed deeply. "What an inviting aroma."

"Cherry pie. You need to sample it. I'm branching into pies now. Market sells out of my doughnuts, muffins, and buns by eight-thirty every morning. He says he needs something for the after-work trade, so I'm experimenting with pies. Don't think of this as calories, think of this as market research."

"Bad pun," Harry teased her.

"Just a tad." Mim held her fingers close together as Miranda blithely ignored her and cut out a full portion. As she did so, a drop of cherry sauce plopped on a letter.

"Clumsy me."

"Don't worry about it," Little Marilyn instructed her.

Mrs. Hogendobber placed the knife on the pie plate, then bent over. She carefully wiped the letter with a napkin. "Hmm."

"Really, Mrs. Hogendobber, don't worry about it."

"I'm not, actually." Miranda handed the letter to Harry. "Queer."

Harry studied the airmail envelope from France, postmarked St. Tropez, 1988. "Always wanted to go there."

"Where?" Mim inquired.

"St. Tropez."

"One of Aysha's. I don't think she missed a city in France."

"Look closer." Mrs. Hogendobber pointed to the postmark.

Harry squinted. "The ink."

"Precisely." Mrs. Hogendobber folded her hands, as happy in Harry's progress as if she'd been a star pupil.

"What are you two talking about?" Mim was nosy.

Harry walked over and placed the letter in the elder Marilyn's lap. Mim pulled out her half-moon glasses and held the letter under her nose.

"Look at the color of the ink." Harry cast her eyes around the piles of letters for another one from France. "Ah, here's one. Paris. Look at the color here. This one is from Kerry."

"Different, slightly but different." Mim removed her glasses. "Aren't inks like dye lots? This letter is from Paris. That one from St. Tropez."

"Yes, but postal inks are remarkably consistent." Harry was now on her hands and knees. She pulled out letters. "The letters from 1986 are genuine. But here, here's one from Florence, December 1987." Harry handed that letter to Little Marilyn while giving her one from Italy the year before.

"There really is a shade of difference." Little Marilyn was surprised.

Within seconds Harry and Mrs. Hogendobber were on their hands and knees tossing the letters into piles segregated by year.

"You two are fast. Let me help." Little Marilyn joined them.

"Want to work in the P.O.?" Harry joked.

Mim stayed in the chair. Her knees hurt and she didn't want to admit it. Finally they had all the piles sorted out.

"There's no doubt about this. Kerry's postmarks are authentic. Aysha's are authentic until 1987. Then the inks change." Harry rubbed her chin. "This is strange."

"Surely, there's a mistake." Mim was confused by the implication.

"Mim, I've worked in the post office since George took over in 1958. This postmark is forged. Any good stationer can create a round stamp. That's simple. Aysha nearly matched the inks, probably from the postmarks on letters she'd received from Little Marilyn and Kerry in Europe, but different countries have different formulas. Well, now, think of stationery itself. Haven't you noticed how the paper of a personal letter from England is a bit different from our own?"

"Then how did the letters get here?" Big Marilyn asked the key question.

"That's easy if you have a friend in Crozet." Harry crossed her legs like an Indian. "All she had to do was mail these letters in a manila envelope and have her friend distribute them."

"Much as I hate to admit it, when George was postmaster, he let a lot of people behind the counter. We do too, to tell the truth, as you well know. It wouldn't take much to slip these letters into the appropriate boxes when one's back was turned. Some of the letters are addressed to Little Marilyn in care of Ottoline Gill."

"Well, I guess we know who her friend was," Harry said.

"Why would her mother participate in such subterfuge?" Mim was astounded. But then, Mim was also secure in her social position.

"Because she didn't want anyone to know what Aysha was really doing. Maybe it didn't fit the program," Harry answered.

"Then where was she and what was she doing?" Little Marilyn, eyes wide, asked.

Little Marilyn turned over the letters to Rick Shaw that night. He emphatically swore everyone to secrecy when he arrived. Mim demanded to know what he was going to do about it, where it might lead, and he finally said, "I don't know exactly, but I will do everything I can to find out why. I won't set this aside—just trust me."

"I have no choice." She pursed her lips.

After he left, the group broke up to go home. Quietly pulling aside Harry, Little Marilyn nervously asked, "Would you mind terribly—and believe me I understand if you do—but if not, would you mind if I asked Blair to drive over to Richmond with me for the symphony?"

"No, not at all."

"You see, I'm not sure of your status—that's not how I meant to say it, but—"

"I understand. I'm not sure either."

"Do you care for him?" She didn't realize she was holding her hands tightly. Another minute, and she'd be wringing them.

Harry took a deep breath. "He's one of the best-looking men I've ever laid eyes on, and I like him. I know you like his curly hair." She smiled. "But Blair's diffident, for lack of a better word. He likes me fine, but I don't think he's in love with me."

"What about that fight at the party?"

"Two dogs with a bone. I'm not sure it was as much about me as about property rights."

"Oh, Harry, that's cynical. I think they both care for you very much."

"Tell me, Marilyn, what does it mean for a man to care for a woman?"

"I know what they say when they want something—" Little Marilyn paused. "And they buy presents, they work hard, they'll do anything to get your attention. But I'm not an expert on love."

"Is anybody?" Harry smiled. "Miranda, maybe."

"She certainly had George wrapped around her little finger." Then Little Marilyn brightened. "Because she knew the way to a man's heart is through his stomach."

They both laughed, which caused Mim and Mrs. Hogendobber to turn to them.

"How can you laugh at a time like this?" Mim snapped.

"Releasing tension, Mother."

"Find another way to do it."

Little Marilyn whispered to Harry, "I could bash her. That would do it for sure."

Harry whispered back, "You'd have help."

"Mother means well, but she can't stop telling everyone what to do and how to do it."

"Will you two speak up?" Mim demanded.

"We were discussing the high heel as a weapon," Harry lied.

"Oh."

Little Marilyn picked up the thread. "With all this violence—guns, strangling—we were talking about what we would do if someone attacked us. Well, take off your heels and hit him in the eye. Just as hard as you can."

"Gruesome. Or hit him on the back of the head when he runs," Harry added.

"Harry." Mim stared hard at her feet. "You only wear sneakers."

"Do you remember Delphine Falkenroth?" Miranda asked Mim.

"Yes, she got that modeling job in New York City right after the war."

"Once she hailed a cab and a man ran right in front of her and hopped in it. Delphine said she held on to the door and hit him so many times over the head with her high heel that he swore like a fishmonger, but he surrendered the cab." She waited a beat. "She married him, of course."

"Is that how she met Roddy? Oh, she never told me that." Mim relished the tale.

Harry whispered again to Little Marilyn, "A trip down Memory Lane. I'm going to collect Mrs. Murphy and Tucker and head home."

Once home, she called Cynthia Cooper, who was already informed of the bogus inks and postmarks.

"Coop, I had a thought."

"Yeah?"

"Did you go by Hassett's to see if anyone there remembered Kerry buying the gun?"

"One of the first things I did after Hogan was killed."

"And?"

"The paperwork matched, the driver's license numbers matched up."

"But the salesman—"

"He'd gone on vacation. A month's camping in Maine. Ought to be back right about now."

"You'll go back, of course."

"I will—but I'm hoping I don't have to."

"What are you up to?"

"Can't tell."

44

Cynthia Cooper never expected Frank Kenton to be attractive. She waited in the airport lobby holding a sign with his name on it. When a tall, distinguished man approached her, an earring in his left ear, she thought he was going to ask for directions.

"Deputy Cooper?"

"Mr. Kenton?"

"The same."

"Uh—do you have any luggage?"

"No. My carry-on is it."

As they walked to the squad car, he apologized for how angry he had been the first time she phoned him. Gruff as he'd been, he wasn't angry at her. She declared that she quite understood.

The first place to which she drove him was Kerry McCray's house. Rick Shaw awaited them, and as they all three approached the front door, Kerry hurried out to greet them, Kyle right behind her. Frank smiled at her. "I've never seen you before in my life."

"Thank you. Thank you." Tears sprang to her eyes.

"Lady, I haven't done a thing."

As Frank and Cynthia climbed back into the squad car, Cynthia exhaled. "I'm half-glad Kerry isn't Malibu and half-disappointed. One always hopes for an easy case—would you like lunch? Maybe we should take a food break before we push on."

"Fine with me."

Mrs. Hogendobber waved as Cynthia cruised by the post office. The deputy pulled a U-turn and stopped. She ran into the post office.

"Hi, how are you this morning?" Miranda smiled.

"I'm okay. What about yourself?"

"A little tired."

"Where's Harry and the zoo?"

"She's up at Ash Lawn with Little Marilyn, Aysha, and Ottoline."

"What in the world is she doing there, and what is Aysha doing there? Norman's hardly cold."

Mrs. Hogendobber frowned. "I know, but Aysha said she was going stir crazy, so she drove up to gather up her things there as well as Laura Freely's. Marilyn's lost two docents, so she's in a fix. Anyway, she begged to have Harry for a day, since she knows the place so well. Harry asked me and I said fine. Of course, she's not a William and Mary graduate, but in a pinch a Smithie will do. Little Marilyn needs to train a new batch of docents fast."

Cynthia stood in the middle of the post office. She looked out the window at Frank in the air-conditioned car, then back to Mrs. Hogendobber. "Mrs. H., I have a favor to ask of you."

"Of course."

"Call Little Marilyn. Don't speak to anyone but her. She's got to keep Aysha there until I get there."

"Oh, dear. Kerry's out on bail. I never thought of that." Miranda's hand, tipped in mocha mist nail polish today, flew to her face. "I'll get right on it."

Then Cynthia darted into Market Shiflett's, bought two home-made sandwiches, drinks, and Miranda's peach cobbler.

She hopped in the squad car. "Frank, here. There's been a change of plans. Hang on." She hit the siren and flew down 240, shooting through the intersection onto 250, bearing right to pick up I-64 miles down the road.

"You'll love the peach cobbler," she informed a bug-eyed Frank.

"I'm sure—but I think I'll wait." He smiled weakly.

Once she'd maneuvered onto I-64, heading east, she said, "It's a straightaway for about fifteen miles, then we'll hit twisty roads again. I don't know how strong your stomach is. If it's cast iron, eat."

"I'll wait. Where are we going?"

"Ash Lawn, home of James Monroe. We get off onto Route 20 South and then hang a left up the road past Monticello. I'm hit-ting ninety, but I can't go much more than forty once we get on the mountain road. Another fifteen, twenty minutes and we're there." She picked up her pager and told headquarters where she was going. She asked for backup—just in case.

"She's a real cobra."

"I know."

Cynthia turned off the siren two miles from Ash Lawn. She drove down the curving tree-lined drive, turning left into the parking lot, and drove right up to the gift shop. "Ready?"

"Yes." Frank was delighted to escape from the car.

Harry noticed that Little Marilyn was unusually tense. She hoped it wasn't because she was failing as a docent. Harry shepherded her group through the house, telling them where to step down and where to watch their heads. She pointed out pieces of furniture and added tidbits about Monroe's term of office.

Mrs. Murphy and Tucker had burrowed under the huge box-woods. The earth was cooler than the air.

Aysha was underneath the house collecting the last of Laura Freely's period clothing as well as her own. Ottoline was helping her.

Cynthia and Frank walked to the front door as nonchalantly as possible. Harry was just opening the side door to let out her group as Cynthia and Frank entered through the front.

As it was lunch hour, the visitors to Ash Lawn who would be in the next tour group, which was Marilyn's, had chosen to sit under the magnificent spreading trees, drinking something ice cold.

Harry was surprised to find Cynthia there.

"This is Frank Kenton from San Francisco."

Harry held out her hand. "Welcome to Ash Lawn."

"It's okay, Harry, you don't have to give him the tour." Cynthia smiled tensely.

Little Marilyn, having been warned by Miranda, contained her nervousness as best she could. "Should I call her now?"

"Yes," Cynthia replied.

The candlesticks shook in their holders as Little Marilyn walked by. After a few minutes she returned with Aysha and Ottoline.

Aysha froze at the sight of Frank.

"That's Malibu," he quietly said.

"No!" Ottoline screamed.

Aysha spun around, grabbed Harry, and dragged her into the living room. Ottoline slammed the doors. When Cynthia tried to pursue her, a bullet smashed through the door, just missing her head.

"Get out of here, all of you!" Cynthia commanded.

Marilyn and Frank hurried outside. Marilyn, mindful of her duty, quickly herded the visitors down to the parking lot. The wail of a siren meant help was coming.

Mrs. Murphy leapt up. *"Mom. Mom. Are you okay?"*

Tucker, without a sound, scooted out from under the boxwood and shot toward the house.

Mrs. Murphy squeezed through the front door which was slightly ajar. Tucker had a harder time of it, but managed.

Cynthia was crouched down, her back to the wall by the door into the living room. Her gun was held at the ready. "Come on out, Aysha. Game's up."

"I've got a gun in my hand."

"Won't do you any good."

Aysha laughed. "If I shoot you first it will."

Ottoline called out, "Cynthia, let her go. Take me in her place. She's lost her husband. She's not in her right mind."

Cynthia noticed the cat and dog. "Get out of here."

Mrs. Murphy tore out the front door. Tucker waited a moment, gave Cynthia a soulful look, then followed her feline friend.

"Tucker, around the side. Maybe I can get in a window."

They heard Harry's voice. "Aysha, give yourself up. Maybe things will go easier for you."

"Shut up!"

The sound of Harry's beloved voice spurred on both animals. Mrs. Murphy raced to the low paned window. Closed. Ash Lawn was air-conditioned. Both cat and dog saw Harry being held at gunpoint in the middle of the room.

Ottoline stood off to the side of the doors.

"Tucker, these old windows are pretty low. Think you can crash through?"

"Yes."

They ran back fifty yards, then turned and hurtled toward the old hand-blown window. Tucker left the ground a split second before Murphy, ducking her head, and hit the glass with the top of her head. Mrs. Murphy, her eyes squeezed tight against the shattering glass, sailed in a hairbreadth behind Tucker. Broken glass went everywhere.

Aysha whirled and fired. She was so set on a human opponent, she never figured on the animals. Tucker, still running, leapt up and hit her full force, and she staggered back.

Ottoline screamed, "Shoot the dog!"

Mrs. Murphy leapt up and sank her fangs into Aysha's right wrist while grabbing on to her forearm with front and hind claws. Then she tore into the flesh for all she was worth.

Aysha howled. Harry threw a block into her and they tumbled onto the floor. Tucker clamped her jaws on a leg. Ottoline ran over to kick the corgi.

Mrs. Murphy released her grip and yelled, *"The hand, Tucker, go for the hand."* Tucker bounded over the struggling bodies. Ottoline's kick was a fraction of a second too late. Aysha was reaching up to bludgeon Harry on the head. Tucker savaged Aysha's hand, biting deep holes in the fleshy palm. Aysha dropped the gun. Ottoline quickly reached for it. Tucker ran quietly behind her and bit her too, then picked up the gun.

Harry yelled, "Coop! Help!"

Mrs. Murphy kept clawing Aysha as Tucker eluded a determined Ottoline, her focus on the gun.

Coop held her service pistol in both hands and blew out the lock on the doors. "It's over, Aysha." She leveled her gun at the fighting women.

Harry, a bruise already swelling up under her left eye, released Aysha and scrambled to her feet. She was struggling to catch her breath. Ottoline ran up behind Coop and grabbed her around the neck, but Coop ducked and elbowed her in the gut. With an "umph" Ottoline let go.

Aysha started to spring out the door, but Harry tackled her.

Coop shoved Ottoline over to where Aysha was slowly getting up.

"You were so smart, Aysha, but you were done in by a dog and a cat." Harry rejoiced as Tucker brought her the gun.

"It's always the one you don't figure that gets you." Cynthia never took her eyes off her quarry.

Rick Shaw thundered in. He grasped the situation and handcuffed Aysha and Ottoline together, back to back, then read them their rights.

"Ow." Aysha winced from where Mrs. Murphy and Tucker had ripped her hand.

Harry squatted down and petted her friends. She checked their paws for cuts from the glass.

"Why?" Harry asked.

"Why not?" Aysha insouciantly replied.

"Well, then how?" Cynthia queried.

"I have a right to remain silent."

"Answer one question, Aysha." Harry brushed herself off. "Was Norman in on it?"

Aysha shrugged, not answering the question.

Ottoline laughed derisively. "That coward. He lived in fear of his own shadow." Ottoline turned to Rick Shaw. "You're making a big mistake."

Aysha, still panting, said, "Mother, my lawyer will do the talking."

Harry picked up a purring Mrs. Murphy. "Aysha, your letters to Marilyn from St. Tropez and Paris and wherever—you faked the postmarks and did a good job. But it's much harder to fake the inks."

Ottoline grumbled. "You can't prove that in a court of law. And just because I delivered fake postcards doesn't make my daughter a criminal."

Aysha's eyes narrowed, then widened. "Mother, anything you say can be used against me!"

Ottoline shook her head. "I want to make a clean breast of it. I needed money. Stealing from a bank is ridiculously easy. Crozet National was very sloppy regarding their security. Norman was putty in my hands. It was quite simple, really. When he weakened, I strangled him. As he slowed by the canning plant I popped up out of the back seat and told him to pull over. He was harder to kill than I thought, but I did have the advantage of surprise. At least I didn't have to hear him whine anymore about what would happen if he got caught."

Mrs. Murphy reached out with her paw, claws extended. *"Aysha, are you going to stand there and let your mother take the rap?"*

"I hate cats," Aysha spat at the little tiger who had foiled her plans.

"Well, this one was smart enough to stop you," Cynthia sarcastically said.

"That's enough." Rick wanted to get mother and daughter down to the station to book them. He pointed toward the squad car. As they were handcuffed back to back, walking proved difficult.

"Did you kill Hogan Freely too?" Harry asked Ottoline.

"Yes. Remember when we were in Market Shiflett's? Hogan said he was going to work late and bang around on the computer. He was intelligent enough that he might have—"

"Mother, shut up!" Aysha stumbled.

"What if Hogan had figured out my system?" Ottoline said, emphasizing "my."

"There is no system, Mother. Norman was stealing from the bank. Hogan threatened him. He killed Hogan and his accomplice inside the bank killed him. Kerry *was* his partner. He betrayed me."

"He did?" Ottoline's eyebrows jumped up. She thought a second, then her tone changed as she followed Aysha's desperate line of reasoning. "What a worm!"

"Aysha, we know you worked at the Anvil. You can't deny that." Harry, still quietly seething with anger, argued as she followed them to the squad car.

"So?"

Ottoline went on rapidly, babbling as though that would get the people off the track. "I had to do something. I mean, my daughter, a *Gill*, working in a place like that. She was just going through a stage, of course, but think how it could have compromised her chances of a good marriage once she returned home, which she would do, in time. So I begged her to write postcards as if she were still in Europe. I took care of the rest. As it was, she had drifted away from Marilyn and Kerry so they didn't know exactly where she was. Sending fake postcards wasn't that hard, you see, and her reputation remained unsullied. I don't know why young people have to go through these rebellious stages. My generation never did."

"You had World War Two. That was rebellion enough."

"I'm not that old," Ottoline frostily corrected Harry.

"Ladies, these are good stories. Let's get to the station house and you can make your statements and call your lawyer," Rick prodded them.

Frank Kenton followed Cynthia. As he opened the door to her squad car he gave Aysha a long, hard look.

Defiantly, she stared back.

"I'll live to see you rot in hell." He smiled.

"I like that, Frank. There's a real irony to that—you as a moral force." Aysha laughed at him.

"Don't lower yourself to talk to him," Ottoline snapped.

"She lowered herself plenty in San Francisco," Frank yelled at Ottoline. "Lady, we'd have all been better off if you hadn't *been* a mother."

Ottoline hesitated before trying to get in the back seat of the squad car. Rick held open the door. The way the two women were handcuffed, they couldn't maneuver their way into the car.

"This is impossible." Aysha stated the obvious.

"You're right." Rick unlocked her handcuffs.

That fast, Aysha sprinted toward the trees.

"Stop or I'll shoot!" Rick dropped to one knee while pulling his revolver.

Cynthia, too, dropped, gun at the ready. Aysha made an easy target.

Tucker dug into the earth, flying after Aysha. Passing the human was easy for such a fast little dog. She turned in front of Aysha just as Rick fired a warning shot. Harry was going to call the dog back but thought it unwise to interrupt Tucker's trajectory.

Aysha glanced over her shoulder just as Tucker crouched in front of her. She tripped over the little dog and hit the ground hard.

Cynthia, younger and faster than Rick, was halfway there, when a wobbly Aysha clambered to her feet.

"Goddamned dog!"

"Put your hands behind your head and slowly, I said slowly, walk back to the squad car."

Ottoline, crying uncontrollably, slumped against the white and blue car. "I did it. Really. I'm guilty."

"Shut up, Mother! You never listen."

A flash of parental authority passed over Ottoline's face. "If you'd listened to me in the first place, none of us would be in this mess! I told you not to marry Mike Huckstep!"

"I don't know anyone by that name!" Aysha's whole body contorted with rage.

Ottoline's face fell like a collapsed building. She realized that in her frantic attempt to save her daughter she had spilled the beans.

45

Reverend Jones was the last to join the little group at Harry's farm for a potluck supper hastily arranged by Susan. He greeted Mrs. Hogendobber, Mim, Little Marilyn, Market, Pewter, Ned, Blair, Cynthia, Kerry McCray, and her brother, Kyle.

"What did I miss?"

"Idle gossip. We waited for you," Mrs. Hogendobber told him. "Fair's the only one missing. He'll come when he can."

"Did you ever find out how Aysha transferred the money?" Susan eagerly asked.

"Yes, but we don't know what she's done with it, except for the sum she transferred into Kerry's account. She fully intends to hire the best lawyer money can buy and serve out her jail term if she doesn't get capital punishment. She'll probably be out on good behavior before she's fifty, and then she'll go to wherever she's stashed the money." Cynthia sounded bitter.

"How'd she do it?" Mim asked again.

"There was a rider attached to the void command in the Crozet National computer. Remember all the instructions for dealing with the Threadneedle virus? Well, it was brilliant, really. When the bank would void the command of the virus to scramble files, a rider would go into effect that instructed the computer to transfer two million dollars into a blind account on August first. The money didn't leave the bank. Later Aysha or Norman squirreled it out. For all we know, it may still be in that blind account, or it may be in an offshore account in a country whose bankers are easily bribed."

"Where was Mike Huckstep in all this?" Blair was curious.

"Ah..." Cynthia smiled at him. She always smiled at Blair. "That was the fly in the ointment. She had everything perfectly planned, a plan she undoubtedly stole from Huckstep, and he shows up at Ash Lawn just before her trap was set to spring. She wasn't taking any chances and she was shrewd enough to know the death of a biker wouldn't pull at many heartstrings in Crozet. She coolly calculated how to get away with murder. She told him she was enacting his plan. He signed the bank cards willingly, thinking the ill-gotten gain would be pirated into his account. They'd be rich. Norman inserted the account information into the system, not knowing who Mike really was. Meanwhile, Aysha told Mike she wanted him back. He didn't know she was married to Norman, of course. She told him how awful she'd felt running out on him, but she was afraid of total commitment, and when she realized her mistake she couldn't find him—he'd moved from Glover Street, where they used to live. She suggested he pick her up on the motorcycle and they could cruise around. Bam! That was it for Mike Huckstep, her real husband. Not only is she a killer and a thief, she's a bigamist."

"How did he find her?" Harry wondered.

"He knew her real name. Aysha got a break when he showed up at Ash Lawn strung out like he was. He called her by the name he knew best. Of course, Ottoline is claiming Huckstep must have been killed by a drug dealer or some other low life—anyone but her precious daughter."

"So, Coop, how did Huckstep find Aysha?" Susan asked.

"Oh," she said, smiling, "I got off the subject, didn't I? He must have tapped into our Department of Motor Vehicle files or he could have zapped the state income tax records. The man seems to have been, without a doubt, a computer genius."

"Imagine if that mind had been harnessed to the service of the Lord," Mrs. Hogendobber mused.

"Miranda, that's an interesting thought." Herbie crossed his arms over his chest. "Speaking of his mind, I wonder what provoked him to look for her."

"Love. He was still in love with her, despite all," Blair firmly stated. "You could see that the day he came to Ash Lawn. Some men are gluttons for that brand of punishment."

"We'll never really know." Cynthia thought Blair's interpretation was on the romantic side.

"Takes some people that way," Kerry ruefully added to the conversation.

"Guess he got more and more lonesome and—" Susan paused. "It doesn't matter, I guess. But what I can't figure out is how he knew to go to Ash Lawn."

"Yeah, that's weird." Little Marilyn recalled his visit.

"My hunch is that Aysha bragged about her pedigree, that old Virginia vice. She probably said she was or would be a docent at Monticello or Ash Lawn or something like that. I doubt we'll ever truly know because she is keeping her mouth shut like a steel trap." Cynthia shook her head. "In fact, if it weren't for the way Ottoline keeps letting things slip, we wouldn't know enough to put together a case."

"Poor Norman, the perfect cog in her wheel." Kerry's eyes misted over.

"Why couldn't Mike put his plan into effect?" Little Marilyn asked.

"A man like that wouldn't have friends inside a bank. He

needed a partner who was or could be socially acceptable. I suppose the original plan entailed Aysha working inside a bank," Mim shrewdly noted.

"Aysha decided she could pull it off without him," Cynthia said. "When he showed up she shrewdly told him she'd found a dupe inside the bank. They could be in business pronto. Although Mike probably did love her as Blair believes, she couldn't control him the way she could control Norman. And she definitely had her eyes on the whole enchilada."

"I keep thinking about poor Hogan. There he was in Market's store, telling us he was going to work late that night, telling Aysha." Susan shivered, remembering.

"He scared her for sure. The fog was pure luck." Cynthia glanced over at Blair. He was so handsome, she couldn't keep her eyes off him.

Little Marilyn noticed. "Thank God for Mrs. Murphy and Tee Tucker, they're the real heroes."

"Don't let it go to your head," Pewter chided.

"You're out of sorts because you missed the fireworks." Mrs. Murphy preened.

"You're right." Pewter tiptoed toward those covered dishes in the kitchen.

"Has she shown any remorse?" Mrs. Hogendobber inquired.

"None."

"Ottoline says Aysha is being framed. She insists that Kerry is the culprit while she killed Norman to spare her daughter a dreadful marriage." Mim rose to signal time to eat. "But then, Ottoline always was a silly fool."

"Whose blood was on the saddlebag?" Harry asked.

"What blood?" Mim motioned for Little Marilyn to join her. "I don't know anything about blood."

"A few drops of blood on Mike Huckstep's saddlebags." Cynthia checked her hands and decided she needed to wash them before eating. "Aysha's. She must have had a small cut."

By now the humans had invaded the kitchen. Much as they

wanted to wait for Fair, their stomachs wouldn't. Besides, with a vet, one never knew what his hours would be.

Little Marilyn had cooked crisp chicken.

"Don't forget us," came the chorus from the floor.

She didn't. Each animal received delectable chicken cut into small cubes. As the people carried their plates back into the living room, the animals happily ate.

Miranda asked, "What about Kerry?"

"Aysha was slick, slick as an eel." Cynthia put down her drumstick. "First she used the term *Threadneedle* because she knew Kerry worked for a bank in London, near the Bank of England, on Threadneedle Street. She figured by the time we unearthed that odd fact, Kerry's neck would be in the noose. Aysha had a fake driver's license made with her statistics and photograph but with Kerry's name, address, and social security number, which she pulled out of the bank computer in Norman's office. She bought the gun at Hassett's that way."

"Fake driver's licenses?" Miranda was surprised.

"High school kids are a big market—so they can buy liquor," Harry said.

"How would you know that?" Miranda demanded.

"Oh—" Harry's voice rose upward.

"It's a good thing your mother is not here to hear this."

"Yes. It is." Harry agreed with Miranda.

"But why would Aysha kill Norman? He was her cover," Marilyn wanted to know.

"She didn't," Harry blurted out, not from knowledge but from intuition and what she had observed at Ash Lawn.

"Norman chickened out after Hogan's murder. White-collar crime was all right, but murder—well, he was getting very shaky. Aysha was afraid he'd crack and give them away. Ottoline, terrified that her daughter might get caught, really did strangle him. I'm sure the old girl's telling the truth about that, although we don't have any proof."

"So Ottoline knew all along." Harry was astonished.

"Not at first." Cynthia shrugged. "When Mike Huckstep's body was found, Ottoline got her first seismic wake-up call. When Hogan was killed, she had to have known. Aysha may even have told her. Like I said, Aysha denies everything and Ottoline confesses to everything."

"She killed to protect her daughter." Mim shook her head.

"Too late. And planting the weapon in Kerry's Toyota—that was obvious and clumsy."

"Then it was Aysha driving the motorcycle out from Sugar Hollow?" Harry remembered her close call.

"Yes." Cynthia finished off a chicken wing as the others chatted.

"You know," Mim changed the subject, "Ottoline was forever Aysha's safety net. She never let her grow up in the sense that the woman was never accountable for her actions. The wrong kind of love," Mim observed. "Hope I didn't do that to you."

Her daughter answered, "Well, Mother, you'd be happy to live my life for me and everyone else's in this room. You *are* domineering."

A silence descended upon the group.

Big Marilyn broke it. "So...?"

They all laughed.

"Did you think it was Aysha?" Pewter spoke with her mouth full.

"No. We just knew it wasn't Kerry. At least we were pretty sure it wasn't," Tucker replied.

"I'm happy we're alive." Murphy flicked her tail. *"I don't understand why humans kill each other. I guess I never will."*

"You have to love them for what they are." Tucker snuck over to sniff Pewter's plate.

Pewter boxed Tucker on the nose. *"Watch it. I don't have to love a poacher!"*

"You take so long to eat." Tucker winced.

"If you'd eat more slowly you'd enjoy it more," Pewter advised.

They heard the vet truck pull up outside, a door slamming,

then Fair pushed open the screen door. The friends, intent on their dinners, greeted him. Then one by one they noticed.

"What have you done?" Mrs. Hogendobber exclaimed.

"Curled my hair a little," he replied in an unusually strong voice. "Didn't come out quite the way I expected."

"Might I ask why you did it?" Harry was polite.

"Works for Blair." He shrugged. "Thought it might work for me."

Dear Highly Intelligent Feline:

Tired of the same old ball of string? Well, I've developed my own line of catnip toys, all tested by Pewter and me. Not that I love for Pewter to play with my little sockies, but if I don't let her, she shreds my manuscripts. You see how that is!

Just so the humans won't feel left out, I've designed a T-shirt for them.

If you'd like to see how creative I am, write to me and I'll send you a brochure.

> Sneaky Pie's Flea Market
> c/o American Artists, Inc.
> P.O. Box 4671
> Charlottesville, VA 22905

In felinity,

SNEAKY PIE BROWN

P.S. Dogs, get a cat to write for you!

Don't miss the new mystery from

RITA MAE BROWN
and
SNEAKY PIE BROWN

Whisker of Evil

Now available in hardcover
from Bantam Books

Please read on for a preview...

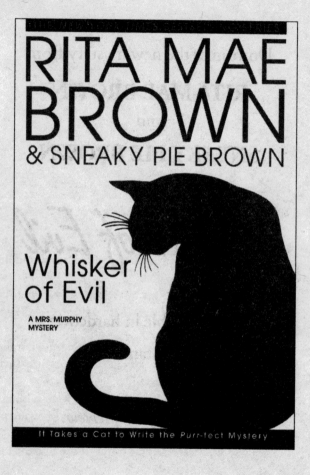

RITA MAE BROWN
& SNEAKY PIE BROWN

Whisker of Evil

**A MRS. MURPHY
MYSTERY**

Whisker of Evil

on sale now

Barry Monteith was still breathing when Harry found him.
His throat had been ripped out.

Tee Tucker, a corgi, racing ahead of Mary Minor
Haristeen as well as the two cats, Mrs. Murphy and Pewter,
found him first.

Barry was on his back, eyes open, gasping and gurgling,
life ebbing with each spasm. He did not recognize Tucker
nor Harry when they reached him.

"Barry, Barry." Harry tried to comfort him, hoping he
could hear her. "It will be all right," she said, knowing perfectly well he was dying.

The tiger cat, Mrs. Murphy, watched the blood jet upward.

"Jugular," fat, gray Pewter succinctly commented.

Gently, Harry took the young man's hand and prayed,
"Dear Lord, receive into thy bosom the soul of Barry
Monteith, a good man." Tears welled in her eyes.

Barry jerked, then his suffering ended.

Death, often so shocking to city dwellers, was part of life here in the country. A hawk would swoop down to carry away the chick while the biddy screamed useless defiance. A bull would break his hip and need to be put down. And one day an old farmer would slowly walk to his tractor only to discover he couldn't climb into the seat. The Angel of Death placed his hand on the stooping shoulder.

It appeared the Angel had offered little peaceful deliverance to Barry Monteith, thirty-four, fit, handsome with brown curly hair, and fun-loving. Barry had started his own business, breeding thoroughbreds, a year ago, with a business partner, Sugar Thierry.

"Sweet Jesus." Harry wiped away the tears.

That Saturday morning, crisp, clear, and beautiful, had held the alluring promise of a perfect May 29. The promise had just curdled.

Harry had finished her early-morning chores and, despite a list of projects, decided to take a walk for an hour. She followed Potlicker Creek to see if the beavers had built any new dams. Barry was sprawled at the creek's edge on a dirt road two miles from her farm that wound up over the mountains into adjoining Augusta County. It edged the vast land holdings of Tally Urquhart, who, well into her nineties and spry, loathed traffic. Three cars constituted traffic in her mind. The only time the road saw much use was during deer-hunting season in the fall.

"Tucker, Mrs. Murphy, and Pewter, stay. I'm going to run to Tally's and phone the sheriff."

If Harry hit a steady lope, crossed the fields and one set of woods, she figured she could reach the phone in Tally's stable within fifteen minutes, though the pitch and roll of the land including one steep ravine would cost time.

As she left her animals, they inspected Barry.

"What could rip his throat like that? A bear swipe?" Pewter's pupils widened.

"Perhaps." Mrs. Murphy, noncommittal, sniffed the gaping wound, as did Tucker.

The cat curled her upper lip to waft more scent into her nostrils. The dog, whose nose was much longer and nostrils larger, simply inhaled.

"I don't smell bear," Tucker declared. *"That's an overpowering scent, and on a morning like this it would stick."*

Pewter, who cherished luxury and beauty, found that Barry's corpse disturbed her equilibrium. *"Let's be grateful we found him today and not three days from now."*

"Stop jabbering, Pewter, and look around, will you? Look for tracks."

Grumbling, the gray cat daintily stepped down the dirt road. *"You mean like car tracks?"*

"Yes, or animal tracks," Mrs. Murphy directed, then returned her attention to Tucker. *"Even though coyote scent isn't as strong as bear, we'd still smell a whiff. Bobcat? I don't smell anything like that. Or dog. There are wild dogs and wild pigs back in the mountains. The humans don't even realize they're there."*

Tucker cocked her perfectly shaped head. *"No dirt around the wound. No saliva, either."*

"I don't see anything. Not even a birdie foot," Pewter, irritated, called out from a hundred yards down the road.

"Well, go across the creek then and look over there." Mrs. Murphy's patience wore thin.

"And get my paws wet?" Pewter's voice rose.

"It's a ford. Hop from rock to rock. Go on, Pewt, stop being a chicken."

Angrily, Pewter puffed up, tearing past them to launch

herself over the ford. She almost made it, but a splash indicated she'd gotten her hind paws wet.

If circumstances had been different, Mrs. Murphy and Tucker would have laughed. Instead, they returned to Barry.

"I can't identify the animal that tore him up." The tiger shook her head.

"Well, the wound is jagged but clean. Like I said, no dirt." Tucker studied the folds of flesh laid back.

"He was killed lying down," the cat sagely noted. *"If he was standing up, don't you think blood would be everywhere?"*

"Not necessarily," the dog replied, thinking how strong heartbeats sent blood straight out from the jugular. Tucker was puzzled by the odd calmness of the scene.

"Pewter, have you found anything on that side?"

"Deer tracks. Big deer tracks."

"Keep looking," Mrs. Murphy requested.

"I hate it when you're bossy." Nonetheless, Pewter moved down the dirt road heading west.

"Barry was such a nice man." Tucker mournfully looked at the square-jawed face, wide-open eyes staring at heaven.

Mrs. Murphy circled the body. *"Tucker, I'm climbing up that sycamore. If I look down maybe I'll see something."*

Her claws, razor sharp, dug into the thin surface of the tree, strips of darker outer bark peeling, exposing the whitish underbark. The odor of fresh water, of the tufted titmouse above her, all informed her. She scanned around for broken limbs, bent bushes, anything indicating Barry—or other humans or large animals—had traveled to this spot avoiding the dirt road.

"Pewter?"

"Big fat nothing." The gray kitty noted that her hind paws were wet. She was getting little clods of dirt stuck be-

tween her toes. This bothered her more than Barry did. After all, he was dead. Nothing she could do for him. But the hardening brown earth between her toes, that was discomfiting.

"*Well, come on back. We'll wait for Mom.*" Mrs. Murphy dropped her hind legs over the limb where she was sitting. Her hind paws reached for the trunk, the claws dug in, and she released her grip, swinging her front paws to the trunk. She backed down.

Tucker touched noses with Pewter, who had recrossed the creek more successfully this time.

Mrs. Murphy came up and sat beside them.

"*Hope his face doesn't change colors while we're waiting for the humans. I hate that. They get all mottled.*" Pewter wrinkled her nose.

"*I wouldn't worry.*" Tucker sighed.

In the distance they heard sirens.

"*Bet they won't know what to make of this, either,*" Tucker said.

"*It's peculiar.*" Mrs. Murphy turned her head in the direction of the sirens.

"*Weird and creepy.*" Pewter pronounced judgment as she picked at her hind toes, and she was right.

Welcome to the charming world of

MRS. MURPHY

Don't miss these earlier mysteries...

THE TAIL OF THE TIP-OFF

When winter hits Crozet, Virginia, it hits hard. That's nothing new to postmistress Mary Minor "Harry" Haristeen and her friends, who keep warm with hard work, hot toddies, and rabid rooting for the University of Virginia's women's basketball team. But post-game high spirits are laid low when contractor H.H. Donaldson drops dead in the parking lot. And soon word spreads that it wasn't a heart attack that did him in. It just doesn't sit right with Harry that one of her fellow fans is a murderer. And as tiger cat Mrs. Murphy knows, things that don't sit right with Harry lead her to poke her not-very-sensitive human nose into dangerous places. To make sure their intrepid mom lands on her feet, the feisty feline and her furry cohorts Pewter and corgi Tee Tucker are about to have their paws full helping Harry uncover a killer with no sense of fair play....

"You don't have to be a cat lover to enjoy Brown's 11th Mrs. Murphy novel.... Brown writes so compellingly... [she] breathes believability into every aspect of this smart and sassy novel." —*Publishers Weekly* (starred review)

CATCH AS CAT CAN

Spring fever comes to the small town of Crozet, Virginia. As the annual Dogwood Festival approaches, postmistress Mary Minor "Harry" Haristeen feels her own mating instincts stir. As for tiger cat Mrs. Murphy, feline intuition tells her there's more in the air than just pheromones. It begins with a case of stolen hubcaps and proceeds to the mysterious death of a dissolute young mechanic over a sobering cup of coffee. Then another death and a shooting lead to the discovery of a half-million crisp, clean dollar bills that look to be very dirty. Now Harry is on the trail of a cold-blooded murderer. Mrs. Murphy already knows who it is—and who's next in line. She also knows that Harry, curious as a cat, does not have nine lives. And the one she does have is hanging by the thinnest of threads.

"The[se] mysteries continue to be a true treat."
—*The Post & Courier* (Charleston, SC)

CLAWS AND EFFECT

Winter puts tiny Crozet, Virginia, in a deep freeze and everyone seems to be suffering from the winter blahs, including postmistress Mary Minor "Harry" Haristeen. So all are ripe for the juicy gossip coming out of Crozet Hospital—until the main source of that gossip turns up dead. It's not like Harry to resist a mystery, and she soon finds the hospital a hotbed of ego, jealousy, and illicit love. But it's tiger cat Mrs. Murphy, roaming the netherworld of Crozet Hospital, who sniffs out a secret that dates back to the Underground Railroad. Then Harry is attacked and a doctor is executed in cold blood. Soon only a quick-witted cat and her animal pals feline Pewter and corgi Tee Tucker stand between Harry and a coldly calculating killer with a prescription for murder.

"Reading a Mrs. Murphy mystery is like
eating a potato chip. You always go back for more....
Whimsical and enchanting...the latest expert tale
from a deserving bestselling series."
—*The Midwest Book Review*

PAWING THROUGH THE PAST

"You'll never get old." Each member of the class of 1980 has received the letter. Mary Minor "Harry" Haristeen, who is on the organizing committee for Crozet High's twentieth reunion, decides to take it as a compliment. Others think it's a joke. But Mrs. Murphy senses trouble. And the sly tiger cat is soon proven right...when the class womanizer turns up dead with a bullet between his eyes. Then another note followed by another murder makes it clear that someone has waited twenty years to take revenge. While Harry tries to piece together the puzzle, it's up to Mrs. Murphy and her animal pals to sniff out the truth.

And there isn't much time. Mrs. Murphy is the first to realize that Harry has been chosen Most Likely to Die, and if she doesn't hurry, Crozet High's twentieth reunion could be Harry's last.

"This is a cat-lover's dream of a mystery.... 'Harry' is simply irresistible.... [Rita Mae] Brown once again proves herself 'Queen of Cat Crimes.'... Don't miss out on this lively series, for it's one of the best around."
—*Old Book Barn Gazette*

CAT ON THE SCENT

Things have been pretty exciting lately in Crozet, Virginia—a little *too* exciting if you ask resident feline investigator Mrs. Murphy. Just as the town starts to buzz over its Civil War reenactment, a popular local man disappears. No one's seen Tommy Van Allen's single-engine plane, either—except for Mrs. Murphy, who spotted it during a foggy evening's mousing. Even Mrs. Murphy's favorite human, postmistress Mary Minor "Harry" Haristeen, can sense that something is amiss. But things really take an ugly turn when the town reenacts the battle of Oak Ridge—and a participant ends up with three very real bullets in his back. While the clever tiger cat and her friends sift through clues that just don't fit together, more than a few locals fear that the scandal will force well-hidden town secrets into the harsh light of day. And when Mrs. Murphy's relentless tracking places loved ones in danger, it takes more than a canny kitty and her team of animal sleuths to set things right again....

MURDER ON THE PROWL

When a phony obituary appears in the local paper, the good people of Crozet, Virginia, are understandably upset. Who would stoop to such a tasteless act? Is it a sick joke—or a sinister warning? Only Mrs. Murphy, the canny tiger cat, senses true malice at work. And her instincts prove correct when a second fake obit appears, followed by a fiendish murder...and then another. People are dropping like flies in Crozet, and no one knows why. Yet even if Mrs. Murphy untangles the knot of passion and deceit that has sent someone into a killing frenzy, it won't be enough. Somehow the shrewd puss must guide her favorite human, postmistress "Harry" Haristeen, down a perilous trail to a deadly killer...and a killer of a climax. Or the next obit may be Harry's own.

MURDER, SHE MEOWED

The annual steeplechase races are the high point in the social calendar of the horse-mad Virginians of cozy Crozet. But when one of the jockeys is found murdered in the main barn, Mary Minor "Harry" Haristeen finds herself in a desperate race of her own—to trap the killer. Luckily for her, she has an experienced ally: her sage tiger cat, Mrs. Murphy. Utilizing her feline genius to plumb the depths of human depravity, Mrs. Murphy finds herself on a trail that leads to the shocking truth behind the murder. But will her human companion catch on in time to beat the killer to the gruesome finish line?

"The intriguing characters in this much-loved series continue to entertain." —*The Nashville Banner*

PAY DIRT

The residents of tiny Crozet, Virginia, thrive on gossip, especially in the post office, where Mary Minor "Harry" Haristeen presides with her tiger cat, Mrs. Murphy. So when a belligerent Hell's Angel crashes Crozet, demanding to see his girlfriend, the leather-clad interloper quickly becomes the chief topic of conversation. Then the biker is found murdered, and everyone is baffled. Well, almost everyone...Mrs. Murphy and her friends Welsh corgi Tee Tucker and overweight feline Pewter haven't been slinking through alleys for nothing. But can they dig up the truth in time to save their human from a ruthless killer?

"If you must work with a collaborator, you want it to be someone with intelligence, wit, and an infinite capacity for subtlety—someone, in fact, very much like a cat....It's always a pleasure to visit this cozy world....There's no resisting Harry's droll sense of humor...or Mrs. Murphy's tart commentary." —*The New York Times Book Review*

MURDER AT MONTICELLO

The most popular citizen of Virginia has been dead for nearly 170 years. That hasn't stopped the good people of tiny Crozet, Virginia, from taking pride in every aspect of Thomas Jefferson's life. But when an archaeological dig of the slave quarters at Jefferson's home, Monticello, uncovers a shocking secret, emotions in Crozet run high—dangerously high. The stunning discovery at Monticello hints at hidden passions and age-old scandals. As postmistress Mary Minor "Harry" Haristeen and some of Crozet's Very Best People try to learn the identity of a centuries-old skeleton—and the reason behind the murder—Harry's tiger cat, Mrs. Murphy, and her canine and feline friends attempt to sniff out a modern-day killer. Mrs. Murphy and corgi Tee Tucker will stick their paws into the darker mysteries of human nature to solve murders old and new—before curiosity can kill the cat...and Harry Haristeen.

"You don't have to be a cat lover to love *Murder at Monticello*." —*The Indianapolis Star*

REST IN PIECES

Small towns don't take kindly to strangers—unless the stranger happens to be a drop-dead gorgeous and seemingly unattached male. When Blair Bainbridge comes to Crozet, Virginia, the local matchmakers lose no time in declaring him perfect for their newly divorced postmistress, Mary Minor "Harry" Haristeen. Even Harry's tiger cat, Mrs. Murphy, and her Welsh corgi, Tee Tucker, believe he smells

A-okay. Could his one little imperfection be that he's a killer? Blair becomes the most likely suspect when the pieces of a dismembered corpse begin turning up around Crozet. No one knows who the dead man is, but when a grisly clue makes a spectacular appearance in the middle of the fall festivities, more than an early winter snow begins chilling the blood of Crozet's Very Best People. That's when Mrs. Murphy, her friend Tucker, and her human companion Harry begin to sort through the clues...only to find themselves a whisker away from becoming the killer's next victims.

"Skillfully plotted, properly gruesome...and wise as well as wickedly funny." —*Booklist*

And don't miss the very first

MRS. MURPHY

mystery . . .

WISH YOU WERE HERE

Small towns are like families. Everyone lives very close together . . . and everyone keeps secrets. Crozet, Virginia, is a
typical small town—until its secrets explode into murder.
Crozet's thirty-something postmistress, Mary Minor
"Harry" Haristeen, has a tiger cat (Mrs. Murphy) and a
Welsh corgi (Tee Tucker), a pending divorce, and a bad
habit of reading postcards not addressed to her. When
Crozet's citizens start turning up murdered, Harry remembers that each received a card with a tombstone on the front
and the message "wish you were here" on the back. Intent
on protecting their human friends, Mrs. Murphy and
Tucker begin to scent out clues. Meanwhile, Harry is con-
ducting her own investigation, unaware that her pets are
one step ahead of her. If only Mrs. Murphy could alert her
somehow, Harry could uncover the culprit before another
murder occurs—and before Harry finds herself on the
killer's mailing list.

"Charming . . . Ms. Brown writes with wise, disarming wit."
—*The New York Times Book Review*

RITA MAE BROWN

___56497-8	**VENUS ENVY**	$7.50/$10.99 in Canada
___38040-0	**BINGO**	$19.00/$28.00
___27888-6	**HIGH HEARTS**	$6.99/$9.99
___27573-9	**IN HER DAY**	$6.99/$9.99
___27886-X	**RUBYFRUIT JUNGLE**	$7.50/$10.99
___27446-5	**SOUTHERN DISCOMFORT**	$6.99/$9.99
___26930-5	**SUDDEN DEATH**	$6.99/$9.99
___38037-0	**SIX OF ONE**	$12.95/$19.95
___57224-5	**RIDING SHOTGUN**	$6.99/$9.99
___56949-X	**DOLLEY:** A NOVEL OF DOLLEY MADISON IN LOVE AND WAR	$6.50/$8.99
___34630-X	**STARTING FROM SCRATCH:** A DIFFERENT KIND OF WRITER'S MANUAL	$19.00/$28.00
___37826-0	**RITA WILL:** AN AUTOBIOGRAPHY	$14.95/$22.95

Please enclose check or money order only, no cash or CODs. Shipping & handling costs: $5.50 U.S. mail, $7.50 UPS. New York and Tennessee residents must remit applicable sales tax. Canadian residents must remit applicable GST and provincial taxes. Please allow 4 – 6 weeks for delivery. All orders are subject to availability. This offer subject to change without notice. Please call 1-800-726-0600 for further information.

Bantam Dell Publishing Group, Inc.
Attn: Customer Service
400 Hahn Road
Westminster, MD 21157

TOTAL AMT $_____
SHIPPING & HANDLING $_____
SALES TAX (NY, TN) $_____

TOTAL ENCLOSED $_____

Name _____

Address _____

City/State/Zip _____

Daytime Phone (_____) _____

RMB 4/04